LOOSE GRAVEL

Also by David P. Holmes

Fiction
Secrets
Emily's Run

Non-fiction
Salt of the Earth

LOOSE GRAVEL

David Holmes

To Mary K—

Thank you

Dep Holmes

6-27-11

NORTH STAR PRESS OF ST. CLOUD, INC.

Saint Cloud, Minnesota

First Edition, June 2011

Printed in the United States of America

Published by
North Star Press of St. Cloud, Inc.
P.O. Box 451
St. Cloud, Minnesota 56302

www.northstarpress.com

I humbly express my gratitude to the wonderful people who have worked to allow me be who I am today:

My father, Albert Fenton Holmes, for instilling the gifts of love and understanding.
My wife, Lois (Smedly), for being my beacon and staying by my side.
Corinne and Seal Dwyer of North Star Press, for seeing something the others didn't.
My son Jeff, for his amazing artistic talents in creating book covers.
Connie Anderson, for being a friend and advisor.
And
Charlotte Westby, who opened the first door for me.

LOOSE GRAVEL

CHAPTER 1
INDISCRETIONS

June 11, 8:00 p.m., Gull Lake, Brainerd, Minnesota.

IT ALL STARTED WITH ISABELLE'S JEALOUSY, fueled by her unstable mental condition. If she had left it alone, nobody would have gotten hurt, and nobody would have died. Now, she sat hidden in the roadside bushes facing the front of the large white house, waiting for the chance to steal a gun to murder her mother.

Dressed in a black Dacron jumpsuit, she was a shadow blending well with the impending darkness. A black knit ski mask was rolled up, exposing her face, her excessive blond hair tucked up inside. Also black, the running shoes were tied tightly.

Except for the two guards, nobody was home now, not even the maid or cook. The dogs had been taken for training yesterday, and Lenny and Vicka were in Chicago. However, this was not a place to be caught breaking into. The thought of what Lenny would do to anyone invading his privacy to this extent was chilling. The house would normally be empty, but with the dogs gone, the guards inside were taking advantage of their boss's absence.

10:30 p.m. It was as dark as it was going to get, and time to do this. One guard had left half an hour ago, leaving the other one still inside. This couldn't wait any longer. Blood was pounding in her temples like a kettledrum, but there was no turning back. A quick check of the strap around her thigh ensured the thin eight-inch knife was in its scabbard securely in place. She reached up and rolled the ski mask down over her face, her eyes peering through the only two holes in front. Nervous spasms of breath captured the heat behind the mask, increasing her dread to a frightening level.

Cautiously moving from her position in a slow creep out of the cover of the shrubbery, she crouched for the two hundred foot run across the open expanse of lawn to the house. Her goal was the patio at the rear of the mansion where she knew she could scale the wall to enter the upstairs bedroom window. With the sensitive alarm system, entering any other part of the ground floor was not an option,

Breaking into a fast dash, she ran toward the house. The motion sensors set off the spotlights, prompting a verbal push, "Oh shit, faster." Grunting her last effort, she prompted herself, "Move your ass. My God, move." Throwing her body against the foundation, she lay motionless near the portico, waiting, pressed tightly against the concrete wall.

The front door opened exposing a massive man in his underwear. Stepping off the porch into the yard, the sight of the Uzi cradled in his arm was all he needed to chase away any intruder . . . except for the one hiding in the shadows. She fingered the handle of the knife on her thigh, just in case. If she was discovered, she could quickly pull the ski mask off. He would recognize her. Distracting and seducing him would be easy, before she killed him.

Annoyed, the big man went back into the house to shut off the lights. He snarled, "Fucking cats."

When the yard fell into darkness, she knew he had turned off the sensors, adding to her advantage. Waiting and listening, there was only dead quiet, and it was time to move again.

Inhaling through the mask, her hot breath was repellant yet stimulating. Carefully rising, Isabelle stealthily crept along the building towards the back of the mansion to where the patio was. Underwater lights in the pool gave off a soft eerie green illumination and guided her to where she needed to be. Cautiously looking into the patio she froze. She hadn't planned on what she saw. *"I can't stop now. I have to do it anyway."*

An unexpected character had been inserted into the scheme. To the edge of the stone patio, a nude female was reclining on a chaise lounge, her back to Isabelle.

The woman had long, thick, blonde hair that cascaded over her shoulders and the padded lounge. Quickly checking for the guard to come back, she needed to gamble that the girl would be alone for a few more moments. Creeping closer, Isabelle was startled when the blonde sensed someone near her.

The voice coming from the naked woman was deep and sultry, heavy with a guttural accent, "Grotzke, would you be a dear and get me . . ."

Whatever she wanted, she wasn't going to get it. Or need it. Reaching around from the back of the lawn chair, Isabelle's fingers clamped themselves around the soft neck and squeezed the blonde's throat, pulling her tightly against the chair. To bring a swift finish to this, the knife came out of the scabbard silently piercing through the chairs webbing and cushion, penetrating deep into her body, making her death surprisingly easy. There was no real struggle, just a gasping with her arms and legs convulsing in protest. They soon stilled. Propping up the limp body back into position in the lounge, Isabelle was finished and ready to continue with her plan. A noise from within the house startled her. With the prowess of a cat, Isabelle glided across the patio to the wall behind the door. Pressing against the building she waited, becoming no more than a shadow.

The patio door opened. Behind it, Isabelle stood still, the knife poised. Grotzke was naked now and evidently expecting some kind of contact with the girl. As he padded across the flagstone deck, Isabelle marveled at the sculptured physique, his muscles rippling and bulging with each movement of his broad body. The same body that she had held in her arms, between her thighs, and in her mouth, for the pornographic stardom in front of Lenny's camera. She knew Grotzke intimately and knew he needed to be feared.

Padding up to the lounge chair, his request came out as a command, "Petra, come on. We can take a dip."

Petra lay motionless, irritating him. Harsher with his demand, "Come on, bitch, into the pool." Confused at the total lack of response, he knelt down next to her and wasn't alarmed until he looked at her gaping mouth and wide, frightened eyes staring motionlessly at nothing. Petra's warm blood running along his leg threw his senses into alert, but his alarm was not quick enough.

The knife slid across his throat so clean and fast he didn't feel it, until his own blood flooded his chest, and Petra's breasts. Although in shock, he knew exactly what happened, as he had done the same thing to others. He just never knew who his killer was. The reason this was happening just didn't matter. On his knees, next to the girl, he seemed almost frozen in place. Isabelle gave him a gentle nudge, and he slowly toppled forward to lie across her. An irritating screech came from the metal legs as the lounge moved from the intrusion of his bulk.

Admiring her handiwork, Isabelle ran her fingers across the muscular flesh of Grotzke's back down to his buttock. Her sneer turned into a sinister chortle of laughter as she assaulted him with a final insult, plunging the knife deep into that buttock. A final slur enforcing her dominance, she muttered, "Pig."

Rolling up the ski mask, she took in a clean welcomed breath of air and turned to enter the mansion, grateful she no longer had to scale the wall.

Isabelle floated silently through the lavish, cloistered house, absolutely certain where she needed to go. Ascending the curved white marble staircase to the second floor, she knew exactly which bedroom to choose. In the huge carpeted chamber she knew so well, she opened the double doors to the walk-in closet. A soft light came on. Feeling up on the shelf, she found the gun in the shoebox right where it was supposed to be. Pushing the box back, the .32 Beretta Tomcat went into her pocket before reaching out to snatch one of Vicka's dresses from the rod full of expensive designer clothing. Stepping to the window overlooking the glowing green of the patio below, she waved her hand frivolously and grinned at the morbid scene she had left, uttering, "My, my, what a mess. Ta-ta, Lenny."

Turning to leave the bedroom, she ran her fingers over the huge circular bed, recalling the times she had lain there posing for Lenny's camera, opening her body for all of them to ogle and marvel. Lenny and his wife, Vicka, the cameraman, Grotzke and the others, they were all there to relish her. The crown for the naked princess was especially sweet when her mother stood by jealously watching her own husband having sex with his stepdaughter, all caught on video. Becoming one of Lenny's favorite models, she took advantage of everything she could, and now, her plan was to implicate him with murder. The game she was playing teetered on the edge of insanity, and the possibility of getting Lenny Cherasky blamed for what she was doing, just made it more exhilarating.

If Isabelle had been as alert as she was vengeful, or had taken into consideration her fragile mental state, she would have never left her bloody footprints trailing through Lenny's house. Also, she would have never entered into this madness in the first place.

Hurrying out to one of Lenny's cars, a quick stop at the control panel opened the iron gates, and the Volvo sped to the next site of this insane plan.

THE TRAFFIC WAS SPARSE at this time of night. With the fresh air rushing through the window, Isabelle felt a dreamy euphoric feeling wash through her. Slipping a disc into the slot on the dash, the beating strains of the Cranberry's tune, "Dreams," rolled from the stereo.

Totally oblivious emotionally to what she had just done, Isabelle looked forward to what was going to be a fun night. There was no way to top this one. Chuckling to herself, a sick limerick danced from her lips, "Mommy's gonna die, Mommy's gonna die." Her lips puckered into a grin as the stolen Volvo pulled her closer to madness.

June 12, 1:30 a.m., Minnetonka, Western Minneapolis suburb.

SITTING IN THE CAR DOWN the block from Gordon's house, Isabelle inspected the Beretta. She pulled back the slide to make certain there was a round in the chamber. Her long delicate fingers fondled the knurled butt of the pistol, worshiping the power it gave her. There was no remorse or guilt, after all. It was her mother that had pushed it this far.

The sneer on her lips twisted into vicious arrogance, "I can hardly wait to see her face. You can't top this one, old woman." As a brutal afterthought, "Fuck you too, Gordy."

Carefully, with sadistic pleasure, she clicked off the safety to make the weapon ready. Taking a deep breath to steady her nerves, she exited the car and walked in the darkness to Gordon Marks's house. The gun dangled precariously from her gloved fingers with the dress rolled up under her arm.

Gordon's house came into view, nestled within a dozen others just like it. Deep shadows lay across the front yard, leaving the rear in a silver glow from the moon. Perfect for sneaking, but avoiding suburban gimmicks left on the lawns and sidewalks was crucial. Quick glances at the neighboring houses showed nothing but darkened windows. Down the street, a gray glow came from a large picture window, possibly a case of insomnia kept company by mindless talk shows.

INSIDE GORDON'S HOUSE the gorgeous spring day had mellowed into a warm and calm evening. Windows, left open, welcomed the cool fresh breezes into the bedroom, making the spring evening a part of the love making. The sweat coating their bodies came from their passion, with the cool air floating over them, causing tiny bumps to form on her flesh.

Amy rolled over on top of him, her lips brushing his, whispering, "There's something I want to do, come with me." Straddling his thighs, she pulled him up, putting her arms around his neck, with her tongue playing games against his lips. Caressing his body, sliding her hands over the perspiration, she got off the bed, pulling him with her.

"Amy, what are you doing?"

In the darkness of the bedroom, Gordon couldn't see the mischievous grin on her face, but he had a notion she was up to something. Amy chuckled, "Don't worry. Whatever it is, you know it will feel good. Come on," she urged, pulling him out of the bed. Like a puppy, he followed her through his house, into the kitchen, and out the back door to the patio.

Whispering hoarsely to avoid detection, "Amy, the neighbors will see us."

Still holding his hand, she tugged on him until he relented, following her to the grassy back yard. "Who cares? Don't be such a poop, Gordy, it's the middle of the night and everyone is asleep." It was time for thirty-six-year-old Amanda Freeman to throw the wrench into Gordon Marks's life. The curtain was up and the act had begun with Amy setting up another victim to pay for what happened so many years ago.

Gordy stared at her as she twirled her naked body around his yard, arms outstretched, bathed in the silver glow of moonlight. Her blonde hair, usually tied into a ponytail, was swinging freely as she danced to the tune of seduction. Finally landing at his picnic table, she hoisted herself to the top. Arms propped behind her, legs straddling the redwood stained wooden planks, she cooed, "Come on old man, are you going to turn me down?"

Spellbound, Gordy stumbled through the grass to the soft flesh waiting for him perched on top of his picnic table. His fifty-year-old body groaned as he forced it up to cradle himself between her thighs. Amy lay back pulling him with, locking her legs around him. Stretching her arms back, her breasts straining for his touch, she squeezed her legs tighter, locking him helplessly in place.

Reaching an orgasm was not Amy's goal. All she wanted was for this man to relish her, to covet her with passion and carnal lust. To make sure it was done right, it had to happen here, in the back yard. Just as it did way back then, only now, she was the one in control. She was the one who was going to hurt and punish.

The ecstatic moan and shuddering of his body was what she was waiting for, feeling a surge of power rush through her, she squeezed him harder between her thighs. He belonged to her now, knowing she could control him as long as it was fun for her. She had captured another man to add to her string of destruction and broken hearts. The stimulating part of this would be showing Isabelle how easily she had mastered the man, and just how much she would be able to hurt him when he outlived his usefulness. Triumph over her daughter's failure would be sweet indeed.

Gordon Marks, tall and muscular, except for the roll starting to form around his mid-section, was a local radio personality. Hosting a mid-day talk show, he espoused the virtues of marital fidelity, and the evils of liberal politics. His following ranged from angry Democrats and snide Republicans to worshiping housewives. Barely able to make his spousal maintenance payments to two ex-wives, and support checks to his illegitimate son, he looked for vulnerable sources of additional income. Lonely and frustrated housewives seemed to fit the bill. Amanda Freeman wasn't lonely or frustrated. She was just beautiful, and Gordy was infatuated with her.

AMANDA'S (AMY'S) PROBLEMS started when she was raped at age sixteen. She became pregnant but refused to name the father but did want to keep the child. Two years of failed counseling and lost patience from her overly religious parents, left Amy with no other option. If she wished to raise her daughter the best way she could, she would have to do so alone. On Amy's eighteenth birthday, she was told to take her two-year-old child and leave the refuge of her righteous parent's home. For two years Amy had to rely for help on homeless shelters, food stamps, and welfare. Then she met Darrel Freeman. With a degree in computer science, Darrel had a somewhat promising career doing things that nobody else knew anything about. His attraction to the blonde woman with the four-year-old daughter was immediate, though they met in the supermarket. Amy was, quite simply, gorgeous. Even just pushing a cart down the cereal isle, she took his breath away. Two weeks later, he got up the nerve to talk to her, but, surprisingly, she responded.

Amy considered Darrel a mousy nerd. Had she been in any other situation, she wouldn't have given him a moment's notice. But he was employed and had a house to live in. Those two elements were just what she needed after being forced to go on the streets to earn a living. If love was supposed to be a part of her life, she would try to find it after Darrel rescued her and Isabelle.

Just because she had a husband didn't mean Amy needed to quit playing, and her daughter learned the same game Mom played, and that was that beautiful women had power. At twenty, Isabelle used men with as much skill as she was taught, except being younger, she got the cream of the crop, and, from that, learned to expect that she was the more powerful woman. She expected it, yes, but also needed it.

Gordon Marks was one of Isabelle's leftovers. Plain and simple, once he met the pair of them, he favored the less petulant mother over her. Isabelle flew into a rage over being dumped, but gave the impression she had accepted it, leaving the man for her mother to use.

Now, when they were comfortable in the affair, Isabelle could extract her revenge. It wasn't so much that Mom had taken the man that irritated Isabelle, but that her mother and Gordy had too much fun together. Isabelle was not going to be up-staged. Much to the daughter's chagrin, Gordon Marks was on Amy's stringer, hanging helplessly over the side of the boat. A trophy waiting to be gutted.

Isabelle's access to Gordon's house was easy because it was never locked. The shadow quietly opened the front door and slid inside. Deft fingers caressed the smooth deadly steel of the weapon, letting it nestle into her hand. The house was silent and dark, but she had no doubt that Gordon and his lover—her mother—were there. Muffled noises came from someplace, and she assumed it was from the bedroom, the same bedroom that used to be *her* playground. Only now it belonged to her mother. The thought of this caused Isabelle to mutter, "You conniving bitch."

Cautiously lifting feet on the thick carpeting, she silently moved to the bedroom door. There she caught the aroma from the effects of spent love making hanging in the air. The sweat and secretions of passions expelled in the room were obnoxious to her, yet stimulating. Moonlight glowed softly on the wet, rumpled sheets and pillows strewn across the bed and onto the floor. An almost empty bottle of cheap cream sherry sat on the nightstand, but there were no glasses.

Isabelle bent over to pick up a small, delicate pair of thong panties. She held them up to the moonlight for a closer inspection. A cheap perfume wafted from them, making them as repellent as they were enticing. The closet door stood ajar, so reaching in to slip the stolen dress onto a vacant hanger was simple. Isabelle had to marvel at how smoothly her plan was falling into place. "It's just so fucking easy, and you two are just so fucking stupid." Moving to the hallway and glancing into the bathroom, it was obvious they weren't in there, though she might have assumed the two would be showering the aftermath of their passion away.

Strains of distant voices drew Isabelle's shadow through the house to the kitchen where the remnants of dinner and dirty dishes had been left. Standing at the open doorway looking into the moonlit yard, she saw them. Their two bodies were on the picnic table, with Gordon's rear end and Amy's raised legs forming a silver sculpture in the moonlight.

Through a seditious grin, she quietly castigated her mother, "My my, Mommy, that's a new twist. In the yard again, is it? Come on, bitch, get over it. Isn't it ironic, Mommy, that it was in a place like this I was conceived and where you are going to die?" For the last ten years, Isabelle's disgust at being conceived in a rape, her hatred had mounted for her mother, which had now reached the tipping point.

To Isabelle's chagrin, she remembered the shelters and the cold days wandering the streets with her mother looking for work and a place to sleep. She had always felt like a spare part that didn't fit anyplace, shunning kids' and offers of friendship. At age ten her place in life became more focused, as the attention from her stepfather showed her that if she gave men the right signals, she could get things she wanted. Watching her mother flirt with men, occasionally bringing them home, she understood that using sex was the answer to security. At age fifteen, she dated and traded men with her mother, comparing notes afterward on how foolish they could make them look. But that was all in the past.

Carefully placing one foot in front of the other, the shadow crept closer to the erotic display in the yard. The motion of the two bodies had slowed from the gyrations of Gordon's orgasm to caressing and relaxing. Her mother's legs were wrapped around his waist while she rubbed his back and smiled as he kissed her breasts.

They were wrapped in their own world. Nothing outside it mattered until Gordon felt the muzzle of the gun press against his temple. Amy, sensing Gordon's change in movement, opened her eyes, her expression of satisfaction and pleasure turning to shock at seeing Isabelle hovering over them. Gordon jerked his head up at the same time Amy screamed. The pistol exploded with the bullet mushrooming through Gordon's brain, tearing out the other side of his skull. Two more shots quickly following the first. Death was swift, but not until Gordon's instantaneous thought that it was Amy who had shot him.

In terror, Amy pushed against the dead man lying on top of her, rolling him over the side of the wooden table top. Screeching and flailing her arms and legs, she scrambled her way off the end of the table slipping on her lover's brain matter and blood, thudding on the ground next to the remnants of Gordon Marks. Pushing back to get away from the dead Gordon and the girl with the gun, Amy wildly waved her arms, still screaming.

Amused at the sight of the naked woman's animations, Isabelle calmly told her, "Oh, shut up, you little whore. The game's over, Mom. I'm going to work alone now. You've got my boyfriend, and I've got you're husband. I've got it all, and you lose."

As Isabelle raised the pistol at her cowering mother, Amy climbed to her feet scuffling backwards with her arms wrapped around her face and head. Leaning forward her legs pinching together, was the only protection she had. Her screaming had escalated to pleading, "*No, no, no, please.*"

Fire spat out the muzzle of the pistol, sending Amy to the ground with a bleeding hole in her stomach. She felt the slug slam into her abdomen and bury itself deep within her body. Before she realized she was critically wounded, the fear of what was happening was what forced her to the ground. Her voice feeble, she squealed, "Izzy, no, not this."

Though Isabelle squeezed the trigger three more times, nothing happened. The slide had locked open, and the Barretta was demanding more ammunition. This part of the game was over for Isabelle as she disconnected her mind from what she had done. Oblivious to the dead man, and her mother writhing in the grass, the gun slid from her hand to land on the ground next to the mush that used to be Gordon Marks's head.

Isabelle then turned and left the yard, leaving the gun as the defining connection to Leonid Cherasky. Back in the Volvo, she fired the car into life, and jammed the accelerator to the floor, screeching away from the house. She would abandon the car in a few blocks.

The screaming and gunshots caused every single residence surrounding Gordon's house to light up. Directly next door, Mrs. Douglas hung out the window calling to her husband, "Wally, what is it? Wally?"

Walter Douglas shouted back, "Shut up, Marsha. Call 911. Hurry."

Other neighbors joined Walter in Gordy's back yard peering at the naked bodies, careful to stay away and not destroy evidence or touch anything gory. The latest episode of CSI aired that evening, making everyone an expert.

The naked woman moaned in the damp grass, holding her hands over the blood escaping from her body, saturating her fingers. Whimpering a plea to the gathering crowd, "Please help me."

Walter Douglas knelt beside her, putting his hand on her shoulder, offering what he could, "The ambulance is on the way. You're going to be taken care of real soon." The feel of her nakedness made him uncomfortable, yet he managed to look at the flow of her flesh with a perverse level of pleasure.

The only reply she could give him was a wheezing sigh and another plea for help before she closed her eyes and became silent.

The sirens, flashing lights, and bustling officials called an end to the quiet spring evening in Gordon Marks's back yard. The usual scene was put into play with witnesses questioned and the forensics squad bending over Gordon's body. It looked like a double homicide at first until a detective looked up from Amy, calling out, "Detective Bruntz, this one is alive."

Detective Harold Bruntz, leaning against the fence gate, had been watching the efficient confusion under the floodlights that had been set up. Not quite reaching five-foot-seven in height, his massive girth strained the strength of the cedar-wood fence post. His huge hand came up and pointed to the EMT crew waiting at the edge of the yard. A voice that rattled deep in his throat commanded them, "Get that one and wrap her up. I want to see if she can talk before you take her."

Running in with their stretcher and bags of gadgets and medicine, they took about a full minute to get the IVs plugged into her, and made ready to slide her into the ambulance. Her dignity restored by a sheet, Bruntz bent over Amy, asking, "Ma'am, do you know who did this?"

Amy's head slowly rolled from side to side, her lips mouthing a silent, "No."

Detective Bruntz lifted the sheet to scan her from breasts to the wound in her abdomen, noticing she was clean-shaven under the smear of blood. He asked the EMT, "Is there an exit wound?"

The young man in a hurry to get the patient to the ER, quickly said, "No, she still has the slug."

Nodding and waving the EMT off, Bruntz went back to the crime scene. The detective gave his partner an obvious order, "Keep forensics here all night. Be sure all the evidence is bagged. Meet me here tomorrow morning."

His partner, Jim Haggard, would have appreciated some help from Bruntz. In a frustrated, antagonistic slur, Jim blurted, "You wouldn't want to stay and help a little bit would you?"

Growling, Harold answered, "You don't need me. I got something else to do. See you tomorrow."

Detective Haggard knew all too well what Bruntz's agenda was. Disgusted with his partner's attitude, Haggard was, in truth, relieved to see the senior detective leave the scene, which of course put him in charge.

Detective Bruntz waddled off to his rusty Plymouth. The driver's door creaking open, and the springs groaned as he sat down. In truth, he was hiding from the frenzy in Gordon's house. At one time, Harold would have been at the center of the show, directing traffic, assigning tasks and comfortable as the ring master. Things were different now, and he was smart enough to stay out of the way while younger, more aggressive detectives did the grunt work.

Staring out the windshield at the commotion, he wondered how many times he'd seen people's lives shattered by foolish acts that could have been avoided. How many stories had he been compelled to listen to about monstrous dealings of infidelity, lying and stealing. Harold Bruntz just could not understand how the human race got so fucked up.

Shaking his head, he knew he couldn't hide from it. Lighting his cigar and downing the last of the half pint, he understood completely that he was one of the vilest offenders of human vices. The only difference now was that he could sit back and watch others do it.

Harold Bruntz had something more important than Gordon Marks's murder to take care of. He ran the story through his head again, just like Flo gave it to him, yesterday. "*He wouldn't pay me, Hal. Then he beat the crap out of me.*" He cranked the Plymouth to life and drove off to find his target, a two-bit hood with the street name of Jimmy Jeepers. Harold's closest and only true friend, Florence Widholm, had granted Jeepers a satisfying sample of her profession, and he stiffed her. In Harold's book, that was not a good thing to do. Worse, the punk had hit her, bringing Bruntz's temper to a boil. In Harold's book, nobody hit a woman. Especially his woman.

In the blighted area near Chicago Avenue and Thirty-Eighth Street in the bowels of Minneapolis, he parked in the shadows behind the old red-brick apartment building. Clenching the soaked cigar between his teeth, he entered the rear, quietly moving to the dark corridor in the basement. At Jimmy's door, he paused for a moment, listening for sounds inside. Assured that James J. Piper was asleep, Harold put his shoulder to the door and forced it open. There was only one room in the apartment, with the metal framed bed in the center.

A whore sat up with a start, the remnants of Jimmy's elation clinging to her chin, and screamed. Harold knew her on the street as Pammie and didn't want her running around with this tale wagging from her mouth. In a swift movement that belied his bulk and plodding demeanor, Harold grabbed a fistful of hair at the back of her head, and pulled her face close to his. With a growl that emanated from deep within his huge body, "You keep your mouth shut, and I'll let you live."

The fear in her eyes was all Harold needed. As soon as he released her, she gabbed her clothes and raced naked into the hallway to a much safer place.

Jimmy Jeepers, also naked, came bounding off the bed on the attack, but came to a dead stop when Harold's fist buried itself into his gut. "Ooooh, Jesus," he groaned, doubling over, sinking onto the mattress.

Grabbing Jeepers by the cheek, Harold snarled at him, "You stiffed Flo for ten bucks."

Frantically pleading, Jimmy yelped, "Ow, let go, man. That hurts." Jimmy's efforts to wrench loose from Harold's grip only resulted in tearing his cheek. Reeling back, Jimmy grabbed his face, shrieking, "Oh, shit, man. I'm bleeding."

Calm and in control, Harold ordered, "Get me Flo's money."

"Oh, God, you bastard. Yeah, sure, here." Jimmy Jeepers fumbled with his wallet, pulling out a twenty, his shaking hand holding it out.

"That's not enough." Under protest, Harold recovered two-hundred-twenty dollars. As jimmy was straining to hold his dismembered face together, Harold's fist came crashing into it. Jimmy went tumbling back, bouncing off the metal head board to collapse on the filthy mattress. Looking over the mess that had been carnal passion just moments ago, Harold left Jimmy Jeepers with a firm message, "If I have to come back, you're dead, prick."

Back in the Plymouth, Harold found another half pint of Old Mister Boston under the seat, and drove home, the vision of Amanda Freeman's naked body at the crime scene planted in his mind.

LEAVING THE ABANDONED VOLVO for the police to find, Isabelle waited for her boyfriend to pick her up. Sliding in beside him, she leaned over to give him a thank-you kiss. Stripping out of the jumpsuit, he had a change of clothing waiting for her.

Richard Olson was as much of a puppet as the rest of Isabelle's prisoners. He would crawl through snake shit and eat ground glass if she asked him to, but he was not stupid. He knew what things were right and what were wrong, and this thing they were doing had a bad smell to it. Curiosity pounded for attention in his head, forcing him to nervously ask, "What are we doing, Izzy? What just happened?" His objections to her escapades were lost in her cooing for his servitude.

She shut off his prying by running her hand over his leg, followed with, "Nothing, honey. We're just playing a trick on someone. Take me up to Brainerd to get my car, and I'll spend the night with you." Slouching down in the seat, her feet up on the dashboard, she smiled at the righteous thing she had just done. Running her hands over the silken tanned softness of her legs, braced up in front of her, the only justification she needed raced through her mind, "*Now, I'm the most beautiful one. Nobody will ever want her more than me.*" Isabelle thought she had just murdered her mother. She had administered the ultimate revenge with no way for Mom to show her she was better.

During the long silent trip to Brainerd, her mind took her to her stepfather and the life the two of them could share now. She had been told of the prize that awaited them, and she had no intention of sharing it. When she finishes with him, he could join the scrap heap with the rest of them, along with the small life now growing in her body.

Oblivious to the terrible thing she had just done, she turned to her boyfriend and asked him a question he didn't dare answer. "Dickey, you don't mind doing these things for me, do you? If you love me more than anybody, you don't."

CHAPTER 2
THE CLOWN

Detective Harold Bruntz had been a cop for over thirty years. Much to the disappointment of his colleagues, he avoided retirement because there was nothing else he knew, nothing else he desired to do. Unless he got fired, there was no way to get rid of him, and with thirty years of tenure, that was unlikely.

If Bruntz gave up eating for a few weeks he could tip the scale at about 285 pounds. His five-foot-seven height accented by his weight made him look like a clown. His belly stuck out farther than his bulbous, blue-veined, red nose, which also accentuated his pock-marked face. A thinning mop of unruly hair sat on top of his head and hadn't seen a comb or a squirt of soap since the barber refused to cut it unless he washed it first. Cheap cigars, cheap whiskey, and a cheap woman were the only accessories in his life. He reeked of every foul smell that came out of his two-room apartment.

Harold Bruntz held the dubious record of having more partners than anyone in the history of Minnesota law enforcement. Each newly assigned partner would devise imaginative schemes to get themselves transferred as quickly as possible. The justification to management was the obnoxious odors rolling off him. In spite of the objections from Harold's counterparts, the real reason to separate themselves from him was the way he ran his investigations. His co-workers could never understand why this detachment from humanity was kept employed at the city's expense, until they worked on a ball busting case with him. However, in reality, it was his unorthodox and blundering methods of solving crimes that turned partners off. Harold Bruntz would bull his way through a problem using any method that was handy at the time—strong-arm, verbal intimidation, or just plain planting false evidence. If Harold had a suspect in his sights, it was kiss-your-ass-goodbye time. The truth was important to him; he just didn't spend a lot of time looking for it.

His methods were unorthodox, unrefined and, quite often, illegal. It came to be known that Harold had one speed, but he was reluctant to use it. Frustrated chiefs, mayors, and commissioners had removed him from just about every case he'd been involved in, only to beg him to return and finish the work where others had failed.

He was a pariah to everyone except his cheap woman.

Florence Widholm was a prostitute living in the same building as Harold. Once a high-class call girl getting up to one thousand dollars a night, she had succumbed to age, now specializing in ten-dollar acts of fellatio. She could have earned more if she'd stop using an abundance of make up and black eye shadow, but that was her niche, and she was comfortable.

No matter how old Flo got, she would always be a beautiful woman. A wild tangle of naturally black hair surrounded a sensuous face that spelled out her message. Her visage had followed the sagging breasts and underarms, but she held a regal dignity that would compel a man to use her. However, the men she usually came in contact with were the ones who couldn't afford intercourse with a younger woman.

Occasionally, if Flo was short on rent money she'd give Harold a freebie to pay it for her. The rent came to more than Flo's price, but Harold considered it his charitable act.

Five nights a week, Harold would eat cold canned beef stew or hash, saving the sixth meal for a pizza with Flo. The seventh meal didn't count because he was too drunk to remember to eat. Tonight would be his seventh meal night. Last night was a seventh meal night also, but who was counting?

June 12, 9:00.a.m.

Waking up the next morning, Harold wasn't surprised to find himself still in the upholstered chair he had been in last night. His pants were around his ankles, with his boxers resting on top of them.

Considering the filth and stains embedded in them as good enough for another day, he pulled the underwear and trousers into place. Stepping over Flo's snoring, naked body sagging on the floor, he stumbled into the area known as the kitchen to swish the scum from his mouth with a full swig of raw cheap whiskey. No point to waste any, he swallowed, grimacing until the burn left his throat.

Flo's underpants were on the floor next to her aged and misshapen body. With a great deal of effort he knelt down and put Jimmy Jeepers money into the folds of cotton before stepping into the sunshine of another day, and the business of another case.

Stopping at a gas station for a bag of doughnuts and a cup of coffee, he was ready to start working, if he could only remember where he was supposed to go and what the case was all about. His cheeks puffing out from an overfill of doughnut, he recalled the young woman with the shaved pubic region, and went to work.

Bouncing off the curb in front of Gordon Marks house, he almost ran over an officer keeping guard on the scene. The officer took note of the doughnut crumbs resting in Harold's glasses, hanging by a cord around his neck, and the fresh coffee stain on his wrinkled shirt. Smirking at the notorious clown, the officer acknowledged Harold by giving him the extension of his middle finger and a snide greeting, "Good morning, Detective Bruntz."

Harold responded by muttering, "Yeah, and fuck you too," and forced his bulging body under the yellow perimeter tape.

Meeting Jim Haggard in the living room, he expected a run down on what forensics had discovered. However, Detective Haggard could only offer speculation, telling Harold the basics. "The dead guy is Gordon Marks. He's the blow-hard on the radio always screaming at people. The radio station wants all the details so they can run some kind of special on him."

Harold burped, then asked, "What about the woman?"

Recoiling from Harold's breath, the detective told him, "Her name is Amanda Freeman. I can only assume she was his pincushion and her husband didn't like it. He's one of those computer guys, and I thought you'd like to go roust him out a little bit. It's obvious he caught them, and *bam*, to the moon, Alice."

Looking around the sparsely furnished room, Harold asked, "What else did you find?"

With an incredulous shrug of his shoulders, Detective Haggard said, "There was nothing else. This guy lived on love and used the house as his diving board. The place was spotless."

The collection of evidence contained the perfumed panties, the gun, four spent shell casings and the almost empty bottle of wine. Shuffling through the bed-room, Harold asked, "Did they scan the sheets for semen?"

Upset at the absurdity of the request, Detective Haggard answered, "Why? We know they were in here."

Without looking at his partner, he said, "When you get the full scan of the sheets, plus any that are in the laundry, bag them. Check for prints and DNA on the wine bottle."

With that done, Harold waddled into the back yard. On his hands and knees, Detective Bruntz circled the picnic table like a dog looking for a place to pee. Hoisting his frame upright, with a great deal of difficulty, Bruntz pointed to the turf, telling his partner, "That looks like a shoe print in the grass. They were both barefoot and this is smaller than the trampling done by our guys. Get a picture of it and make a plaster cast." Gazing over the mess on the top of the picnic table, Harold instructed, "Get a swab of the semen spots and the guy's brains. Make a map of the table to ID where the samples came from."

Looking towards the spot where Amanda Freeman had been shot, he guessed the killer never went over that far, so he turned away from it, saying, "Get the lab on that stuff. Check the casings and weapon for prints. I'm going to the hospital."

Leaving his partner standing dumbly in Gordon's back yard, Harold went back into the house. Detouring back to the bed room, he thumbed through drawers and checked the closet. About to leave, his eye caught on a dress hanging in the closet. Detective Haggard followed to see what was getting so much attention.

Harold mumbled, "Hmm, I don't think the dead guy could fit in this, and its way too expensive for Mrs. Freeman. Bag this also." He gave the Armani tag a quick check, noticing a dark strand of hair attached to the shoulder. "Look here, there's a hair to be taken."

Bending closer, then repelling at some foul odor wafting from Harold, Jim Haggard gasped, "Where, what hair?"

Holding the garment up to the light, irritated, Bruntz admonished, "There, try looking a little bit. Unless the guy was a transvestite, there's someone else connected now. Put a tape on this place and keep a guard here. There's more shit lying around we need to find. Get to the lab and meet me back here tonight. I'll be at the hospital."

In the living room, Harold got back on his hands and knees, peering at the carpeting. His partner behind him said, "I thought you were leaving. Now what?"

"The killer could have left a foot print in the carpet we might have compared to the one in the yard. Too late. Nothing in here now but the shit we dragged in."

Propping his glasses on the end of his nose, Harold peered closely at the carpet where he was kneeling. Snapping his fingers over his head, he commanded, "Give me some scissors." Impatiently snapping again, "Now, for Christ sake."

Taking a pair of tiny cutters from the forensics kit, Haggard added his annoyance, "Here. Jesus, man. Give me time to move."

Struggling to get upright again, he handed Haggard a carpet fiber pinched in the jaws of a tweezers, grunting, "Looks like blood, get DNA on it."

The flabbergasted partner mumbled, "How do you find shit that nobody else can see?" He squeezed open a tiny manila envelope to accept the blood sample left from the shoes of the careless Isabelle.

Harold's disgust came out as a grin. He added, "Check the dishes and crap in the kitchen to see if a third person was eating here."

Grumbling at the complacent attitude of the younger detectives and officers, Harold felt he was going to be working this case by himself. Admonishing his partner, Harold told him, "Somebody was murdered here, Jim. Have enough respect for the guy to be sure all the evidence is found before we come along and fuck up the crime scene."

Detective James Haggard held utter contempt for his partner, seriously objecting to whatever directions Harold gave him. Jim understood that these clues should have been covered as a matter of routine, but working with Harold Bruntz forced him to work with animosity and below a normal level of competence. The seasoned master of the detective squad did nothing else but make Jim Haggard look bad. Lashing back, Jim said, "If you'd stick around to help we'd . . ." He realized that his words went nowhere as Bruntz was walking away, ignoring him.

Outside, Harold tore the parking ticket off his car, throwing it at the smirking policeman on guard, telling him, "Prick." He got into his Plymouth Reliant, ground it into life and drove ahead of the smoke billowing from the tail pipe. About ten feet later, he quickly pulled over to the curb and let it diesel itself into silence.

The cop on guard at Gordon's house called out, "Hey, Bruntz, you get lost already?"

Ignoring the chiding, Harold pointed down the street, telling him, "Try being a cop instead of a comedian, smart-ass. The killer had to leave somehow, so walk about two blocks to see if there's any obvious sign of a car taking off. Probably skid marks."

With that in place, Harold walked the gutter in the opposite direction. Finding nothing, he went back to his car to see the policeman trotting towards him, yelling, "Hey, Bruntz, there are some skid marks up there." He turned and pointed to where he came from.

Bruntz said, "Good, set some markers out and tell Haggard to get pictures of them. Nice work."

As he struggled to get back into his Plymouth, the policeman called after him, "Sorry about the ticket."

Taking a used cigar from the dashboard, he muttered, "Yeah, sure." Soon, the interior of the Plymouth was engulfed in smoke.

PARKING IN A DOCTORS ONLY SPOT, Harold plowed his way through the main entrance, cigar smoke circling wildly around his head. A woman in a power suit ran up, excitedly telling him, "You can't smoke in here."

"Huh? Oh, yeah, sorry." He took it from his mouth, a trail of saliva following it to the woman's hand. He said, "Thanks," leaving her with a disgusted sneer on her face and a wet cigar in her hand.

After checking registration, he made his way to the second floor where he was pleased to see a guard at the door. He told him, "Don't let anyone in until I'm done."

Dragging the foul odor of the cigar with him, he entered and let the door close behind him. There was a man sitting next to the bed holding the victim's hand. "Are you Mr. Freeman?"

Standing, "Yes, I am." Darrel Freeman was unusually ordinary. His dumpy body was a shade under six feet. He had a receding hairline and a face that could be forgotten easily, a definite mismatch to the beautiful woman lying in the bed.

He had a confused wrinkle to his forehead and was about to ask a question, when Bruntz told him, "Come with me," and Harold escorted him to the hallway and the guard.

"Keep this man here until I come out. I want to question him after I talk to his wife."

Inside, he took Mr. Freeman's chair and sat close to the victim. She had tubes and wires running into her body, and held a gray vacant look to her face. Blinking slowly, she appeared to be staring into space. In spite of the drawn, sick appearance of the woman, she struck Harold as being an extremely beautiful person. Before speaking, he stared at her, captivated and thinking back to seeing her naked body under the EMT sheet, disregarding the blood.

"I'm Detective Bruntz. I'm here to find out what happened last night. Are you up to talking?"

Turning her face to Harold, she slowly said, "I told some people already." Her attempt to give him a *go away* look fell short.

Using an unnecessary brusqueness to hide his attraction to her, he bluntly let her know what the rules were, "Well, that doesn't count. I'm the one who's going to put the story together, and I'm the one you're going to talk to. First, let me tell you, I don't want to have to wade through lies and bullshit to get the truth. If you lie to me I'm going to start looking at you as an accomplice. Do you understand?"

Taken back by the detective's abruptness, Amy knit a wrinkle into her forehead and said, "Yes, I have nothing to hide. I'm the one who got shot."

Detective Bruntz took out his note book, but avoided using a pen. It was just a gimmick to give the suspect something to focus on. "How long have you and Mr. Marks been having the affair?"

Turning her face away, she said, "I don't want to talk about that. My husband is right outside."

"Mrs. Freeman, if I wanted to I could have him in here while I ask you these questions. I put him outside so you could answer me candidly. If you don't cooperate, I'm going to put you in handcuffs and arrest you as an accomplice."

She flashed a worried look. "All right. I'll tell you all I can."

Waving his hand in front of her, he anxiously said, "Answer my question then. How long?"

Sullenly, the words almost a whisper, "It really wasn't an affair. We've only done it a few times."

"A few times in how long a time span?"

Her response was weak and far from convincing, "About six months."

Physically, Amanda Freeman was a strong woman. When it came to flirting and manipulation, she was clever and devious. However, confronted by a police officer, she had no resistance. Wilting under the interrogation, she reconsidered her answer. Correcting her statement, she mournfully added, "We've been doing it regularly for six months."

With total lack of diplomacy, one of the reasons Harold was so unpopular, he blatantly asked, "Your pubic area is clean shaven. Are you promiscuous? Do you screw a lot of men?"

Startled, the woman strained to sit up, wincing with the strain on her wound. Objecting with a great amount of indignation, "I beg your pardon. That's no business of—"

He gruffly cut her off, "Everything about you and what you do is my business, Mrs. Freeman. You were involved in a murder. If you want me to believe you're innocent of any participation, you'll answer all of my questions." He paused to let that sink in, then firmly repeated, "Do you screw a lot of men?"

Falling back to the pillow, tears rolling down her cheeks with her arm over her face to hide the shame, she gave in to his intimidation and quietly answered, "Yes."

"I want their names."

Protesting, she pleaded with a sobbing, "I can't do that. Most of them are married. This is going to ruin my own marriage."

Gently putting his hand on her arm, he softly said, "Mrs. Freeman, you ruined your own marriage the first time you cheated on your husband. The men you've slept with are all suspects, and I need their names." Amy's flesh was warm and soft under his touch and he wanted to feel more of her, but pulled away before she became alarmed.

It took her awhile through the sniveling, and this time he used a pen to record the names she reluctantly gave him. At eight, he felt compassion for her, saying, "That's enough, I can deal with this." He knew that in reality he would probably never bother with the list of names. A routine he considered boring and mundane.

He looked at her again, asking, "Mrs. Freeman, do you have any idea who pulled the trigger? Did you see anything that might identify them?"

The time it took for her to answer him put enough suspicion into his mind to think this case was not just a simple shooting. Rolling her head back and forth, she said, "No. It was too dark." A moment later, she moved to face him, compulsively blurting out, "They spoke to me. I was yelling and they called me a whore and told me to be quiet." After she said it, she wished she hadn't. The emotional pain of Isabelle trying to kill her leaked to the surface and hurt more than the bullet wound in her stomach.

At last, a good connection to a real person, he asked, "Was it a man or woman?"

Amy looked out the window, her fingers over her lips, her voice trailing, "It was dark. I couldn't tell you. I don't know."

There was a vacancy to her answer that disturbed him. He could sense a hole where more was hidden that she didn't want to talk about. He knew the next question was not necessary, but he asked it anyway to satisfy a carnal craving of his own, "Amanda, have you ever received money for having sex with any of these men?"

Her forehead wrinkled with her eyebrows squeezing a burning glare from her watering eyes, she adamantly cried out, "For Gods sake, no."

"Well, the shooter called you a whore. It could be someone connected to that. A pimp or a jealous competitor."

Her mind writhing in shame, Mrs. Freeman wailed, "Please, *no*. I'm not . . ." Whimpering the rest of her plea, "I'm not a whore. Oh, God, leave me alone." She turned her face away, openly sobbing.

With over thirty years experience interviewing suspects, Harold had a reasonable understanding of human nature. Looking at the response from her, he had to believe what she said. "Okay, we'll leave that alone, for now."

As a last thought, he asked, "One more thing . . . was there anyone else with the two of you? Did anybody eat dinner with you, or join as a third party in the sex?"

Crushed by the implication, she weakly wailed, "No. Please go away."

Getting up, he answered, "Just asking," convinced she was truthful again.

Leaving the woman in tears, he turned to compassionately offer, "Mrs. Freeman, I think you and your husband should find a counselor or somebody. Save what you've got. This may just make the two of you closer."

In the hallway, he led a nervous Darrel Freeman to a waiting room. Inside, he said, "Mr. Freeman, sit down."

With the table between them, Harold plunged into the inquisition. "How long have you known about your wife's indiscretions?"

Darrel's face drained of color, and wringing his hands, he answered, "I wasn't aware of her doing this. She said it was just a mistake and it was only this once. She told me he smooth-talked her and got her drunk, almost raping her."

Adjusting to the gap in their stories, Bruntz asked, "When was the first time you discovered your wife was cheating on you?" Bruntz thought there was more to this story than he was being told, with his gut feeling telling him things were going to get very deep before any light came on.

Darrel answered with an overly convincing self-righteousness. "Just late last night when the hospital called me. They said she had been shot. Have there been more times?"

Averting the question, Harold asked, "Do you own a gun?"

"No, I don't like guns. I shot a .22 when I was a boy, but it frightened me. I haven't touched a gun since."

Bruntz asked, "You were at home when you got the call?"

"Yes. I was asleep on the sofa waiting for Amy to come home."

Harold considered his next question but asked it anyway. "You're kind of a nerdy guy, and your wife is a babe. Wouldn't that lead to trouble between the two of you?"

Offended, Darrel said, "Trouble? I don't . . ."

"Mr. Freeman, your wife was shot fucking another man. You'd have to be an idiot to not see that as a problem. Did you shoot them?"

Alarmed, Darrel blared, "Good God, no."

Harold, standing up, ordered the rising Darrel, "No, you sit there. I'll be back."

The guard at Amanda's door, anxious to break the boredom of routine, asked Harold, "What do you think, Bruntz?"

"They're both hiding something. For just being shot, the wife seems bothered by another problem." Nodding his head towards the waiting room, "He keeps staring at his hands. He's evasive. Make sure nobody goes in there and don't let him out for anything. If he has to pee, get a nurse to give him a cup. If he has to shit, tell him to squat in the corner."

Moving to a window at the end of the hallway to get a cell phone signal, Bruntz called the desk sergeant, "Have someone get down here quick to check Mr. Freeman for gun shot residue." Slipping the phone into his pocket, Harold glanced at the door to Mrs. Freeman's room. It wasn't just the naked body that bothered him; it was her, the woman. Her face, the voice, the eyes or the blonde— it didn't matter. He had to suppress a curious sensation running through his head and gut. He didn't want it to happen, but the attraction was there anyway.

He understood the distance between them, him being a mule and she was a racehorse. He was a cop and she was a suspect. She was beautiful and he wasn't. Two creatures that could never fit, yet she had crawled into his mind worming her way to depths deep enough to avoid being pulled out.

CHAPTER 3
DO-SI-DO, Y'ALL CHANGE PARTNERS

DARREL FREEMAN WAS CLEAN of gun shot residue, but was kept on the list of possible suspects. According to Harold's logic, "Anyone with a bar of soap can beat a GSR test."

Back at the station house, Harold made a file of all the information he had up to this point. A list of items sent to the lab was put in the folder, with a space to write in what was discovered by the scientists.

Attempting to read Harold Bruntz and understand his unkempt demeanor, one tended to see total chaos. However, in his own inimitable way, he was methodical about putting details together. It wasn't something he could share with anyone as it still looked like chaos. But, most of the time he was in control. Now was not one of those times. A gnawing anxiety crept across his mind, hinting that there was something else he was supposed to do, but he couldn't zero in on it. Mrs. Freeman's shaved pubic area came back to him, but that had nothing to do with anything, other than his own fantasy.

Standing up, thinking he was ready to go home, his name was bellowed across the squad room, "Bruntz, get in here." The glass door to Lieutenant Warner's office rattled shut as an exclamation to the command. Snickers and guffaws floated through the dusty space of the squad room from cops glad they weren't the ones being summoned.

The file labeled *Gordon Marks* was brushed off his desk when he turned to respond, causing him to step on the sheets of paper strewn across the floor. Turning to the lieutenant's door, he answered, "Yeah, be right there." On his hands and knees, recovering the pages, Harold quietly mumbled, "Prick."

A solitary, carefully concealed voice rang out, "Hey Bruntz, Mama's calling."

Pulling himself upright, he flashed his middle digit to his cohorts.

Holding the manila folder, his shoe print emblazoned on the side, he stepped into the office of Lieutenant Robert Warner. Warner's boss, Captain Faye Hilksman, was sitting behind Bob's desk, a glass of whiskey in her hand. Dressed in a wrinkled dark blue suit, her short bobbed hair was designed to make her appear like a woman, yet close enough to be seen as a good old boy. The hardened lines etched into her face came from too many years of street fighting in the name of justice. If asked, she could display biceps with enough bulges to win a modicum of respect. The flab hanging from her waist and chin was fallout attributed to liquor, and the last half of her career behind a desk.

Harold, standing alone in front of his superiors felt like he was waiting for someone to tie a blindfold over his eyes. Next would come, "Ready, aim . . ." With his shirt tail hanging out, his fly half open and his grease splattered tie loosely knotted around his sagging neck, Harold Bruntz could hardly give a rats dump what anyone thought of his appearance. He looked for a place to sit down, but there was none, and he was not going to be offered one. Standing in front of the firing squad, he sniffled and unenthusiastically said, "Captain Hilksman, nice to see you." Looking at Lieutenant Warner, he added, "You called?"

Staring in bewilderment, the Captain took a gulp of whiskey, and asked, "Jesus Christ, Bruntz, you look like shit. Did you have a hard day?" Her voice was hard enough to drive a nail into concrete, and her soured lips were ready to pull it out again.

Understanding that he was about to get keelhauled, he mumbled, "No, just working." He held up the *Marks* file, saying, "Putting it all together."

Lieutenant Warner interrupted the captain's obvious stream of insults to inquire about the case. In a softer tone, he asked, "What have you got so far, Hal?" Bob Warner tolerated Harold Bruntz and his lack of self respect because he knew that at the end of a grinding case, the disheveled man would bring it to a closure. Unfortunately, Harold Bruntz was just too easy to make fun of.

Bruntz opened the file to display the papers inside to prove that he indeed did have something to show them, including his footprint. "Here's all the stuff in the lab, a list of suspects, and my interviews with the Freeman's."

The captain stood up, a dour sneer contorting her mouth, spouted, "I thought Mr. Freeman was the prime suspect. You've got him locked up don't you?" The whiskey had worked its way to her brain, slurring her words.

Harold eyed the half empty bottle, licking his lips, "No, he's out. Probably home now. His wife will be getting released from the hospital some time soon, and they've got a few issues to work out."

Leaning forward, she snarled, "*OUT?* The man shot his wife's lover, you moron. Arrest the bastard and close the case. That radio station is raking us through the coals for not acting sooner." Unwilling to contain her contempt, she added, "And stay away from the photographers. If they see your messy ass they'll really have something to crow about."

Bob Warner interrupted, "Faye, ease up, hear him out." Turning to Harold for an answer, the lieutenant urged him to satisfy the captain. "What's your feeling about this, Hal?"

Harold shrugged his shoulders, telling them both, "We can't prove he did it, yet."

That was not nearly enough to stem the fury coming from the captain. "Bruntz, we need someone in jail. He did it, trust me."

Standing firm, Harold said, "He was clean on the GSR test, and talking to him he didn't know what his wife was doing. He does now." Looking straight at the Captain, he plowed into her with strong logic that he was so good at. "Unless you were there to see it happen, you can't yell guilty. Wait until the lab gets some answers. There's some evidence and foreign blood residue we need to identify. Falsely arresting someone and then have them walk is going to make you all look as stupid as you think I look."

The reality of the candid comment hit home, sending Captain Hilksman back into the chair. The only logical thing she could think of was to mutter, "Get the fuck out of here."

As the glass door rattled shut, Captain Hilksman looked up at Lieutenant Warner, hissing, "How long is it going to take to get that bum out of here. I want him fired."

Pleading for common sense, he answered, "Be reasonable, Faye. His record is the best in the precinct. He solves cases; that's what he's supposed to do."

"He's a fucking pig. I promoted Jim Haggard to take his place." With a wry smile, she added, "And, he's got an awesome butt. With an ass like Jim Haggard has, this office will look good again."

Irritated at the ludicrous comments, Warner barked, "Well, if you like Haggards ass, go grab the damn thing. But, Bruntz can't just be fired. We'd have the union crawling all over us." After a leering pause, Warner added, "And he's damn good at what he does."

The captain's next comment came as a whiskey slur, "I don't give a shit. Let the son-of-a-bitch clean the bathrooms. Just get rid of him."

With that rebuff behind him, Harold casually went home, completely forgetting that he was to meet his partner, Jim Haggard, at the crime scene.

SHUFFLING AROUND IN HIS KITCHEN, he took a half-empty can of beef stew out of the refrigerator, dropping a lump of meat on the floor for the cat to savor. The rest he ate cold out of the can. Planting himself in the large, thread-bare stuffed chair, he sat silently staring at the dead gray screen of the TV set. The broken rabbit ears offset the scene, with his mind wandering to the Freeman family. At this particular moment, he was more concerned about the fidelity issues between them than he was of the murder of Gordon Marks. His thoughts were brought to the unpleasant memory of his ex-wife, Gladys, and the clean, clear vision he kept of her walking out of his life forever. The greasy stained wallpaper and threadbare carpeting that surrounded him were as compelling as the silence that pounded into his mind. His head slumped with a small drop of moisture oozing from the corner of his eye. The mangy, large gray cat, jumped onto his lap demanding to be scratched.

June 13, 9:00 a.m.

WAKING UP THE NEXT MORNING, it was easy for Harold to get ready for work, as he walked out of his apartment wearing the clothing he never took off last night. The only thing different, was a few more wrinkles, a new assortment of cat hair, and a stronger odor from the crevices of his body. He knew he had two different colored socks on, but it just wasn't very important.

Checking at the hospital, he found out Mrs. Freeman had been sent home with her husband. Moving his Plymouth Reliant into traffic, he headed for their home in the suburbs.

THE SUBURBAN TWO-STORY was quiet on the outside, but filled with tension inside. Amanda Freeman, laced with a painkiller, did the best she could to have a conversation with her daughter, cautiously aware of Isabelle's fragile mental instability, especially when it came to men. "Izzy, what were you thinking? You could have killed me, sweetheart, and now the police are asking questions. Do you have any idea how serious this is?"

Totally ignoring the gravity of murdering Gordon Marks, Isabelle sat on the arm of the sofa running her fingers through her mother's hair. "What are you worried about? You didn't die, and he was a worthless prick. You should be happy he's dead. I am."

"Izzy, you shot me, and Gordon is dead." Deathly afraid of exploring her daughter's motivation, Amy asked, "Did you want me to die? You should really get back into treatment. What you did was not right."

Isabelle's mindset held her above reproach. She considered herself just too far removed to worry about a simple thing like murder, and was resentful of the implication that there was anything unbalanced in her mental capacity. Clenching a shock of her mother's hair, she angrily spouted, "Well, screw you and the treatment idea. The therapist is a stupid pervert. As for Gordon, Mom, he's dead, forget it. Besides, I thought you liked playing the game with a little danger in it. Don't you think that killing these assholes is the ultimate challenge?" Isabelle's patent pout formed into a sinister sneer, twisting her mother's head to the side to establish her point.

Astonished, and sick to think that she would take the game to this level, Amy tried to reason with her. "Isabelle, stop and think about what you did. If—" She wasn't given a chance to finish. The doorbell shattered the conversation.

Isabelle quickly moved to the door to escape her mother's rhetoric.

In response to Harold pushing the button, the Freeman front door opened, exposing the breath-taking vision of a tanned young woman. Staring at Harold for a long moment, the young woman's lips parted with the question floating out, "Yeah?"

Dumbfounded, the detectives eyes ranged over the woman, assessing, appraising. The tank top strained across her breasts, and Harold was mesmerized by the illusion that they actually pointed up. The ragged bottom edge of the brief top had been cut strategically to give a fleeting glimpse of the bottom of those breasts. His ogling lowered to the bare mid-section flaunting her navel and several inches of bare flesh beneath it. From there, the cruise took in the short cotton cut-offs exposing the bottoms of her buttocks. From her long flowing blonde hair, down her legs to her bare feet, she had, *Look at me, I'm a babe,* written over every inch of her body. The assembly of soft curves shifted her weight so her legs were slightly separated.

As far as Harold could see, there were no panty lines, and definitely no bra straps. As she moved her arms, he could see the well-toned muscles under her flawless skin. Her abdomen rippled, pulling away from the waistband of her shorts. Harold was tempted to reach out and stick his hand into that gap of clothing.

She spoke again. "If you're a Jehovah's Witness, go away." Her voice had a soft spoiled-brat tone that Harold could imagine smelled like baby powder.

Willing his tongue to soften up enough to allow him to speak, Harold said, "No, I'm not." He fumbled with his badge, dropping it on the stoop. He bent over and picked it up, coming up with it, his gaze followed the flow of flesh from the floor to her deep-blue eyes. Holding it up for display, he said, "I'm Detective Bruntz. I came to see Mrs. Freeman."

Giving him an opportunity to appreciate her a moment longer, she turned, yelling, "Mom, some fat cop here to see you." He had grown accustomed to insults, but this one burned a bit deeper.

Darrel Freeman came to the door, "Detective Bruntz. What do you want? Amy is resting."

Harold could have left then because there was really nothing more he had to ask that would clear up anything. He just wanted to ogle Amanda Freeman some more, and now, with the young girl standing so close, he needed to satisfy his lust. "I'd appreciate just a few minutes, Mr. Freeman. You know, clean up some details."

With the fleshy girl floating behind, Darrel led him into a modestly furnished living room. The morning news was on the TV set, with a video of Gordon Marks's house airing. A reporter was holding a microphone to her mouth trying to get the police sentry to give her some ground-breaking news flash. Instead, she got a surly, "Go on, get out of here."

Darrel reached out with the remote, shutting it off. The sudden silence became uncomfortable and very obvious.

Darrel broke the stillness, saying, "It's all over the news. I hope no reporters come here."

Harold smiled, adding, "Yeah, they're all vultures." With a slight chuckle, he said, "The governor called them jackals. You might as well get ready for them." He glanced at the blonde girl, wishing she would get naked, and got a blank stare in return. She had placed herself on the arm of the sofa next to Mrs. Freeman. Her bare legs were straddling the arm, with Harold imagining her doing that to him.

Amanda was propped up, covered with a blanket, holding a cup of coffee. She looked surprised enough to see him to almost spill her cup. Catching herself staring, she said, "Detective Burns, I didn't expect to see you. What is it?"

He corrected her, "Bruntz. The name is Bruntz." He handed her the official police business card with his name, phone number, and precinct location. She gave it a cursory once-over before discarding it on the end table. "I just had a few more things to cover. Would you mind?"

Not wishing to go into detail in front of her husband, she decided she had better cooperate, hoping this man had enough decency to guard the information she gave him concerning her actions. "I suppose. Would you like some coffee?"

Smiling, he said, "That would be nice. Thank you."

She looked at the Barbie doll in the skimpy shorts, asking her, "Isabelle, would you get a cup of coffee for him?"

With no indication of yes or no, Isabelle slid out of the room giving Harold a derisive glance that he took as contempt and mockery. Harold had no idea if he was going to get the coffee or not.

He turned to Darrel, using his official police intimidation to control the scene, "Mr. Freeman, would you leave us alone, please?"

Uncertain, Darrel got up, saying, "Uh, I suppose so. I'll be in the kitchen."

Isabelle came in with a steaming cup, making a point to slide her fingers over his hand as she passed it to him. Leaning forward to be certain, he enjoyed the cleavage between the soft rounded mounds of her breasts, she lingered a moment beyond what was necessary. Their eyes locked, and Harold became hypnotized by a deep cerulean that no artist could ever match. If his voice would work, he wanted to ask if she would have sex with him when he was done. However, the absurdity of that was obvious.

Amy told her daughter, "Izzy, please leave us for a while."

As Izzy walked out with her butt cheeks working the short-shorts up into her crevice, Harold swallowed hard to dismiss the sight. The tattoo of a ladybug, between the top of the shorts and the left dimple, seemed to wink at him.

Harold absently commented, "Nice looking girl." He wondered if Flo would want a ladybug on her ass. Getting back to business, he turned to her, asking, "Is it okay if I call you Amanda?"

The coffee cup to her lips, she nodded approval, though, clearly, she wanted him to go away.

He took note of the drained coloring in her face and the sallow pallor around her eyes. She held her cup with both hands, and was obviously very weak. He politely asked, "Shouldn't you still be in the hospital?"

Surprised at his concern, she answered, "They got the bullet out and stitched up a bunch of things. Nothing vital was damaged, just a lot of flesh torn up, so it's just a matter of healing. I have to be careful of internal bleeding. They said I was lucky, but I don't know."

Harold added, "Or maybe the shooter was just a bad shot?"

Talking into her cup, Harold strained to listen, "Yeah, maybe."

Prodding deeper, he asked, "Is it possible that the person really didn't want to kill you?"

Harold's instinct was pulling him closer as he watched her face fall. The weak response, "I don't know." He backed off for a moment, until she quietly repeated, "I don't know—I hope so."

Trying very hard to avoid spilling on himself, he took a sip of coffee, and then asked, "Amanda, how did you meet Gordon Marks?"

Staring into the cup on her lap, she answered, "I met him through my daughter. Please don't involve her in this, I still haven't told Darrel everything. He suspects it went deeper, but he's staying with me—so far."

"Do you recall any more about the voice, or seeing the figure that held the gun?"

She paused, and then answered, "No, it was dark, and I was scared to death."

There was a hesitation to her answer that disturbed him, but he would pry into that at another time. Just observing her uncertainty made his trip here worthwhile.

He had placed himself on the sofa next to her so he could keep his voice low. "I don't think the case will be helped in any way by dragging your dirty laundry into the open. I can't promise that at a later time, it won't come out, but I don't think it would be from me. Have you considered a counselor? Sooner or later some of it is going to show up. It might be better for you to be honest now."

Upset at his inference, she abruptly said, "Detective, please leave my family affairs to me. I know what I have to do."

That signaled the end of his interview, and crushed his fantasy of Amanda Freeman and her shaved pubic region. Getting up, he told her, "I hope you get better real soon. Thanks for seeing me."

He turned to leave, when she said, "Thank you. I know what you're trying to do, and I appreciate it."

As his last bit of advice he said, "Anything you can think of would make this all go easier. There are little details the mind can forget, but it's all important. Don't hesitate to call me."

Smiling, he left Amanda Freeman to handle her marital problems on her own. However, instead of going to the front door, he walked to where he thought the kitchen might be. Isabelle was sitting on the counter top with Darrel standing close to her, his hand on her bare leg. Harold placed his cup in the sink, and asked, "Isabelle, would you please walk me out to my car?" Darrel slid his hand away as if nobody saw.

She didn't respond at first, but finally slid down to the floor, pulling the crotch of her shorts out of her butt. Through the sneering pout on her lips, she asked, "What do you want with me?"

Keeping his silence until they got outside, he asked her, "Tell me about you and Gordon Marks." He had difficulty looking at the girl, not wanting to interrupt his interview with lustful ogling of her bare skin parts.

Leaning against his car, folding her arms over her breasts, she said, "We had a good time for a while, until I met a guy my own age and never went back to him." Admitting to getting dumped in favor of her mother was not something she was going to acknowledge.

"How did your mom get tangled up with him?"

She answered snidely, "Does it matter?"

Quick to jump on her sarcasm, he said, "If it doesn't matter, I'll be the one to say so." Abruptly adding, "Answer my question."

Sighing, she rolled out her concocted version of the story. "He was making a fuss about my leaving and came over here one day to see me. Mom was home and that's all it took. She rescued me from him, and had plans to dump him when the time was right."

"The right time? I don't understand."

Leaning against his car with her amazing little butt pressed into it, she showed a touch of indignation, saying "The guy was a pig and thought he owned me. My mom was going to play his strings for a while, and when she had him by the balls, let him know he wasn't going to possess anyone. Mom really turned him on and discovered how to control him. He deserved to get dumped and find out how it felt to hurt someone's feelings."

"He'd done this to others?"

"Of course, he had a long string of women he'd bleed and dump." Bruntz noted her agitation.

With a new twist and possible motive, he asked, "Do you know any of these women?"

She curtly answered, "No, why would I?"

"What was your father's reaction to what his wife was doing?"

She abruptly walked away, calling over her shoulder, "My stepfather? Ask him yourself."

Harold's eyes followed the girl as she slithered to the house. She turned once to give him a sneer of indignation, but continued her sensual exit for his pleasure. This was an exciting moment, sending signals from Harold's brain to his groin, but most importantly, he got a better idea of the games that Isabelle and her mother played with men.

Harold's instinct was a curse at times. If his mind told him to take a look at something, he didn't always know what to question, leaving him confused and upset. Watching the gorgeous assembly disappear into the Freeman house, he felt that this was one of those times. Something was sitting wrong, but he would have to wait until it became obvious. He moved his eyes from the Freeman front door to the spot on his car that held Isabelle's butt. He wanted to kneel in front of the spot and lick it, but he resisted.

Back at the precinct, he thumbed through the case folder and made a copy of all the neighbors' names taken in Gordon Marks's back yard. A useless effort, but the only thing he could think of to do.

Before he could get away, Jim Haggard cornered him, angrily spitting out, "Bruntz, I don't give a shit how many cases you've closed, if you make an appointment to meet me someplace, have enough consideration to show up. If you can't make it, use the fucking telephone. I sat at that goddamn house for three hours waiting for you."

Trying to understand the venum being leveled at him, he finally said, "Was I supposed to . . ." Then it hit him, the thing that made him feel so uneasy. "Oh, no. I'm sorry, Jim. I forgot." Harold tried a smile to cover it, but his partner pushed him aside, walking away with a few choice names trailing after him.

Harold heard his name rolling loudly across the squad room. He looked up to see Lieutenant Warner fuming at his office door, calling, "Bruntz, get your ass in here."

Once in the glass-walled office, with the door clattering shut behind him, he had a bad feeling about this meeting. Bob Warner laid into him. "Harold, I've given you as much leeway as I can. You are just a fuck-up like everyone says you are. Captain Hilksman wants me to fire you just because you look like a homeless bum. Now, Jim Haggard wants to dump you as a partner. That makes seventeen well-respected police officers that have refused to work with you."

Harold truly liked Jim Haggard and felt a pang of disappointment at this news. He looked at his boss, saying, "I'm sorry, Lieutenant. I try working with these guys, but I can't seem to connect. I have trouble with people, and they all turn away. I have my way of doing things, and they have theirs. Are you sure Jim won't change his mind?"

"Hal, if Jim Haggard could get away with it, he'd shoot you."

Harold nervously shuffled his feet, saying, "Couldn't we try it again?"

The lieutenant's answer was adamant, "No. But, I might have a solution."

With a thread of hope dangling in front of him, Harold brightened up, "Sure, whatever you want."

"There's a replacement coming from vice. She's been exposed and threatened, so we're going to bring her in-house. She'll be working a desk and give you a hand when you need something traced or tracked down. Take her out into the field with you whenever you can."

Not comfortable with the proposed change in partners, Harold protested. "Lieutenant, I've never worked with a woman before. I don't think this is a good idea."

The lieutenant stuck his snarling face into Harold's. "Bruntz, I don't give a shit what you think. You're getting a partner." Lieutenant Warner picked up the phone and barked, "Send her in."

A sinking feeling of despair and loneliness swept over Harold, leaving a gnawing pain in his belly. Getting used to a new partner was bad enough, but he had deep reservations about working with a woman. Before Harold could plead his case, the hard-eyed look from the lieutenant shut him up.

The opaque glass door to Lieutenant Warner's office rattled open, and Harold Bruntz' life was about to change.

CHAPTER 4
Yo-Yo

June 13, Late afternoon.

AROLD'S NEW PARTNER STEPPED into the lieutenant's office with all the grace and dignity of Genghis Kahn raping twelve million square miles of Asia. Yolanda Brown was taller than Harold, weighed in at 125 pounds max, and gave the impression she was permanently stoned. Her hair just did what it wanted to, looking like long tight black springs sprouting from her head. Her gait was set in a high torque with her leaning forward as she moved, looking as if momentum was pulling at her. She was absolutely unable to stand still for any time at all without her entire body twitching and snapping with a nervous edge. She looked as if she was going to take off in a sprint, jumping at the starting line.

Harold smiled slightly, afraid to look at her directly. Pleading with his boss, "Lieutenant, I'm not sure . . ."

Yolanda glared at him, her dark eyes resembling the muzzle end of a twelve-gauge double-barrel, eyebrows leveled into a pounce-and-kill shape. She snarled, "What are you afraid of, asshole? Won't work with a woman, a sister? Come on, you white piece of fuck, spit it out, and I'll shove it up your honkey ass." Her fists were balled. Harold certain he was going to get hit if he reacted badly.

Lieutenant Warner stepped between them, calling out, "Hey, hey, come on you two. Let's just talk and work this out. Officer Brown, you shut up and keep the racial crap out of this. Bruntz, you just shut up."

Thinking he had gained control, Warner continued, "All right, now. Listen, both of you have hit a dead end as far as keeping your jobs on this police force. You two learn to work together, or punch out and go home, for good." Bob Warner's look was fierce enough to cover the bullshit he was feeding them.

Yolanda's motors slowed down, putting the agitation into neutral. She shuffled with her arms back and forth from her rear pockets to being folded over her chest. Harold just sank within himself, slumping in defeat, having no other choice. His sigh of resignation was loud enough to draw Yolanda Brown into battle formation.

A stern redress from Lieutenant Warner came out as a hiss, "Brown, calm down."

Lieutenant Warner sat behind his desk. "All right, that's better. We've got a high profile case that needs to get solved, and you two are going to be at the front of it. With the case load on the other officers, we're stretched too thin to give you a lot of personnel support. Bruntz, take Yolanda and brief her on what we know so far. Officer Brown, pay attention and be ready to help Detective Bruntz however he needs you. When you aren't in the field with him, you'll be filing and shuffling papers to help the rest of the officers."

Done with his speech, Lieutenant Warner ordered, "Now, get the hell out of here and bring me Gordon Marks's killer." He leaned forward on his desk, with a too-busy-to-answer-questions act of rustling papers.

The two officers looked at each other, nodding acceptance of their situation and left the office, leaving a sullen cloud behind. Harold looked back, giving the lieutenant one last mournful look of despair. All he got in return was a granite-faced rejection.

Moving through the office door at the same time, Harold and Yolanda squeezed in the frame together; doing a comedic dance until Harold relented, giving her room to leave gracefully.

Watching the bizarre scene, shaking his head in disbelief, Warner muttered, "Oh, God, no." He picked up the phone and punched his numbers. Captain Faye Hilksman answered. Bob told her, "They took it."

From the other end of the connection, her response was, "Good, when they fuck this up enough, we can fire both of them."

After a moment of silence, Captain Hilksman added, "You free tonight?"

Slowly shaking his head, not wanting to, he said anyway, "Yeah, sure, why not?"

BOTH THE NEW PARTNERS sat at Harold's desk, the Marks folder open in front of them. He started to explain the details, until she interrupted him, "Yo-yo. Call me Yo-yo."

Confused, he gazed blankly at her and muttered, "Huh?"

"My name, you bone head. My name is Yo-yo. You ever call me Yolanda and I'll stick my foot up your white ass. Excuse me, your *fat* white ass."

Thinking of all the things she had recently promised to shove into his rectum, he smiled, saying, "Yo-yo. Sure." Getting back to the file, he said, "It's too late now, but tomorrow maybe you could press the lab to finish the work on the evidence they have. It's all we have to work with, so far. Then you can interview all the guys Mrs. Freeman was boinking." Happy to avoid those mundane jobs, he added, "That would be a good place for you to start. And we need to find out more about Mr. Freeman. With his wife's long list of indiscretions, he is sitting high on my list of suspects."

Without a warning, Yo-yo grabbed his shirt sleeve and tugged, pushing her face close to his. In the instant this happened, he didn't have time to decipher her look as either fear or panic. Recoiling, thinking she was going to launch an attack, she surprised him with a plea, "Just one thing, man. Take me with you, please. I can't stay in here fucking with papers and shit. You take me with, and I'll even treat you decent."

Yo-yo's idea of treating Harold to anything was vastly different from what he imagined. Thinking her offer was as good as it was going to get, he said, "Yeah, sure. We can be partners, okay?" Smirking, Harold offered a touch of humor to accept his new partner, "That's better than you sticking stuff up my ass."

Her less than sincere response was, "Yeah, whatever. Just don't leave me here with the chicken-shit stuff. I ain't no good at that, man."

Hesitating a moment, he got serious. "You know, I'm not the most liked guy here. Everyone thinks I'm a pig and have a good time making fun of me." His gaze moved from the floor to look directly into her eyes.

Sitting back, she looked at him with a frown, saying, "Can you blame them? You look like shit, man. You don't smell too good neither."

Accepting her assessment, he quietly confessed, "I guess I'm not a neat type person. I just don't think much about it. Not since . . . well, I just don't."

Yo-yo Brown surveyed her new partner for a few moments, telling him, "That's cool. I'll get used to it—maybe. I heard some skittle about you from some other guys. None of it too good, but you got some credentials with 'em." Her next action surprised him when she stood up with more of a command than a question, "Come on, Bruntz, we got something to do."

Following her lead, he allowed himself to be pulled out of the station house and into the street. It was early evening by then, peering up and down the darkening street, she asked, "Where's your car?" He pointed.

Both seated in the Plymouth, he questioned, "Where we going?"

With an air of confidence and finality, she told him, "Your place. Come on, boy, move it, or did you forget where you live?"

He looked at her with a concerned knit to his forehead, not sure if that was a joke or an insult.

She waved him off, telling him, "Don't mind my mouth, Bubba. I can be a smart ass, but you'll get used to it. I ain't as bad as I used to be." With a prideful smile, she added, "No shit, mu-fuck, I used to be mean and nasty. Yeah, one bad mother-fucker."

Harold glanced over, wondering how she could have been any worse. Nodding acknowledgement, Harold drove home with his new partner, confused as to why.

Leading her up the creaking stairs of his apartment, covered with years of grime, he apologized for the squalor. "This isn't the nicest place, but it's cheap. The neighbors are nice. Friendly."

"Don't worry about it, man. It's your home. I grew up in shit like this, only we didn't have no doors, just some curtains or blankets hanging. My line of work brings me into all kinds of places, you know? No shit man, this ain't bad."

Harold shuffled, and Yo-yo bopped, to his door. Her last comment was quiet and not meant for anyone, "Not like my digs, but still your mu-fuckin home."

Harold, teetering on total ignorance said, "I don't know why you wanted to come here. I don't have anything to offer you."

"Don't worry about it, man. Where's the bathroom? Hell, there ain't but two rooms to look in, I'm sure I can find it."

Raising his hand, he pointed, "Uh, right there. The door doesn't close real tight."

"I don't care if it's got a door. Come on, boy, your doing this with me."

Yo-yo's cryptic comments did absolutely nothing to clear up Harold's confusion. Tonight, like it or not, Harold Bruntz was going to get a makeover. Yo-yo pushed him into the bathroom, peeling his clothing off, piece by piece. Batting away his protesting arms trying to wave away her intrusion, she muttered, "No shit, man, this funky stuff is contaminated. Don't even wash it, boy. No way. Just toss this shit, mu-fuck."

Down to his boxers and stockings, he held his hands over his crotch, begging, "No, don't. What's going on? Stop this, please."

Stepping back, she asked, "You embarrassed, boy? Shit, man, I'll take care of that." With the speed of a sprinter, and the finesse of a ballet dancer, Yo-yo shed her clothing, standing stark naked in front of the trembling Harold. The light-brown tint of the flesh clinging to her slender frame formed an erotic pouring of velvety rich milk chocolate. Her movements were as fluid and sensuous as a sonnet from a cello, her strings vibrating in a poetic flow of lust. Yolanda Brown was a babe.

The helpless man just managed to mumble, "Oh my."

Staring at the lean and hardened, dark shimmering body of the undercover prostitute, Harold Bruntz became a robot. She bent down pulling his boxers and stockings off, leaving the blob of a man vulnerable to whatever she wanted to do with him.

Taking him by the arm, she stepped into the grimy bathtub, turned on the water and pulled the curtain shut. The spray of cold water, turning warm, covered his bulbous body with Yo-yo gently washing every part of him, and then sending him through a rinse cycle. Harold's hand instinctively came up to her body, but he pulled it back, uncertain. Recognizing his move, she took his hand and placed it on her small breast, telling him with softness to her voice, "Go ahead honey, touch what you want." She reached below his paunch to prove that touching was all right. Her face close to his, she purred, "Now, doesn't that feel good?" Her next treatment was with a razor and a generous application of soap to his face.

Breathless, Harold was barely able to nod his head, his eyes the size of dinner plates while Yo-yo finished her project.

Stepping from the tub, she held the only towel she could find. Yo-yo said, "Now, Detective Bruntz, you're clean and if you're going to work with me, you're going to stay that way. I don't need no stink-hole man making me sick." Her comments faded into a dissertation meant for herself to hear and understand. "No shit, man, no stinky man is going to work with Yo-yo." Taking a meteoric moment to flash her childhood past, she lamented to herself on her abhorrence of poverty and squalor.

Stepping out behind her, dripping on the floor, Harold still breathless, asked, "What just happened? I'm not sure that partners are supposed to get that close."

"What do you mean, *what just happened?* Weren't you paying attention, boss?" She tossed the towel to him, and calmly said, "That's what I do, honey. Now you know who and what I am. Some people are good at cooking, I'm good at making men happy. They put me into undercover, but I was right at home playing the game because I was damn good, and loved it."

Hiding his girth behind the wet towel, he asked, "You got made? Someone discovered you were a cop?"

Pulling the towel away from him, she said, "Yeah, some goon I busted in a sting a few years ago recognized me and said I was gonna be his ho' or he would rat me out. I got pissed and kicked his gonies up into his brain. The next day I was a target and had to get out." Plopping the towel on top of his head, she blotted the water out. Stepping back she brushed the mop to the side that favored the part, muttering, "Yeah, now that's a good thing. Lookin' good, bro."

Officer Brown scanned the medicine cabinet for deodorant, but only came up with a can of FDS. Turning to him with a quizzical knit, she had to ask, "Now what the fuck do you need with this?" holding it up to him.

A leftover from his friend, Flo, he said, "Oh, that's for someone else."

Confused, she asked, "You don't do kinks do you?"

Embarrassed, Harold took it from her and put the can away, "No, it's not mine."

Yo-yo retrieved it to apply a coating to his arm pits. "I don't care whose it is, boss, you still need some no-stinky."

Satisfied with the clean up, Yo-yo took Harold's hand, and said, "Now come on, let's go see how fucked up your bedroom is."

While Detective Harold Bruntz was being transformed into a happy and clean human being, for a reason yet unknown to him, there was something else happening in another part of town.

Parked in darkness in front of the Freeman garage, Richard Olson was getting laid by the beautiful Isabelle. Arms and legs wildly flying and wrapping around whatever was handy, they were hampered by the constraints of the back seat of his Oldsmobile. Loud lip smacking noises, moans, and grunts, and foggy windows left no uncertainty as to the activity taking place. An occasional, "Oh, Isabelle, my God, oh my God," was the only language exchanged, until Isabelle decided it was time to ram this game into another gear. It was show time. Whispering in his ear at the same time she was devouring it, "Do you like doing this, Dickey?" Her comment was rhetorical, knowing the only possible answer.

In a steamy whisper, she kept on with her intimidation, "Do you love me? If you promise to never look at another woman, we can do this forever."

Now, Isabelle's mind entered the uncontrolled world of mild retardation that had become the only detraction to her being absolutely perfect. Her genes were tainted, sometimes separating her actions from common sense, which her therapist had no cure or control for. A familiar game was about to take place—Isabelle the puppet master.

Tearing Dickeys shirt from his body, he wriggled his arms out of the sleeves while Isabelle worked on the belt and zipper. In a wild frenzy, clothing flew with the skill of inept contortionists. Shoes, socks, and underwear were kicked under the seat with little concern.

Holding his head to her lips, she whispered, "Get out, honey, there's something I want to do. You're gonna love it."

Dickey was out of control at this point, allowing Isabelle to do anything she wanted with him. Confused, Dickey looked through the fogged window and could only manage to stupidly utter, "Huh?"

"Go on, open the door, dummy."

Dickey crawled over his girlfriend, feeling conspicuous and very naked, wondered just how much he was going to consent to before going home. Isabelle got out, putting her arms around him, softly whispering into his ear, "This is going to feel so good." The feeling of her soft warm flesh pressing against him turned him into a mindless pawn.

In the darkness in front of the garage, Isabelle's milky naked body floated in a surreal dance, her arms over her head twirling slowly, her hands flowing outward in a pirouette, blending with the music that only she could hear. Gliding to the rear of the Oldsmobile, she held her hand out, her misty voice telling Dickey, "Help me up."

Mesmerized, the only thing worming its way to Dickey's lips was, "Huh?"

She pulled him to her, whispering, "Help me up, on the car. You're going to make love to me on top of the car."

Richard Olson standing dumbfounded in the driveway, turned to the street right in front of this display. "Isabelle, somebody's going to come by."

Isabelle's mind in the bizarre world that guided her actions, told him, "Let 'em look, they can see me too. You love me, don't you! You can see how beautiful I am. How could anyone not want to make love to me."

"Isabelle, this isn't right, we need . . ."

Dickey's logic on morality and being exposed naked to the street was interrupted by the explosion. The .357 slug tore his head from his neck and plastered the contents of his skull over the front of Isabelle.

The deafening detonation of the revolver made Isabelle's body shudder, not comprehending what had happened. The oozing matter was running down her body, between her breasts, puddling in her navel, to cover her stomach. Her smooth creamy flesh was covered with red splotches where skull chunks had bombarded her.

On its way through Richard's head the slug lost momentum but tumbled far enough to bury itself into Isabelle's shoulder. The impact did little more than push her back slightly. In shock, not aware of the piece of lead embedded in her flesh, she was totally bewildered. Her first reaction was the sound of the familiar voice, paralyzing her. Her body turned to ice, her arms and legs trembling, and she pushed herself back against the body of the Oldsmobile. Her lips quivered while her jaw rattled in fear, mindlessly mumbling, "You! What . . . what . . . have you done?"

The hoarse whisper back spat out, "You sick little bitch. You think you can fuck with me and get by with it? You're a fruitcake with tits, and you're *sick.* "

There it was again, the inference to her being mentally deranged. Incensed at the allegation that she was less than perfect, and mentally deficient, Isabelle recoiled. The remnants of Richard covering her body were of little concern in her outrage. She could not tolerate this repugnant insinuation. Not from this person. Moving away from the car she snapped and growled, "Don't you dare say that—don't ever say that again." She tried to bring her right arm up to strike out, but something was terribly wrong. The throbbing in her shoulder was making her stomach jump as the pain settled in.

The second explosion shattered her chest, throwing her body against the trunk lid, her arms splayed to the side. She remained suspended, her eyes wide and still glaring with anger, until she slid down over the bumper to sit on top of her boyfriend's body. In a grotesque display of gore and carnage, her legs spread open for everyone to see. The one fantasy she wanted fulfilled.

Lights came on in the neighbors homes with frantic calls to 911.

June 14, 7:00 a.m.

GETTING UP FIRST the next morning, Yo-yo found Florence Widholm sitting at Harold's kitchen table. Surprised, Yo-yo exclaimed, "Who the fuck are you and what you doing here, girl?"

Looking up, Flo calmly said, "I saw Hal was busy so I just made some coffee. Want some?"

With a big question mark in her face, Yo-yo cautiously said, "Yeah, sure. I'll have some coffee. So who are you? You his wife or something?" She took the coffee offered to her, nodding her thanks.

"No, I'm Flo. I'm just a friend and neighbor. Hal doesn't have a wife."

Nodding, Yo-yo said, "Oh, that's cool." Assessing Flo some more, Yo-yo said, "You just come in and make coffee? Huh. What happened to your face?" She motioned her cup to the damage inflicted by Jimmy Jeepers.

Putting her fingers to her bruised cheek, Flo quietly said, "Nothing, just fallout from the job."

Sipping her coffee, question still in place, but slipping away, Yo-yo looked at Flo with curiosity. The woman was showing the strains of old age wrinkles and weight gain, but she sported a beautiful head of coal black hair that was messy in a well kept way. Flo had an air of arrogance about her, but used it in a sensual fashion to make an older woman very desirable. The familiarity crystalized into recognition, and when Yo-yo connected the dots, she smiled and said, "Say, honey, I know you. You're Flo the blow."

The calmness remained, but the smile faded. "Yeah, I'm Flo."

Yo-yo got excited, "No shit, man. You're famous, girl."

Flo nodded, quietly answering, "Yes, I suppose I am. I recognized *you* right away. They call you, uhm—I'm sorry, I can't place your name."

Excited, Yo-yo said, "That's okay, honey, I'm Yo-yo. Yo-yo Brown. Man, I'm happy to meet you."

Calmly answering, Flo said, "Yo-yo, that's right. Now I remember."

The two chatted for a few minutes exchanging names and war stories.

Dressed in a Hawaiian sport shirt he didn't know he had, and a clean pair of khaki pants, Harold found his way into the kitchen and armed himself with a cup of Flo's coffee. He gently rubbed the back of Flo's head, which Yo-yo understood to be a warm and friendly greeting. "Flo, this is my new partner, Yo-yo Brown."

The smile came back. Flo said, "We've been talking. We know each other from way back."

In a cryptic exchange between Flo and Harold, she told him, "I got her something, Hal. It's on the table—don't forget."

All emotion and care about anything drained out of Harold's face as he looked at the floor, then back to Flo, saying, "Thanks. No, I won't forget. I'll go there today. It's today isn't it?"

Nodding, Flo somberly answered, "Yeah, it's today."

Harold's telephone rang. Coming back into the kitchen, he looked at Yo-yo, telling her, "We have to go. There's some shit at the Freeman house."

In the car, with the portable bubble blinking on top, Harold said, "You and Flo seemed to hit it off. She's a nice lady."

Excitedly, Yo-yo said, "Don't you know who that is? That's Flo the blow, man. She's famous."

Knowing of Flo's reputation, Harold tried to down-play it, "Doing what she does shouldn't make someone famous. What's so special?"

Amazed at her partner's ignorance, Yo-yo said, "It's just her, man. She's been around forever, and I know lots of girls that have been in lock-up with her. She used to have class, man. Real class and that makes her something special in the world I know about." Looking out the window, recoiling at the traffic they were careening through, she quietly added, with a level of respect, "Yeah, she's special." Yo-yo had her hands on her legs, pressing tightly, but she was unable to stop the nervous twitching.

Harold put a defensive edge to his partner's comment, "Yeah, she's special, all right, and she still has class."

Yo-yo wouldn't allow him to eat or drink coffee while he was driving, so his stomach was constantly gurgling. Amused at the sounds emitting from his gut, she asked, "You ain't gonna fart are you?"

The twinkle in his eyes and the lifting of his hip, told her he was trying.

Disgusted at his ploy, she said, "Well, just don't crap in your pants. I cleaned you up once, and that's gotta last awhile."

H AROLD BRUNTZ AND HIS PARTNER arrived at the chaotic crime scene in front of the Freeman garage. His old partner, Jim Haggard, was avoiding him, so Harold had to chase him down. Totally oblivious to any animosity that Jim carried, Detective Bruntz got right into it. "Jim. Jim, wait."

Upset at being disturbed and confronted by Harold, Jim couldn't avoid him any longer. "Yeah, okay. What is it?"

Detective James Haggard was about to learn, again, that Harold Bruntz was a business man when it came to cases he was working on. "Jim, like it or not, I'm in charge of this case. I don't care what you think of me. I've been putting up with insults and rejections since before you were born, and I'm not going to let your ego get in my way. Tell me what I need to know and keep your attitude out of it."

Absorbing the rebuff, Jim said, "Sorry, Bruntz. I just couldn't work with you anymore. You do better alone, and I was just getting pissed every time you came near me."

That wasn't what he was asking for, but Harold said, "Oh, yeah. Sorry, Jim, I got the same story from every partner I ever had. Okay, about this," he waved his arm over the crime scene, "What do you know about all of this?"

"We just got here and don't know much at all. The girl was getting pumped on the trunk lid, and wham-o, they're both dead. It looks like someone blew his head off, and then did the girl. Her dad heard the shots and came running out, but says he didn't see anyone else."

Jim opened his note book, "Let's see, oh yeah. The dad say's the girl was seeing a shrink for some mental disturbances, and he wasn't too surprised by her getting naked in front of the house. He say's she liked to scare people with stuff like that and was kind of schizo. Her mother came out and saw the mess and went ballistic. She's been in the house screaming since we got here."

Registering the update, Harold turned away with Jim calling after him, "Hey Bruntz, where'd you get the clown suit?"

Looking down at the colorful shirt hanging over his belly, Harold just shrugged.

Yo-yo was looking over the bloody pile of nude people when Harold ambled up to her. With great difficulty, he lowered his huge frame to kneel next to her, asking, "Anything stand out?"

She held up the .357 caliber revolver, dangling from her latex covered finger, by the trigger guard. "This is it, so far. The gun was laying in the mush from the victims. We'll get the lab to work it over, but being left behind like this I doubt there's anything on it besides guts and blood."

Looking at the mutilated remains of Isabelle, Harold felt a pang of regret. Pointing to her, he told Yo-yo, "I met her. She's Mrs. Freeman's daughter. I talked to her earlier, and she seemed a little dim to me. Nice tits, but not much for brains. Anyway, Haggard says she had some mental problems."

Yo-yo gave him a slight accepting nod, saying, "Yeah well, now those nice tits are hamburger." She stood up, extending a hand to help Harold, and stepped to the rear door of the Oldsmobile. Peering inside, she listed the logistics of the scene. "This part is pretty simple. They were getting it on in here, and then moved it outside. The clothing was taken off with a lot of hurry and force, not much concern over being neat. And look at this. It was crammed under the driver's seat." She held up a set of black Dacron tights, a knit cap with blonde hair strands attached to it, and a pair of black sneakers with traces of blood on them. Of special note was the slim leather scabbard. Dropping the clothing into evidence bags, Yo-yo did the labeling and handed them over to the forensics crew.

Stripping off her latex gloves, she stepped back and said, "What happened in the car was just a boy and girl getting it on. They either got out on their own to do the hump-hump in front of the neighbors, or the person with the cannon forced them out."

Harold had put the same scenario together long before Yo-yo went on with her version. He told her, "Yeah, you hit it all just right. The answer may be in the black stuff and the blood on the sneakers, and we need to compare this shit with the Gordon Marks thing. With the same family involved, I'm seeing a tie-in. Stay close to the lab on that. Good job, Yolan . . . I mean, Yo-yo."

"Nice save, boss. But, getting back to this mess, it just ain't right. The answers we got all fit, except for the *why*. Poor kids. This is just plain grizzly, man. The dude pulling the trigger could've done the same job with a .22." Hefting up the .357, she added, "These things should be outlawed. There ain't nothing more deadly."

Impressed with his partner's proficiency, he asked her, "Will you get on the phone and have a psychiatric specialist sent over here? See if a woman is on call, and they need to get here yesterday." Harold took a brief moment to stare at the gruesome sight, contemplating the remnants of Richard, mumbling, "Well, I hope he at least he enjoyed his last moment."

Entering the Freeman house, he recalled the vision of Isabelle in her short-shorts the first time he saw her. Threading his way through policemen, he found Amanda sitting on the floor of the living room, backed into the corner, her knees pulled up to her chin. Darrel was sitting with her holding her tightly. She was shaking violently and sobbing incoherently, her lips twitching as she stared blankly around the room. Her right hand was flapping aimlessly in front of her.

Darrel made a move to stand up, but Harold told him, "No, stay with her. I've got a medical professional coming that can take care of her." He noticed that both people were in night wear. He picked an officer out of the crowd, telling him, "Make sure they don't go anywhere, and nobody but the shrink goes near them. When they get here, come upstairs and tell me."

There were three bedrooms upstairs. In the bathroom he checked the contents of the waste basket, finding a couple of mini-pads and odds and ends of tissue. An officer had followed him upstairs, so Detective Bruntz handed the wastebasket to him, saying, "Bag this and have forensics take the sink and tub drains apart to analyze the stuff in the traps." He bent over to look closely at water droplets in the sink, saw nothing, and then briefly scanned the shower.

One bedroom held the bric-a-brac that families collect and don't know what to do with. It was unused as a bedroom, but could be a hiding place for who knows what. Family secrets that can't get buried deep enough or stay hidden long enough. The Freeman family had suffered some terrible ordeals, and Harold was going to tear them apart to uncover what he was certain they were hiding.

Isabelle's room was surprisingly neat and well ordered. The bed wasn't made, but still looked like it hadn't been slept in. Mostly out of curiosity and wanting to snoop, Harold browsed through the closet, fingering the trappings of a young girl having fun with life, making men fall in love with her. Briefly checking the drawers and nightstand, he found some papers under the collection of tiny soft underpants. The first one he looked at turned this case in a whole new direction.

Holding it up to the light from the window, he read, *Izzy, I'm sorry for what I did, but you didn't stop me, so I did it. Watching you in the house I know you were teasing me, and there was nothing I could do to stop it. Please don't parade it in front of A. it would ruin our marriage. I fell in love with you, but I know it can't be, so I will leave you alone until you want to do it again. If things work out, maybe we can go away, but I don't know. I will wait for you to decide. I have something that might make you happy. Love, "D"*

The other papers were from men who were also pleading with her to let them make love to her. They all went into an evidence bag. Of special interest in Isabelle's waste basket, he eyed a pregnancy test strip, which was bagged as well.

The next room was Darrel and Amanda's bedroom. The first thing Harold noticed was the rumpled sheets on the bed. One side, the left, was wildly askew with the bottom sheet torn from its tucked in position to follow the top sheet. Whoever slept on that side got out of the bed in one hell of a hurry.

The crime scene investigators arrived, with one of them trailing behind Harold. He instructed the man with the camera to get the bed in a picture and check the sheets for semen deposits. He added, "Check the room to see if anything suspicious is squirreled away. Check the attic, garage, and basement also, and do a semen check on the other bed." He pointed in the direction of Isabelle's room.

The officer from downstairs approached him, saying, "Detective, the shrink is here."

"Okay, thanks." He turned to the forensics officer, "You don't need me here, do you?"

Shaking his head, not looking at Harold, the man mumbled, "No, go ahead. I'll find you if I do."

Downstairs, Harold met with Dr. Wanda Ferber. A tall slender woman with shoulder-length dish-water hair, she was dressed in jogging slacks, a tank top covered by an open-hooded sweatshirt, and jogging shoes that cost more than Harold's car. She was kneeling in front of the still-trembling Amanda, talking softly to her.

Helping Amanda to her feet, Dr. Ferber asked, "Can I take her to her bedroom?"

"No, sorry, we're sweeping it, and it'll be a mess for about an hour. Put her on the sofa."

Detective Bruntz stood up, ordering everyone in the living room, "Clear out, now. We need this room." Holding one officer back, "Stay at the entry and be sure nobody disturbs Mrs. Freeman." He then went into the kitchen and unplugged the telephone so there wouldn't be any phone interruptions. Back in the living room, he asked Dr. Ferber, "Can you stay with her?"

Rejecting Harold's request with a shake of her head, Dr. Ferber told him, "I gave her a sedative. She should drift off for a few hours. I called for a uniformed nurse from the Hennepin County Medical Center to come in and take care of her."

Harold said, "Thanks. This is a crime scene, and she needs to be watched. She's still on the list of suspects."

Hearing that, Darrel voiced his protest, "What do you mean? Her daughter is lying outside dead. Look at the shape she's in."

Taking Darrel by the shoulder, Harold told him, "Put your shoes on, Darrel, you need to go downtown to answer a few questions."

Protesting, Darrel asked, "Why? My wife's in shreds, and I want to be with her." Close to an emotional melt down, Darrel stammered, "Isabelle is . . . poor Izzy is out there. What about her, and the boy?"

"They'll both be taken to the morgue. Your driveway will need some scrubbing, but don't go near it until we tell you." Almost as an afterthought, Harold asked him, "Darrel, which side of the bed do you sleep on?"

Confused and frightened to death, as his hands were pulled behind him, he said, "The left side, near the window. Why?"

With no response from Detective Bruntz, Darrel was handcuffed and taken away, his protests fading with him. Going back to Mrs. Freeman, he was going to ask a barrage of questions, but she was slumped to one side, immobilized by the sedative. Sitting on the same arm of the sofa that Isabelle had graced during his first visit, he stared at the lovely Amanda Freeman. Softly stroking her long blonde hair, he hoped she wasn't aware of his intrusion, his fascination for her becoming stronger.

CHAPTER 5
HAPPY BIRTHDAY

WITH DARREL SECURED in the back seat of a patrol car on his way to the station, still in his pajamas, Harold found Yo-yo squatting in front of the garage. Inquiring about the bodies, he asked, "Did the wagon take them away?"

"Yeah, all the photos were done, and forensics had what they needed." Looking at the growing crowd of spectators, Yo-yo asked a rhetorical question, "What do they find so fascinating about blood and gore? When Isabelle walked around in a tiny top they locked the doors. Now her guts are all over, and they want to see more."

The bodies were on their way to the morgue to be cut apart and analyzed. A large flat bed truck with a lift platform was waiting for permission to pull the Oldsmobile on board to be taken to the forensics lab. A sterile tarp would be draped over it to protect evidence traces, and hide the slime stuck to the rear end.

Surveying the gore hanging on the trunk lid of the Oldsmobile and the red and pink human parts lying on the asphalt driveway, Harold mumbled, "What a waste. What can be so bad that anyone would do this?" The image of Isabelle's tanned, supple body leaning against his car came and went. He glanced at the curious neighbors and shook his head. Bringing his mind back to business, Harold asked, "Anything new to look at?"

"Not much. I bagged Mr. Freeman's slippers; they were just inside the back door and had some dew on them. He was out here, but there's no way to tell if it was before or after the shooting. The neighbors heard the shots, and about ten of them called. The people on both sides of the Freemans said there was always a lot of arguing going on here, and they weren't surprised something bad happened. They all had a few comments on the girl. Evidently she was a flirt and ran around almost naked to tease the old men gawking at her."

Harold wryly commented, "Old men gawking? Who would ever think of doing that?" Back to business, he said, "His slippers, huh? He said he was the one who found the bodies, but why take the time to be so meticulous? "

Yo-yo shrugged, "Beats me."

Grabbing at anything to develop a story that made sense, Harold took out his cell phone to call his precinct desk sergeant. "This is Detective Bruntz," then in response to an ill placed comment from the desk sergeant, he said, "Very funny, just listen for Christ sake. Mr. Freeman is coming in with an officer. Put him in a jump suit and bag his pajamas for evidence. Keep him in an interview room until I get there."

Exasperated at another slur, Harold retorted, "Come on, be a professional for once in your miserable life. We've got dead guys all over the place. Do you realy need to find time to be a comedian? Yes, I said his pajamas."

Yo-yo gave the evidence she had to the forensic crew, and joined her partner at the car. In the driver's seat, Harold clenched a cigar stub in his teeth and a half pint of whiskey was nested between his legs. He hadn't started the car yet, and the cigar was dead. Staring at the open neck of the bottle, he looked up when Yo-yo slammed the door shut. "No shit, mu-fuck, an' I gotta ride with a drunk who's gonna give me second-hand cancer. Do you really gotta . . ."

He interrupted her, softly saying, "Don't nag me, please." Yo-yo's outburst was expected, and it didn't frazzle him. He gave her a look that had a hidden response she wouldn't find the meaning to until later. With soft sagging eyes that held a sad story he moved to start the car and hit the cigarette lighter. The button popped out and he lit the charred end of the cigar, a huge dense fog billowing from his mouth.

With that ritual in place the Plymouth slowly moved away from the Freeman house.

She opened her window to let the foul smoke out, telling him, "Yeah, okay. I'll stay away. You deal with whatever shit you got and I'll just hang on. We going back to the station to bust balls with Mr. Freeman?"

Muttering just loud enough for her to hear, "Yes, but first I've got a stop to make."

"Come on, man. We can't be doing your private shit. We're on a case, boss."

He solemnly answered, "Relax. I have a birthday party to go to."

Sticking her head out the window to escape the cloud coming from Harold's cigar, she mumbled, "Now I know why you're so mu-fuckin' screwed up, man." Her knees and feet were doing their familiar nervous dance. The odor from the cigar was actually pleasant to her, but she wasn't going to let him know that.

Passing through the trendy Uptown area of Minneapolis, Harold slowly circled around Lake Calhoun at the end of Lake Street. A few hundred acres in size, the blue waters were the recreational home to sail boats, canoes, and daring wind surfers. Three lush sandy beaches were the social center for muscle builders and tanned lithe bodies in bikinis. At one time, the prestigious Calhoun Hotel overlooked the bath house on Main Beach, where glimpses of women in the roofless changing rooms were on display for oglers in the third-floor windows.

Harold was in no hurry to get where he was going. Absently telling Yo-yo, "I love driving along this boulevard." Pointing to the shoreline architecture, he lamented, "In the days when the rich actually had money, those homes were the height of society. Now, most are divided into condos and apartments. Too bad. This is a nice area."

Reluctantly, he turned onto Thirty-sixth Street and slid between the stone pillars and iron fence into Lakewood Cemetery. Gradually cruising through the tree-lined lanes, he knew where he was going, but Yo-yo felt he didn't really want to go there. With a show of concern, she kept her mouth shut and enjoyed the ride.

Giant oak trees and lush landscaped green carpeting of immaculate grass were punctuated by towers of monuments bearing family names of past dignitaries and society's finest. Quiet and unhurried, Yo-yo felt she could stroll the narrow lanes of asphalt forever with no fear of getting mugged or raped.

He parked under a huge oak tree and drained the half pint bottle, tossing it into the rear seat. The glove box wouldn't open as it was supposed to, so Harold angrily gave the dashboard a slam with his fist. The door popped open, revealing a spare revolver and two pounds of scrap paper, which fell on Yo-yo's feet. Fumbling through the pile to fish out the package that Flo had given him, he said, "Sorry, I'll pick this up."

Pushing his head away from her feet, she softly told him, "Don't worry about it, man. I'll clean it up. You go do what you gotta do." She looked into his sad eyes, starting to swell with tears. She quietly added, "Go on now."

As she shoved all the stuff back into the glove box, she watched him slowly walk across the grass to a gravesite and fall to his knees. She had the car cleaned up, but waited until his body stopped shaking before she joined him.

Strolling up the grassy slope she sat on the turf beside him and asked, "Who is it, Harold?"

His voice raspy, he slowly answered, "Rachel, my little girl."

Yo-yo leaned over to look at the small stone nestled in the grass, reading *Rachel Bruntz, April 1984 / June 1988 My sweet angel.*

She didn't have to know any more than her partner was in grief. She offered the only sympathy she could dig up at the moment. "She was just a baby, Harold."

Picking at stray blades of grass growing over the plaque, he vacantly answered, "Yeah, just a baby." He opened the paper bag he held, pulling out a small bottle of perfume. He showed it to Yo-yo, saying, "Cachet. It's supposed to be a very nice one. Do you think a seventeen-year-old girl would like that?" Harold's face forced a smile that twitched with agony. His voice held a tremor as he forced out the words, "She'd be seventeen now. Almost a grown-up." The rapid spasms of his chin shook the loose flesh of his neck.

Yo-yo looked deep into the waste-land behind his pale eyes, seeing the pathetic clutter that made up the notorious Harold Bruntz. Touching the bottle with her fingertip, Yo-yo quietly said, "Yes, Harold, she's going to love it. It's a very nice perfume for a seventeen-year-old."

He gently set it on the stone tablet, and his body started shaking again. He tried to hold it back, until he was told, "Let it go, man, let it all out. Let Rachel feel the tears to tell her how much you miss her and still love her."

Rolling over, his inflated stomach keeping him from somersaulting, his heartache came out in a gushing moan, "Oh, God, my baby. I'm sorry, honey. Oh, I miss you so much. Ohhhh."

Yo-yo stood up choking back her own tears and waited patiently, leaning against the fender of the car, giving her partner the dignity of his own privacy. Several minutes later, he stumbled back, wiping his cheeks dry.

She asked him, "Do you want me to drive?"

"No. Thanks but I need to be busy." He hesitated before adding, "Sorry. Please keep this to yourself. I get a lot of crap from every one and couldn't handle being teased about this. It's way too personal for me."

Her voice was quiet and understanding, "Hey, man, it's your private life. I'm glad you shared it with me. There ain't no joke in this anywhere. I'll keep my mouth shut."

They sat for several minutes, both silent for a while before Yo-yo asked, "Can you talk about it?"

He abruptly said, "No."

"That's cool. Okay, that's cool."

Behind a large oak tree overwhelming nearby gravesites, a figure watched the scene at her daughter's headstone. Gladys still held an immense hatred for her ex-husband, loathing him for what he did. However, she knew the pain he was in, feeling compassion for the man. When the Plymouth pulled away, it was her turn to attend the birthday party.

Yo-yo's head was craning as they left the cemetery, excitedly telling him, "Harold, someone else was at Rachel's grave."

Eyes fixed ahead, he said, "Yeah, I know. Leave it alone."

THE TRIP BACK TO THE PRECINCT house was quiet, but not disturbing. When Bruntz had pulled into his spot in the police garage, he shut off the engine, but didn't make a move to get out. Staring at the steering wheel, he paused for a moment, and then quietly started, "She had just turned four. She was the cutest little bug you ever saw. Her head was filled with bouncy blonde curls and she had a smile for everything. I used to read to her every night—her favorite was *Stuart Little*. She used to giggle when we came to the part about Stuart wearing a walnut shell for a helmet. Her giggle was pure happiness, coming from her heart."

He stopped to let the pain of the memory wash away to a spot in his soul where it could come out again—when he could remember and suffer some more.

Taking a deep breath he went on, his voice low and steady, "I was home, supposed to watch her while my wife went to the store. I started drinking and fell asleep. The noise outside woke me up, and I found the front door open. I ran out and saw the crowd in the road. I pushed through them and . . ."

"You don't have to do this. Leave it alone."

Ignoring her, staring blankly out the windshield, he calmly continued, "All I saw were her little legs sticking out of her Winnie the Pooh shorts—the happy face of that little bear staring back at me. The rest of her had been ground into the gravel by a truck. I don't remember anything after that. I was told what an asshole I was and that I acted really bad for a long time, but it's all a blank. The next recollection I have is my wife, Gladys, walking out the door with a suitcase. About a year later, I dunno, maybe it was two, the shrink said I was straightened up enough to go back on the force."

The next few minutes of silence engulfing the car was starting to choke Yo-yo, until Harold looked at her, saying, "Do you know I used to be a champion weight lifter?"

Glad to change the mood, Yo-yo exclaimed, "No shit, man, really?"

"Yeah, I won lots of awards and had my picture in the muscle books. I did a movie with some other muscle freaks. Just a bit part— about ten seconds and six words." He looked at his stomach, "This is what happens when you go to extremes to mess yourself up."

Smiling, she said, "Well, you did a good job at that. You ever think about getting back in shape?"

He pulled himself out of the melancholy, shaking his head, "No, never. Come on, let's see if Mr. Freeman knows anything."

DARREL FREEMAN, IN AN ORANGE jump suit and shackled to a metal table, looked like he'd just been poured from a Cuisinart. Dejected, worried and frightened, he was weakened enough to make him more susceptible to the interrogation.

Yo-yo stood at the observation window listening to the voices as they were recorded. Inside, Harold sat heavily in the opposite chair.

"Detective Bruntz, I've been here all day. My wife is at home sick and my stepdaughter has just been killed. What do you want from me?"

Abruptly, Harold said, "I'll ask the questions, Darrel. You just answer truthfully and everything will be all right."

Opening the manila folder, Harold asked, "What caused you to go into the yard—out to the driveway?"

"I heard a gun shot. It sounded close, so I got scared and ran outside."

"If you were scared, why didn't you call 911? It'd seem that your fear would keep you away. You already told me you didn't like guns."

Shrugging, he said, "I don't know. In those circumstances, who can tell why anyone does anything?"

"Did you know what those circumstances were? Did you know that Isabelle was getting fucked in front of your house? Didn't it make you angry when you saw it?"

Harold showed Darrel the note he had written to her, ensconced in a plastic folder. "You were in love with an extremely beautiful young girl, even had sex with her. We have her sheets in the lab, and I'm positive we're going to find your semen on them. Am I correct?"

Dejected and totally wrung out, Darrel slowly answered, "Yeah, we did it, in her bed." He paused, looking woefully at Harold, "You saw her, Detective. If you were given the chance, wouldn't you do the same thing? Especially if . . . never mind. Yeah we were lovers."

"Isn't something like that difficult to keep a secret? Is that why your wife was having an affair—payback?"

Darrel leaned forward ready to say something, but sat back, looking at the table top. Catching the hesitation, Bruntz said, "What were you going to say, Darrel?"

"Nothing, just nothing."

"How long did it take you to get out to the driveway, Darrel?"

Ignoring the question, Darrel had another concern. "My wife, how is she?"

Thumping his fist on the table, Harold demanded an answer, "Answer my goddamn question. How long did it take you to get out to the driveway?"

Darrel jumped and rattled out a weak response, "I don't know. Not long."

"Bullshit! I timed that trip, Darrel. By the time you heard the shots, got out of bed and figured out what was going on, too much time would have gone by. The police got there almost immediately. You were already there weren't you! You pulled the trigger didn't you?"

With a smug look on his face, Darrel leaned forward, shouting, "No, I didn't. I loved her. I would never hurt her."

Pressing closer, Harold railed on him, "You were angry. Your lover was having sex with someone else, and you killed them both, didn't you? Your wife was almost killed having sex with another man, and you killed him also, didn't you!"

Trying to stand up, Darrel sputtered, "No, you've got it all wrong. I didn't kill anyone."

Pushing Darrel back into the chair, Harold calmed down and asked him, "Why did you take your slippers off when you went back in the house?"

Still befuddled and starting to become incoherent from the intense pressure, he said, "I guess to keep from getting the floor dirty. Doesn't that make sense?"

"You just saw your step daughter with her guts covering the trunk of a car and a dead man with no head lying on your driveway, and you take your slippers off so your linoleum won't get wet?"

Leaning forward, Harold spoke directly into his ear, yet loud enough to be recorded, "The timing doesn't work, Darrel. You got to the bodies almost at the same time they were shot and you claim there was nobody else around. We couldn't find any other footprints leading away from them."

Another gap had to be filled, with Harold asking, "Where was your wife when this happened?"

With a look of genuine disdain, Darrel looked at the detective answering with a slight hesitation, "She was still in bed. She has nothing to do with this."

"Let's look at the evidence, Darrel. The facts are always correct and they don't lie. Your side of the bed was pulled apart as if you got out of it in a big hurry, and your wife's side was neatly folded back. Why did you get out so fast, and if your wife heard the shots why was she so meticulous about getting out of bed?"

Assuming he had Darrel by the short hairs, Harold sat back to see if he would volunteer anything. At that moment, the door opened with an officer sticking his head in to motion for Harold to come outside.

"I'll be right back, Darrel. Think about what I've just laid out for you. Don't be stupid and try covering up the facts."

Stepping into the hallway, he came face to face with Lieutenant Warner. "Pack it up, Bruntz. The DA's going to go for murder one. He saw the girl getting laid and killed them both out of jealousy. He'll also get nailed for the Marks killing because there's enough circumstantial to make it look good. For the slaughter in his driveway, the lab got his prints off the murder weapon, so that part is a slam-dunk. Good job."

Harold didn't care who went to jail for the crime, as long as it was not Mrs. Freeman. He needed to get a statement that Darrel was the only one involved in Isabelle and Richards' murder.

Standing defiantly, Harold said, "Lieutenant, I didn't get a confession yet."

"Don't be a bone-head, Bruntz. Book him for murder one, three counts, and one for assault with a deadly weapon. Go home. It's over."

As Lieutenant Warner was walking away, he was stopped cold by Harold's next comment. "Wouldn't it be better to get a confession?"

"Goddamit, Bruntz, don't pull that shit again. He's going to trial because the DA wants him to. There's enough to put him away and bring this to an end. Don't fuck around with it anymore."

The lieutenant walked away with Harold's loud retort echoing in the hallway, "You got it, Bob. We'll fry the clod."

Yo-yo came out of the observation room asking, "What's that shit all about?"

Still gazing down the hallway, Harold calmly said, "The DA is going to send Mr. Freeman to prison."

Her mind clouded with doubt, she said, "How can he do that?"

"Well, isn't that the way it's supposed to work? We catch the bad guys and they go to jail?"

The frown lines creased her forehead making her hair bounce, "Not when they're innocent. How do we know he wasn't alone and where does Mrs. Freeman fit into this? She was just as close as he was."

Harold took Yo-yo back into the interrogation room with him to confront Darrel, "Mr. Freeman, the district attorney wants to book you for first-degree murder for Isabelle, Richard Olson, and Gordon Marks. What do you think of that?"

His eyes widened in a surprising calm manner, Darrel stammered, "But I didn't do it."

Yo-yo sat on the table next to him, saying, "Maybe you didn't, but you saw who did. You were too close to the scene to not see something. Save your life so you can go home to your wife, she's gonna need you."

He hesitated too long. His voice changed when he spoke, dripping with derision. Darrel contemptuously slurred, "My wife? Do you know how many men she's had sex with? Plenty. I know what she did."

Harold interjected, "Isn't that exactly what you did with Isabelle? You told me your wife didn't have relations with any other men. You lied to me."

Putting his head on the cold metal tabletop, Darrel softly said, "Leave me alone."

Not quite done, Harold asked the big question, "In your love letter to Isabelle, you said you had something that would make her happy. What was that?"

Darrel looked at both detectives with a strange cast of fear, and demanded, "Take me back to my cell. I'm through talking."

June 15

WITH DARREL FREEMAN BEHIND BARS Harold finally had time to look at the reports from the lab on the evidence. His shirt was filled with cigar ashes and coffee stains. Yo-yo came across him like a perfect storm. "No shit, man, can't you stay clean for at least a day? You look like a landfill."

Looking at her over the papers he was reading, he glumly told her, "You're not my mother. Go away. Don't you have some paper work to shuffle?"

Pacing around Harold's desk, her arms flailing wildly, she spat out a retort that Harold heard but ignored. "Yeah, man, I'm gonna go shuffle some paper and all kinds of other shit. I'll just crawl into the mu-fuckin file cabinet, filed under *pissed off*. I'm gonna walk away and ignore what's bothering you as much as it's bothering me."

That last comment got Harold's attention, and his twitch at hearing it was caught by the erratic woman. She pounced on him, straddling his lap with her thin legs on each side of him, sitting on the evidence report. Her hands on his shoulders, she put her face up to his, saying, "You know there's something wrong, don't you? You know that Mr. Freeman is hiding something that scares him enough to spend the rest of his life in jail to avoid." Leaning back, she added, "This ain't closed yet, is it, bubba?"

A woman in handcuffs, walking by with an officer pushing her along, looked at Yo-yo, commenting, "I do a lap dance and get busted. You guys bang in here and it's okay. That's some shit, I want my lawyer."

Giving Harold an evil sneer, the officer said, "Shut up and keep moving."

A grim aura hung over Harold, covering his character with an attitude between confused and upset. Settling back in his chair, with his chin resting on his chest, he had to reveal something to her that could mean nothing less than horseshit.

Taking the cigar out of his mouth so he could speak, Harold told his partner what was in the lab reports. "The prints on the three shell casings from Gordon Marks's yard all had the same pattern— partials. The clip itself also had the same prints. The .357 from the Freeman yard had some smeared prints of Mr. Freeman."

Hoisting herself up to Harold's desk top, she asked, "So, you're saying the prints on the Marks job found a match—that's a good thing, right? Yeah, so who we got? It ain't Mr. Freeman is it? We got him for the mess in the driveway, right?"

"We can get him for killing Isabelle and the Olson boy, but not the Marks job." A cold stare had covered Harold's face, with Yo-yo not sure she wanted to know anymore.

With a heavy sigh, he went on, "I was positive that Isabelle pulled the trigger on her mother, but now . . ."

Shocked, Yo-yo yelped, "Her mother, what kind of shit is that? Young girls don't whack their moms. Well, not much anyway. Why do you say that?"

"There was a tight competition between them trying to see who could destroy the most men. It looks, to me anyway, that the mother got the best of her spoiled daughter, so Isabelle tried to eliminate her.

However, with Isabelle as the last victim, we have a third party. I'm leaning towards Darrel, but with his obvious hanky panky with her, I can't figure out why he'd kill her. It had to be jealousy for boinking the Olson kid in the front yard. Mrs. Freeman is clear of any of it."

Yo-yo's logic was just too strong. "Okay, Sherlock, you're running all over the place and aren't even addressing the involvement of Mrs. Freeman. She was there, in the house, and had a motive also."

Harold's attraction to the beautiful Mrs. Freeman was spinning him out of the picture. He looked at his partner with a sick puppy face, quietly telling her again, "We need to keep Mrs. Freeman out of it."

Her anger erupted in a shout that echoed across the squad room, "*What?* Because she's got a nice ass? You honky son-of-a-bitch, you're gonna pull my foot out of *your* nice ass, which ain't so nice."

Holding his hands up in a calming gesture, he tried feebly to explain, but it still sounded bad. "All right, she's got a nice butt, and I think she's a fox, but please trust me on this. Leave the incrimination against Darrel alone for a while. Those prints on the shell casings at the Marks house bring a new suspect in. If they were involved in the shooting, then Mr. Freeman is into something deeper. Something we don't want to screw with."

Yo-yo's mind was spinning, looking for a place to land. "All right then, whose prints are on the casings from Marks's back yard?"

Harold wished the case would end right here. His goal was to direct the evidence toward Darrel, no matter what the truth was, but another character was about to enter the case, and Harold didn't want that to happen. Not this character anyway.

During his three decades of police work, Harold had worked on the beat in the slums of North Minneapolis, fought with gangs and drug dealers and pimps in the rest of the city. There was no form of violence or blood-covered gore that he hadn't been a part of. When the evidence was too weak to keep a bad guy behind bars, Harold made certain the right trail was left for a conviction. When an arrest was overturned, and there was enough suspicion to follow the criminal, Harold was not beyond his own level of justice. He didn't consider it murder, but rather a finger tipping the scales in the right direction.

There was not very much that could frighten Harold Bruntz. If it was something bad, he either had seen it or had caused it to happen. However, for all that he had been embedded in that had a nasty taste to it, he has managed to keep his distance from the one source of evil that truly did leave him cold.

The world of Leonid Cherasky was not one he wanted to go into.

CHAPTER 6
♫ SAILING, SAILING . . . ♫

YO-YO FELT THE CHILL COME OVER Harold. Getting up from Harold's lap, she stood back, saying, "Maybe I should just go do some filing. Okay?"

He took her hand, leading her into a conference room, closing the door. "Sit down. This isn't going to be good, Yo-yo."

Her legs jumping to a fast beat, she said, "I've been scared before, man, and I don't want to go there again. What's so bad about the prints?"

"They belong to Leonid Cherasky. A car registered to him was found a few blocks from Gordon Marks's house, abandoned. There was trace of blood on the gas pedal that matches a trace sample we got from the carpet fibers in Gordon Marks's house, and from the sneakers found in Richard Olson's car."

Eye's wide at an obvious connection, she spouted, "So this Cherasky guy is tied tight to the Marks killing, as well as the shit in the driveway."

Squashing her enthusiasm, he said, "No. Cherasky is far too removed from getting involved in a murder. He'd have one of his goons do it, and his car would have never been left to be found so easily. It was a plant to turn suspicion to him. The new blood sample could mean there is another victim out there." Harold's hesitation told her there was more.

Prompting him for the rest, "Okay, boss, go on, now what?"

"There's something else."

Yo-yo's arms were waving to keep pace with her voice. "So, spill it, mu-fuck. Am I in a Jeopardy game here? Just tell me without the drama."

"There was an expensive dress in Marks's closet, with a hair from it matching Cherasky's wife's DNA."

"So now we got the Russian dude's wife killing people? Or maybe she was getting poked by Marks also."

"No, it was another plant. His wife would never get involved with that, and if Marks had any sense at all he'd never go near her."

Yo-yo said, "You're just guessing at all this, right?"

"I can't prove it, no. But, Cherasky's far too dangerous to even think about crossing, so this all has to be a diversion to lead away from the real killer."

"And we don't know who that is, do we? Do we? All we got is Mr. Freeman, and since you do your thinking with your dick, Mrs. Freeman is off limits."

"Yes, well, not exactly. I'm going to say that Isabelle did the Marks job because the game she and her mother were playing backfired on her. She's not the first kid to kill a parent, and with the jealousy angle it should stick. We need a statement from Darrel that he was alone and killed Isabelle and the Olson boy."

Yo-yo said, "Maybe we should do the right thing and nail both of the Freemans. As an accomplice, wifie could get off with a lighter sentence. Even better if she rolled on him."

Giving Harold a moment to clear his mind, she looked straight in his eyes, and said, "Just because Mrs. Freeman has a nice ass and you got your weenie tied in a knot for her, you're bending too far the wrong way to keep her out of prison. It's gonna burn you, boss. Besides, she don't give a shit about you. Go with the facts, man. Mrs. Freeman needs to be grilled."

Firm in his answer, Harold said, "No, we go after Darrel. Got that? In the long run, it'll be a whole lot nicer than trying to get Cherasky. Maybe the DA's right and we should just let them take Darrel and be done with it."

Irritated, Yo-yo spat out, "Yeah, and that would put you one day closer to retirement wouldn't it! You know as well as I do that Darrel Freeman ain't gonna burn alone for this." With her nose in his face she strongly added, "Don't we!"

The quiet between them was stifling. Disgusted, Harold admitted, "Why do you have to be so persistent? I got along just fine when I didn't have a partner to justify things to."

Smiling, she answered, "We both want the same thing, bubba. I don't mind bending some rules. And I don't mind putting a good fuck to a bad guy to get him off the street. If Darrel waxed Isabelle and the kid, he'll go down for it. I'll let you deal with the fantasy of you and Mrs. Freeman. However stupid it seems."

Sitting down, crossing her legs to keep them busy, she asked, "Now, what about this new dude? You seem to get the willies talking about this Cher . . . something or other. I heard of him, heard he's supposed to be creepy, but I never dealt with him."

Harold went on to explain his concern, "To work on his level you'd need to crawl in some bad mud. Dealing with pimps, hookers, and druggies is clean compared to the muck surrounding this guy. Lenny Cherasky is the head of the Russian mob in this part of the country. He's supposed to be in Chicago, but there's been a rumor that he keeps a place somewhere up north."

Yo-yo asked, "So, this dude's bad?"

Harold took a breath, saying, "Saddam Hussein and Hitler were bad. Charles Manson's bad. Freddy Krueger was bad. Leonid Cherasky is a bad man's nightmare. He's one of those ruthless sons-of-bitches born totally without a soul or conscience."

"Yeah, so what are we going to do about this Cher . . . guy?"

Irritated, Harold tried correcting her. "Cher-asky, his name is Cherasky. We know Darrel dealt with him by the crap the lab got from his computer. We need to talk to Darrel again to see if we can get Cherasky for any of this." Harold nervously added, "God, I hope not."

Back in the interrogation room, Darrel sat motionless, waiting to be questioned again. Harold entered, sitting across from him. "Good morning, Darrel. Is there anything you need? Are you being treated well?"

Staring at Harold with confusion etched on his face, Darrel asked, "What? Is that what you want to know? You don't care if I'm feeling good or not. What do you want? I want to go home to my wife. If you're concerned about me, let me go."

Small talk over, Harold got to the point. "Darrel, how does Lenny Cherasky fit into your life?"

Stunned, Darrel sat upright. "I don't know him. I don't have to talk to you, you know. I want to go back." His knuckles had turned white from clutching the tabletop, making his lie obvious.

"Darrel, stop and think about what's happening here. You're charged with four capital crimes. Three possible counts of murder in the first degree if we pin the Marks job on you, and definitely the two smeared all over your driveway. The state has every right to seek a death penalty for you, and at the very least, you'll be behind bars forever. Growing old in prison is not like being in a retirement home. You're going to have some queenies cock up your butt and made to suck a hundred more."

Detective Bruntz leaned over the table, "Darrel, whatever you are afraid of now is not going to get any better if you take the fall for someone else. Lenny Cherasky can still get to you in prison. He can also do terrible things to your wife and you'll be helpless to stop it."

Opening the file for Darrel to see, Harold said, "We took your computer from your home and know you've had business dealings with Cherasky. What did you do for him, Darrel?"

Deflating, broken, Darrel said, "All right, I've dealt with Mr. Cherasky. I set up a website for some pornography to be shown on the Internet."

Harold dug deeper, "There's more, Darrel. By not telling me everything, you're lying to me. What's the rest?"

Pausing, Darrel weighed his options, finally saying, "I made a connection to some of his bank accounts. None of it was illegal. He told me he'd pay me cash to do this for him. He gave me twenty-five thousand dollars."

"Where did you do the work?"

"At his house."

Harold growled, "Where's his house, Darrel?"

The poor man was visibly shaking now and hesitated.

Thumping his fist on the table, Harold yelled, "Goddamit, you dumb shit, don't make me bleed you for this. When I say I want information, I want it all. Spit it out." For a moment, Harold thought he had gone too far with intimidation. The man was cringing. However, to have a real connection to Cherasky's location was too exciting, as well as frightening, to loose. At the same time, Harold was painfully aware that he was treading a path he did not want to travel.

Dejected, with no safe place to turn, Darrel mumbled, "His house is up north, on Gull Lake." With a pathetic look on his drawn face, Darrel repeated, "On Gull Lake. I'll write the directions." Writhing in anguish, Darrel moaned, "If he finds out I told you, I'm going to die. What am I going to do? I'm screwed no matter what happens." Looking up, his eyes, red and puffy, he pleaded for help. "What am I going to do?"

"Just tell me what happened, Darrel."

Sniffling back his pride and knowing he had just signed his own death warrant, Darrel stood up, saying, "I want to go back to my cell. If you want to talk to me again, I want a lawyer with me."

June 20, Gull Lake, Minnesota

THE CHERASKY ESTATE SPRAWLED along the northern shoreline of prestigious Gull Lake, in the middle of the posh vacation and resort community of Brainerd, Minnesota. The iron gates barring entrance remained closed, and nobody nearby to inquire about getting in. Armed with a search warrant did nothing to make this trip any easier.

Yo-yo, talking through her manic gum chewing, said, "Okay boss, when does the cavalry show up."

Frustrated, Harold answered, "We'll get in. Don't worry. We just have to find another way."

Her excited response, "Man shit, mu-fuck. We ain't going to get in there unless we drop out of the fuckin' sky. Ain't no way, baby, no way at all. Come on, let's just go home and file papers and shit. Come on, boss, turn this heap around and move out."

Harold turned around all right, but he didn't go home. Touring the lakeshore past estates and palaces considered "cabins" by the wealthy, he stopped at a marina with a huge sign, BOAT RENTAL.

Standing on the dock of the marina, Yo-yo bellowed out, "This is a fuckin' row boat, you bone-head. We's gonna sink out there."

Handing her a life jacket, he stepped into the fourteen-foot aluminum boat, telling her, "Buckle up. It's a state law." Harold's girth was too large to fit into his own life jacket, so he draped it over his shoulders with a bungee cord holding it shut at his waist.

It took her about five minutes to fuss with the straps of the life jacket, until an amused dock worker came over to help her. "Let me give you a hand, miss."

Looking up at the young man, Yo-yo was more than pleased to let him play with any part of her, unable to resist a lewd comment, "Oh, baby, you can do more than fiddle with my straps. Why don't you come with us, honey? We can have a picnic someplace and dump the fat guy."

Laughing his way through the process, the young man said, "Maybe some other time. There, that should be all right. Have a nice day, ma'am." He eyed the revolver holstered to her hip, and the badge clipped to her blouse. Smiling, he backed away.

She called after him, "It'd be nicer if you were to be my guide. I might drown out there."

He smiled his way back to whatever he'd been doing before, when Harold admonished, "If you're done trying to score, can we go now?"

Struggling to get her long slim legs into the tippy boat, she said, "I'd rather be doing this with him than you. Hold the fuckin' boat still, man." She nervously slid down to plant herself in the front seat.

Harold pushed the boat away from the dock and pulled on the starter rope, the small outboard coughing into life with a billowing of blue smoke. Yo-yo, hung onto the gunwales, frantically muttering, "Oh, Jesus. Shit, man. We're gonna sink, I just fuckin' know it."

The five-horse-power outboard pushed them along the shoreline for about a full hour, with Yo-yo spewing out a stream of insults and comments the entire time. Sitting in the small seat at the bow, her legs jumping and twitching, she was being drenched by the splashing of waves against the slow-moving boat. Finally realizing that Harold was hitting the waves on purpose, she launched into a tirade, "Goddamit, you prick, stop that. I'm getting soaked, and this fucking boat is gonna sink. Water's supposed to mix with booze, not to ride on."

On and on she chirped and never shut up, until Harold just couldn't hold back any longer. He burst into a rocking laughter that shook his huge body, causing his arm to swing the steering arm of the motor, dousing her even more. He thought it was hilarious, until he found himself looking at the muzzle of her .38 service revolver.

"Okay, I'm taking it easy. Put that away before you put a hole in the boat."

With a determined sneer, she said, "Stop that splashing shit or I'll put a hole in you and go home alone. You'd sink like a rock and they'd never know I shot your honkey ass. They wouldn't care, neither." Muttering to herself, "Fuckin' white men are all the same. Stupid."

She looked up to see Harold pointing to something at the shoreline. Cautiously turning, she gazed at a huge green lawn that seemed to stretch on forever. Nestled at the crest of the grassy expanse, sat a gigantic house that could have well passed as a luxury hotel. Stark white and ominous, it sported decks, porches, a million windows and a swimming pool.

There was a dock at the waters edge with a large shiny speed boat tied to it. The skinny wooden strips and the chrome accessories gave the craft a bulky look of speed and luxury. Anchored off the end of the dock, tied to a bobbing buoy, was a huge white yacht that sat motionless, the waves lapping against it. The array of decks and nautical trappings loomed over them as they noisily passed it.

Aiming for the dock, Harold's ineptitude at boating brought the small craft bumping into it, jarring the boat as well as the entire dock. Yo-yo, still fearing for her life, bellowed out, "Jesus, shit, man! What the hell you doing? I'm walking back. No shit, mu-fuck."

Harold, busy with his attempts to tie the runabout to the dock, didn't see the two men running towards them. Yo-yo spying them and the assault weapons they carried, reached for her gun. "Hey, boss, we got company."

Harold, used to her bantering, ignored her. This brought out her will to survive. She yelled at him, "Hey, you fat fart, look up for Christ sake. The army's coming at us."

The rope hanging from his hand, Harold looked up at two large men standing on the dock directly above them. Yo-yo had her revolver drawn, but held behind her back. The empty holster strapped to her waist made her a dangerous target for the two men.

Before Harold could explain the purpose to their visit, one man cocked his weapon, pointing it at Yo-yo's head. The other man spoke, "This is private property. Go away and nobody will get hurt."

Harold, fumbling with the folded search warrant, held it up saying, "We came to see Mr. Cherasky. We're with the Minneapolis police department. We have a search warrant."

The nearest man snatched the paper from Harold's hand and stuffed it into his pocket. He stood up, telling Harold, "This ain't Minneapolis, and you got no search warrant. Go away, now."

Harold held up his badge, defiantly announcing, "We are police officers with a search warrant and we're going to see Mr. Cher . . ."

His speech was cut short by a burst of gunfire from the Uzi held by the other man, the spent shell casings clattering on the bottom of the aluminum boat. Yo-yo scrambled to seat herself on the bottom, her .38 pointed at the shooter's head. Wide-eyed and speechless, she was ready to start a war, knowing they were going to die in the process. The Uzi was trained on her, and she knew she was going to be the first to go. She slowly let the hammer back into place, setting the gun on the wet boat bottom, her hands held up to show she was unarmed. Lying on the bottom of the boat, she tried telling Harold, "Get the fuck out of here, man. This ain't where we're supposed to be. Start the fuckin' motor, asshole." She tried to ignore the cold lake water soaking into her clothing.

The man on the dock said, "Listen to her. She's right. There ain't no search warrant, and you ain't coming ashore."

Harold pressed his issue, telling him, "We just want to . . ."

The next burst from the Uzi tore a gaping hole in the bottom of the boat between Yo-yo's legs. She felt the heat of the slugs ripping past her and the tearing of the aluminum. Bubbling up from the holes, the water engulfed them as the boat settled on the bottom. The two police officers treading water in their life jackets, Harold's billowing up around his chin. The man inserted a new clip into the Uzi, and the slide was pulled back to arm and cock it. Another series of bullets came across the water between them and the dock as a barrier. Both Harold and Yo-yo felt the pressure of the bullets as they tore through the water, inches from them.

Helpless, they started paddling themselves away from the dock, looking back to be sure the weapons weren't pointed at them. If they were shot at, they would have died, being unable to dive with the life jackets.

Far enough away so she could start her tirade again, Yo-yo yelled, "Why didn't you draw your weapon? You just fuckin' stood in the stupid boat."

Bobbing a few feet away, Harold didn't answer at first, but then said, "I forgot it in the car."

Too angry to respond, Yo-yo paddled and paddled as far away from him as she could. She was too angry with Harold to remember she couldn't swim and was afraid of the water. A constant barrage of anger welled up in her, "You're a fucking cop and you forgot your gun. Jesus, shit, man. You forgot your fucking gun." Her next tirade came out in a scream that echoed across the lake. "*Damn.*"

Two hours later, cold and fatigued, they crawled ashore at a small beach area in front of a log-sided cabin. Walking past the building, it was obvious there was nobody at home. Dripping wet, they walked the rest of the way around the lake to the marina. Yo-yo made certain she was always a few hundred feet ahead of Harold, not wanting to speak or look at him. Mumbling and swearing at him incessantly, she would reach back to give him the finger every once in a while. Cold and dripping, the two trudged along, her anger growing with each step.

It was late evening now, and the marina was closed. A note was attached to the windshield of Harold's Plymouth explaining that additional charges would be added to his Visa card. His clothing hanging on him, looking pathetic, he stood motionless in the parking lot, Gull Lake dripping from his life jacket.

Thoroughly disgusted and too tired to rail on him anymore, she slumped into the passenger seat and glumly said, "Let's go."

Sitting in the car, he noticed she was still wearing the life jacket. "Do you want help taking that off?"

Reeking of bad mood, her response came out dripping with anger, "Just shut up and leave me alone. Don't ever talk to me again."

He put the key in the ignition, but hesitated. Turning to her he quietly asked, "Are you going to report what happened?"

Her eyes glared through the wet strands of black hair hanging over her face. She snarled, "Didn't you hear me? I said to fucking never talk to me again." In a calmer, yet gloomy answer, she added, "No, no report. Nobody would believe it anyway."

His fingers just couldn't turn the ignition key until he had one more very important question answered. Slowly, he asked, "Are you going to leave me as a partner?"

It took a full minute for the answer come. Looking at the pathetic man sitting next to her, the trip to the cemetery washed through her brain, thinking that if she had been in his shoes she wouldn't have been able to handle something like that. Calmly and slowly, she told him, "I can't, Harold. You're the only one more fucked up than I am. Next to you, I look good."

Her feet vibrated in spasmodic rhythm, her head bopping to a tune nobody else could hear, she knew he was her partner. There was an overriding fact that she couldn't escape, something she might reveal much later in this deadly game. The more she got to know Harold Bruntz, the more respect she gained for him, and of course, she really liked the man. Mumbling to cover her feelings, "Fuckin' white men don't know shit, man."

Looking away from the angry woman sitting next to him, he understood her fury. He wanted to tell her how sorry he was, but held back. A slight smile crawled across his lips, grateful that she was not going to dump him. He still had his partner. Whispering, he abandoned his pride and told her, "I'm sorry."

Listening to his feeble apology she turned her head and covered her mouth to hide her own smile.

CHAPTER 7
VICKA

June 25

O NCE AGAIN, DARREL FREEMAN sat in the interview room, but this time he was not chained and had the company of Melvin Orenstein, a lawyer who suddenly appeared, but not retained by Darrel. The lawyer's employer had an interest in Darrel, needing to save him from the law. Orenstein started the conversation with, "You have the prerogative to interview my client whenever you want, but if it nears the harassment stage I will go directly to the commissioner himself and have you tarred and feathered."

Harold, in an attempt to whitewash his own goal and give everyone a comfortable feeling, sugar-coated his response. "Mr. Orenstein, your client's rights and personal freedom are the most important thing to us at this time. I want you to tell Mr. Freeman just exactly what he is facing with these charges."

Yo-yo turned her head to squelch an impending puke to Harold's honey dripped poppycock.

Mr. Orenstein seemed oblivious to Harold's sweet talk, or didn't care. "Well, we're not sure these charges are going to stick. So far it all looks circumstantial, and you are on a fishing trip." The lawyer, stalling, added, "Detective Bruntz, you're going to have to prove that what happened at my client's house was something other than a vicious murder of two innocent people. You holding Mr. Freeman on a double homicide is nothing more than your inability to prove anything." The lawyer's comments were filled with fluff and bluff, and he was good at it.

"His prints were on the murder weapon, counselor."

Raising his hands in gesture of futility, Orenstein spouted, "One partial smudge. We have experts who will blow that apart."

Harold was just as good at this game as Darrel's lawyer was. "Circumstantial or not, when pictures of the lovely young girl, his wife's daughter, who he had an affair with are shown to the jury, they will stumble over themselves to convict him, especially after they see the condition of her body in the morgue. The girl was his stepdaughter for Gods sake, and the lab report says she was pregnant with his child. How far is that going to go? The love letter alone will turn the jury against him. The DA wants him to take the hit for all of the murders, and even if he's convicted on only one of them, he's going to prison."

The news about Darrel's sexual activity with his stepdaughter, and knocking her up, stunned the lawyer. He leaned over the table to look at the file. Turning his burning gaze back to Darrel, he mumbled, "This was never brought to our attention. I'll need copies of all that and I know I can get that letter ruled as inadmissible." Back to Harold, he sternly asked, "What do you want?"

Looking deeply at Darrel, Harold put on his best *I'm all for you* impression, "Mr. Freeman, it's possible that you didn't kill anyone, but something has you so frightened you're willing to go to prison for it. Give us a chance to help you. Tell us how Leonid Cherasky is involved and this whole affair could turn away from you. I have to convince the DA that somebody else killed them, and if Cherasky was involved, it'd make you look a lot better."

Melvin leaned over to his client, whispering his message, "You really screwed this up. Give him what he wants but leave Cherasky out of it, okay? I don't have to outline who you're supposed to identify as the shooter, do I?"

Turning to the lawyer, Darrel fearfully questioned just who he was supposed to implicate. He held his hand up to mask his response into Orenstein's ear. The lawyer nodded in affirmation.

His face screwed up in question, hoarsely asked, "Are you sure?"

The same sinister response came from the lawyer.

Cupping his hand over his mouth, Darrel leaned to the lawyer's ear, whispering, "I need to keep them away from Amanda."

Grabbing Darrel's shoulder, he sneered, "I don't give a shit about her. You know what to do." Turning to Harold, Melvin Orenstein asked, "What kind of protection can you offer?"

Elated, Harold chimed, "All charges will be dropped, a new identity and relocation. He'll have to testify in court, but he'll have an armed escort for that." Detective Bruntz had no idea if his superiors would go for that or not. At this point he didn't care. Just get the statement, and he'll deal with the details later.

Mr. Orenstein said, "What my client puts in writing here will stand as our last offer to cooperate."

A yellow legal pad was pushed across the table, Harold gladly saying, "Write what you want." Giddy over the new cooperation, Harold added, "Also write down the details of what Mr. Freeman knows about the Gordon Marks killing." Harold's interest in who wounded Mrs. Freeman was incidental now. Eventually, right or wrong, he would name Isabelle as the Gordon Marks shooter. Harold doubted that Darrel's statement would vindicate him, its purpose being to implicate Leonid Cherasky.

Twenty minutes later, the pad was pushed back with two full sides filled, in Darrel Freeman's handwriting. Quickly reading the scribbling, Harold did a double take before rereading the pad. Astounded, he leaned over the table, saying, "What's this shit? You didn't even mention Leonid Cherasky, and who the hell is David Sloan?"

Yo-yo stepped up to the table taking the pad and set it down, equally confused.

Darrel said, "You wanted the truth, and that's what I gave you."

Looking at Mr. Orenstein, Harold said, "We'll check on David Sloan, but where does Cherasky fit into this?"

With a dour frown, Darrel said, "He doesn't. I told you what you wanted to know. I did some business for him and that's all. If you want him, find another way."

Harold got up, telling them, "All right, Darrel. You'll be taken back to your cell."

Reaching his hand out, Harold told Orenstein, "I'll be in contact with you."

The lawyer stopped Harold, saying, "I brought some street clothing for my client. Just in case he needed it." Arched eyebrows and slight smirk.

Back at his desk, Yo-yo asked, "What the fuck's happening, boss? Who's this Sloan guy?"

"I don't know, but I think we're being duped. Cherasky *has* to fit in here, someplace. If Darrel was involved with Cherasky, we need to find out what it was."

He looked at the statement again with the previously unknown name of David Sloan glaring at him.

June 27, Amanda Freeman's house.

Yo-YO AND HAROLD SAT IN AMY'S living room talking to a zombie. The nurse had made coffee to take the edge off, but Mrs. Freeman was borderline psychotic. Harold looked at Yo-yo and nodding towards the nurse. Catching the signal, Yo-yo guided the nurse to the front door, and calmly said, "We need you to wait outside until we're done here. I hope you understand."

"Of course, I'm not going anywhere." She placed herself on the front step and took out a cigarette.

Harold asked, "Amanda, we need you to talk candidly with us. Are you able to do that?"

Looking up, her eyes red and puffy, she nodded and mumbled, "Yes. I can answer your questions. There's no reason to hold back anything now. How's my husband? I can't get out to go see him."

Yo-yo told her, "He's doing as well as he can. He'll be okay."

Harold aberrantly leveled his voice to a calm and soothing tone, hoping she would be relaxed and answer truthfully. He began, "Were you aware that your husband and your daughter were having an affair?"

Amy stiffened, her cup shaking in her hand, said, "I wasn't certain, but I thought there was something going on. Izzy and I sort of did what we wanted with men, either hers or mine. I guess I'm not surprised. After what I did to Darrel, I have no room to find fault with him." Tightening her grip on the coffee cup, her eye's darted enough for Yo-yo to notice.

Yo-yo leaned over to take the coffee cup from Amanda so her shaking wouldn't spill it. She set it on a nearby table, and asked, "Were you aware that Isabelle was pregnant with Darrel's child?" Her tone was firmer than Harold's.

She slowly answered, "Not until I saw the test strip in the wastebasket. Yeah, I knew. She could hardly wait to tell me and grind it in. I know she left it there for me to find."

Yo-yo felt she had a handle on a motive. She pressed for more. "That should confirm that you were aware of the affair. When did you tell her you knew?"

Amanda's answer was not what Yo-yo was fishing for, but was an interesting revelation. Looking up at Detective Brown, Amy quietly said, "Isabelle's had some problems. She was seeing a counselor to work on issues she was embarrassed to talk about."

Harold, asked, "What kind of issues?"

"She had a problem separating right from wrong and just did whatever came to her. She would impulsively do things that hurt people and couldn't understand why there would be a fuss about it. She didn't have any friends because she'd always do snide, deceitful things to hurt them. Her need to hurt people became a real problem, and then it turned to me. She concentrated on hurting me. She was definitely mentally disturbed, and terribly embarrassed about it. Every time the suggestion came up to revisit her counselor, she'd fly into a rage." A vacant look crossed her face, and she mumbled, "Oh, Izzy, what went wrong? It wasn't supposed to be like this."

Harold felt compassion, but Yo-yo had no intention of leaving Amy alone. She had questions to ask and was ready to get answers. In a few moments, Amanda relaxed enough to leave an opening for Yo-yo to start the questions again. "Both you and Isabelle were shot having sex in someone's back yard. What's the connection there? What's the significance of doing that?"

Sighing, Amy said, "This is getting uncomfortable. I should be past the embarrassing stage, but some of this is really personal."

Yo-yo firmly said, "Just answer."

Closing her eyes, she quietly said, "When I was sixteen I was raped in the back yard. It was late at night, and we were making out on the grass. I just wanted to fool around and feel sexy, but he got carried away and said he couldn't stop. He tore my clothes off and forced himself on me. When it was over, I screamed at him and hit him, but he felt so bad he just held me and told me he was sorry. I would have let it go, but I got pregnant, and it all changed. I was totally angry at that and I've had a fantasy about doing it like that over and over. When I got men to do it in the yard I felt like I was raping them to get even."

Yo-yo asked, "What has that got to do with Isabelle?"

Looking up at the face of the female detective, Amy said, "When I thought she was old enough I told her how she was conceived, but that was a huge mistake. With her mental instability she took it to an unnecessary level and found a way to hurt me. She thought being conceived in a rape made her a bad person, and acted bad to fit the impression. She was too smart to be counseled by the therapists. Isabelle fooled a lot of people. She gave the impression of being dumb, an airhead, to fit the blonde image. But, she was brilliant. So smart that she was able to connive and control people, especially men, without them being aware of it. She fooled her analyst. One day she came home laughing about going to his home and telling his wife about an affair they had. She broke up the marriage and thought it was funny. She had an IQ well over 160.

"I know she blamed me for everything and went to extremes to punish me. She became angry and held a deep contempt for me." Amanda put her head in her hands and wept.

Not wanting to loose the momentum, Yo-yo urged, "Keep going, and tell us the rest."

Sniffling into a tissue, she went on, "I tried to get closer to her but the only thing we could relate to was sex and destruction. We made a joke out of men, and the two of us shared a plan to destroy as many as we could. It became a game, and afterward we'd compare notes and laugh at the fools we made of them. Gordon Marks was the best of all. Both of us tore him apart and felt good about it. I'm glad he's dead. Isabelle said the same thing to me. She said she was glad he was dead." The morose comment seemed to drain her emotionally.

Adjusting herself on the sofa, she continued, "She was insanely jealous when I would bring men home and she started acting out. She was acting out what she saw me doing."

Amanda carefully added, "I think she seduced her stepfather at an early age."

Incredulous at what Amanda said, Yo-yo blurted, "Are you telling us that your husband was abusing your child and you let it go?"

Looking up at Harold, her cheeks wet from the grief, asked, "How much do you have to know?"

He reached out to hold her hand, ignoring the fierce glare from Yo-yo. "We need to know all of it. We have to understand what went on."

Pulling her hand away, she said, "We were very close to each other, yet we really never liked one another. Hurting each other became part of the game, and when I took Gordy away from her, she couldn't handle it."

Harold caught the hole and jumped on it immediately. "Wait a minute, are you saying that you stole Marks from her?"

"Yes, I did. Why is that a surprise?"

"Isabelle told me Marks was a cast off, and you took care of him to get him away from her."

Rolling her head slowly, Amy said, "One of her fantasies to justify where she belonged was all about being the beautiful girl that everyone wanted, instead of me. Poor Izzy."

Yo-yo, desperately trying to stay focused, asked, "Do you think it's possible that Isabelle was playing Richard Olson to fit in the game?"

"Why, yes, I suppose she could have. Do you think so?"

Throwing her arms up in frustration, Yo-yo shot the question back to her, "I don't know, what do you think?"

Amanda shook her head, thinking that was a perfect observation. Until Detective Brown asked, "Where did the gun come from? A .357 weighs too much to be kept in a pocket."

Confused at the logic, Amanda just stared dumbly.

The silence in the living room was overwhelming, when Harold asked, "Amy, who is David Sloan?"

If anything was going to derail Amanda, that was it.

June 27, Minneapolis Courthouse.

As Amy was talking to Detectives Bruntz and Yo-yo Brown, Darrel Freeman was walking out of the Minneapolis jail, free on a one-hundred-thousand dollar posted bond.

In the office of Captain Faye Hilksman, Faye was screaming at Lieutenant Bob Warner, "*What do you mean he's out on bail?*"

Cowering from the wrath of his boss, he feebly answered, "I don't know how it happened. Whoever posted bail did it through a judge higher up than we can go. All of a sudden this case is wrapped up in politics."

Livid, both sat down and shared the captain's reserve supply of Canadian Club.

Darrel was aware of who his benefactor was and would have preferred staying in jail. The obligation that went with the bail money was more than he was ready to commit to. As he stood on the steps of the old limestone court house, a black Mercedes pulled up to the curb. The rear door opened, and a man compelled Darrel to get in.

Sitting next to Leonid Cherasky, Darrel numbly said, "Thanks for bailing me out. What do I owe you for it?"

Lenny turned to Darrel, putting a handhold on his leg with the strength of a pipe wrench, saying, "All I want in return is your silence and your will to stay alive. What did you tell the cops?" Lenny's voice came from deep in his throat and sounded like his neck was grinding rocks together.

Leonid Cherasky had been born with a look that frightened people. A stern muscular man in his mid-forties, sporting a gray crew cut, he gave people the impression that he ate concrete blocks for breakfast. He was rich, demanding, and both politically and physically powerful, getting whatever he wanted using fear and intimidation. His main source of income came from drugs, pornography, and the white slave connection to Russia. His base of operations was in Chicago, Dallas, and Las Vegas. Justification for his income was attributed to dealings in pornography on the Internet—sleazy, but not illegal.

He spent time in Minnesota to escape attention from rivals and the law in the more worldly places. Lenny Cherasky was in control of what he did, and ruled his corner of the empire with an iron fist. As feared and contemptable as he was, the Russian mob boss was frightened by Darrel Freeman. Darrel's business was the unknown and mysterious world of information technology, and he knew how to use and control it better than anybody. Lenny made the mistake of allowing Darrel to wander deeply into his personal business, letting him learn things that could ruin him, and now it was time to correct it.

Nervously, Darrel answered, "I didn't tell them anything, but Detective Bruntz has an idea you're connected." Darrel paused, adding, "Did you know Isabelle was killed? She and her boyfriend—right in front of my garage."

Releasing his hold on Darrel's leg, Lenny laughed and answered with a smile, "Little Isabelle killed? That's a good one. What fool would ever waste a nice piece like that? She must have done something very bad, do you think? Be realistic, my friend, someone killed your little girl because she must have done something very bad."

The sadistic grin on Lenny's face made Darrel shrink. Lenny kept up the banter, the European inflection to his voice making him seem more sinister, "Too bad. She was a good fuck. And took a good picture. She just couldn't get enough of that camera poking into all her places."

Suddenly, Lenny's mood darkened making Darrel's stomach churn. "You dip-shit, of course I know she's dead. And I also know that it was my gun used to kill one of her boyfriends, that old guy with the big mouth. How do you think she got hold of a gun hidden in my house, Darrel? You were in there enough to know some things you shouldn't."

Bristling, Darrel did the best he could to stay calm, but Lenny felt the agitation.

"Darrel my friend, you should have never been digging into her, you know that, don't you! If you want some ass, don't get it at home. With all the guys fucking your wife, you can bang all you want with other dames."

Starting to perspire, Darrel said, "Please, leave Amy out of this."

Lenny's expression hardened. "Who killed my bodyguard, Darrel?"

Sitting forward on the seat, Darrel said, "What? I don't know any . . ."

"Relax. I don't think you did it. You don't have the balls for that. But, you might know who did. Do you?"

"Lenny, for God's sake, I'm smart enough to know not to fuck with you. If I had any idea I'd tell you."

Lenny's face turned red, the muscles in his neck stiffening. He growled, "It was your stepdaughter, you dumb shit. She snuck into my house, killed my guard and stole a gun and a car. Her footprints were all over the place. Nobody but a dumb broad like that would leave their footprints in blood for Christ sake. Why would she want to set me up, Darrel?"

"Oh Jesus, Lenny. Are you sure it was her?"

"Oh, Darrel, you ignorant wimp. I have more connections in the police department than that drunken bitch that runs the place. I got the reports before anyone else."

Darrel, desperate for excuses, said, "Isabelle could go nuts at nothing and do whatever she wanted. She tried to kill her mother. How insane is that?" Darrel sat in silence, his guts falling and tumbling inside his stomach, sadly adding, "Amy was with him. My wife was shot having sex with that son-of-a-bitch Marks."

Totally disgusted with Darrel's lack of control over his family, Lenny's advice was sincere, "Darrel, why don't you get pissed enough to do something about it? She's your wife for Chrissake, take charge, my friend."

Darrel felt Lenny staring hard at him, and then answered, almost to himself, "Don't worry about Amy. I'll take care of her."

Cherasky had made his point and curtly changed the subject, "I need you at the house. There are some more entries to make on the computer."

"I already showed you how to do that. You don't need me anymore."

"You can show me again." There was no room for debate, Darrel would do as he was told, like it or not. The thought of going back into Lenny's house shattered his nervous system.

June 27, The Freeman house.

THE MENTION OF DAVID SLOAN brought Amy up from the sofa, "How do you know about him?"

Harold firmly admonished her, "Sit down, Amy. It's my job to know these things. Who is he?"

Amanda Freeman was drained. Her face was ghostly white, she had dark patches under her eyes and was loosing weight. This amazingly gorgeous woman was emaciated and getting worse. She slowly lowered herself back to the sofa, and moaned, "David Sloan is Isabelle's biological father. I've been in contact with him for the last five or six years. When Izzy got curious about him I found him and he wanted to meet his daughter. We picked it up again and have been seeing each other regularly."

Harold said, "His name isn't on the list you gave me. Is there a particular reason you omitted him?"

"I didn't want him involved. He's a decent guy and . . . he's just a decent guy."

This time, Yo-yo stepped into the conversation, "Finish what you were going to say, honey."

Harold shot Yo-yo a glance, his objection to her interfering.

Amy looked at her, and said, "God, do you people have to know everything?"

Yo-yo again, "Yes, honey. We're cops, and we need to know it all. Please make it easy for all of us and answer. Talk here or talk downtown. Either way you're going to talk."

Her head down, Amy said, "I never told anyone he was the father. I was hoping he'd find me and want to do the right thing. But, he waited too long, I guess."

Yo-yo said, "You still saw him after he dumped you? He raped you and dumped you? Are you in love with him?"

Amy looked up with a sad smirk to her blank lips, "Love? Who in hell knows what that is? Yeah we were seeing each other. It's just something that happened. He was off limits to Isabelle in the game we played. She was his daughter, and he wouldn't have let it happen anyway. Izzy would taunt me though. She'd giggle and ask if it would be a turn-on if she had sex with her father."

Harold wrinkled his face at the sickness of that, and asked, "What has been his involvement with Isabelle."

"He'd just talk to her and send a gift now and then."

Harold asked, "Are you familiar with Leonid Cherasky?"

Amanda stiffened, staring into her hands clasped on her lap, and not answering.

Harold got up from his chair and sat on the sofa next to her, taking her cold limp hand into his. Softly, he said, "Amy, you need to help us. Isabelle is dead, and we need to ,bring her killer in so nobody else gets hurt. Gordon Marks was murdered and you could have been killed also."

Amy pulled her hand away and abruptly blurted, "No I wouldn't." She knew immediately she had made a mistake, but couldn't take it back.

Her mind was in a kamikaze dive, and she wanted desperately to be alone. She looked at Harold with pleading eyes, "Please, leave me alone. Maybe you could come back later."

Harold looked up at Yo-yo, and they both understood the revelation that was just given to them.

June 27, the Cherasky Estate, Gull Lake.

T HE IRON GATES TO THE GULL LAKE mansion opened on command to allow the Mercedes entrance. Cruising along the landscaping and green undergrowth, it circled under the portico. A muscular man with a pistol strapped to his chest opened the door to let them out. Darrel stood nervously on the crushed rock drive wishing he could evaporate. As the Mercedes glided away, Lenny nudged Darrel to move, nearly pushing him over.

Entering the spacious and austere living room, Darrel faced a skinny man wearing heavy glasses. The man was nervous and twitchy, and constantly pushing his glasses up onto his nose. He wore a cheap, wrinkled, brown suit accented by a stained tie that would never match anything. If there were a place the skinny man might be comfortable in, this was not it.

Lenny strode directly to the bar and poured a cognac from a crystal decanter. He poured a second one for the other man, ignoring Darrel, who caught the snub immediately.

More of an announcement than an introduction, Lenny's voice boomed, "Darrel Freeman, meet Harry Warden, my accountant."

Darrel and Harry Warden nodded greetings to each other, with the accountant still uncertain why he was here. Harry, a recovering alcoholic teetering on relapse, was uncertain what to do with the alcohol in his hand. Peering through the heavy lenses hanging on his nose, Harry clutched the precious glass, twitching nervously.

Lenny, glass in hand said, "Gentlemen, this way, please," bidding them to follow. Darrel knew where he was headed, afraid the rolling in his stomach was going to erupt. Unlocking the door to his office, Lenny made sure they followed him in. The muscular man with the gun attached to him slid in behind them.

"Darrel, I want you to show Harry everything there is to know about the programs you put into the computer. I'll come back in an hour to see how things are going." Lenny gently pushed Harry towards the desk to be sure he understood that he was going to get involved, like it or not. "Any questions, Darrel?" No answer was expected.

The perspiration was flowing off Darrel, and his eyes became cloudy. He knew Cherasky well enough to understand this could be the beginning of the end for him. "No questions. I'll run him through the same thing I did for you."

"Good." Lenny cracked his knuckles and left, but the henchman stayed, quietly propped in a chair across the room.

June 27, Amanda Freeman's house.

SITTING IN THE PLYMOUTH, outside of the Freeman house, Harold lit a cigar and sat quietly for a minute. Turning to a disgusted and retching Yo-yo, her hand waving away the thick smoke, he said, "You heard that didn't you?"

"Yeah, boss, she knows who shot her. It looks like someone gave her a gut wound to equalize everything. No shit, man, they could have still killed her, or at least crippled her."

Harold had a feeling they were missing something. "I'm not so sure. It was dark, and if the shooter was not used to a pistol, their aim could have been off. Remember, the slide was open and the clip was empty. I'm convinced more than ever it was the girl who did the shooting. She was a spoiled brat not used to being second fiddle, and if she was pissed enough at her mother, she sure as hell would have doused her."

Exasperated, Yo-yo reminded him, "You just heard what she said. She knew she wasn't going to die."

"Or, more likely that she *hoped* she wouldn't die." Something wormed its way into his head, "Think about this. If it was Isabelle who shot Marks, and with the games they were playing, there's a strong chance she wanted her mother dead and to blame it on Cherasky. That would leave her and her stepfather open to do whatever they wanted if Darrel wasn't threatened by Lenny. And, if Amanda implicates Isabelle in the shooting it may affect Darrel's place in all this."

Sneering at his logic, yet finding a sound reasoning to it, she said, "Where do you come up with shit like that?"

"It's what's kept me on the job for thirty years. Instinct. Now, we have a definite connection to Cherasky. I'm still going to nail Darrel for a double homicide, but here's a chance to get that Russian prick out of the way. This Sloan guy might play a part in this, also."

Accepting his explanation, she added, "You might be right, boss, and that means we have to talk to this Cherasky dude and find Mr. Sloan. Of course you know I think you're wrong about Mr. Freeman being the killer."

Disappointed that it came up, he grudgingly answered, "Yeah, I know. We'll get back to Mrs. Freeman later, but for now its *hands off*."

Disturbed by his complacent attitude towards Amanda Freeman, she threw a sour look at him, and then rolled down her window, saying, "Why can't you smoke cigarettes like everyone else?"

"Those things will kill you. We're going back to Lenny's place. We gotta get in there."

Yo-yo sat up from her slouch, wide eyed, "You're fuckin' nuts, man. We almost got killed there."

Harold ground the car to life, ashes piling on his stomach, said, "I got a plan this time."

Yo-yo yelling, "You had a plan last time. Take me back to the station, I got some filing to do."

Ignoring her, the rusty Plymouth rattled its way to the Brainerd Lakes area. Yo-yo turned to her partner and asked, "Okay, bubba, tell me your plan so I can be ready to unscrew it for you."

Chewing on his cigar, Harold absently said, "Give me a minute. I'll think of something." If Harold had been alone on this trip he would have cracked open another half pint to help his mind process better.

Looking hard at him, Yo-yo said, "If it involves water, call the Navy, boss. I ain't going through no more of that shit."

Two hours later, as they approached the iron gates to Lenny's estate, they slowly yawned open to let a car leave. It was a cream-colored BMW convertible, with a dark-haired woman behind the wheel. Harold had to swerve off the road to avoid colliding with her.

Given the choice of speeding through the gates before they closed, or going after Lenny Cheraski's closest connection, he made a decision. Spinning the steering wheel wildly, the little engine in the Plymouth screamed, trying to develop enough power to follow the Beemer. Harold was straining to get the car off the shoulder and back onto the road.

Yo-yo, spilling over from the momentum, yelled, "What the fuck are you doing, man?"

Explaining loudly. "That's Vicka Cherasky, Lenny's wife. If we stand any chance of getting to Lenny, it's going to be through her. Hang on, I don't want to lose her."

Yo-yo sat on the edge of the seat, wide eyed and clutching the dashboard as tightly as she could. She started reaching back for the seat belt, but remembered it didn't work. Her lips stretched tightly across her face, and she moaned, "Ohhh shit!"

Harold had no idea that Darrel had been bailed out, and was at that very minute inside the large white house they were leaving behind.

Weaving in and out of traffic, Harold followed Vicka to the Westgate shopping Center in Brainerd. They spotted her entering a Victoria's Secret shop, so to avoid a scene they waited on a bench in the bustling courtyard. Besides, Harold was just too embarrassed to go in.

Breaking into the boredom of waiting, Yo-yo pointed to the store front, and said, "They got some good shit in there, man. I should go check out some of the slinky stuff."

Harold put his hand out to protest the idea, "Stay right here. What does a cop need that stuff for?"

Moving closer to him to be sure he heard her, she said, "Working with you I'm more than likely going to get bounced off the force and have to go back on the street. A girl needs some decent stuff to get a better price."

A few more minutes floated by with Yo-yo picking up the conversation again, with a teasing smile, "If I went on the street would you do me, boss?"

Shaking his head, he said, "You're not going on the street. Besides, you'd lose money doing it."

Mumbling to herself, yet loud enough for Harold to hear, "What do you know about it? Stupid white men don't know shit, man."

Vicka took less than a quarter hour to pick out a bra and trappings that satisfied her. Coming out of the store she was flanked by Harold and Yo-yo. Startled, she looked at both of them thinking she was going to be kidnapped and got ready to scream.

Harold stemmed off a nasty scene by showing her his badge, and said, "Mrs. Cherasky, we need to talk to you."

Stopping in her tracks, letting the crowd brush past, she said, "I can't tell you anything about anything. Talk to my husband."

Vicka Cherasky was a bit taller than either Harold or Yo-yo. She spoke with a slight European accent and carried an air of elegance with her. Yo-yo thought she'd do very well as a high class call girl, thinking of Florence Widholm.

"We've been trying to do that, but he's pretty well bottled up. There's a coffee shop down the hall. Can we go there and just talk for a few minutes?"

Defiantly, she said, "And if I refuse?"

"Then I'll have to arrest you as a material witness and take you to Minneapolis."

"My husband will have me out in no time."

Harold played his trump card, "Sure he will, but he's going to have to go all the way to Minneapolis, wait until tomorrow and go through the process of getting you released. Do you really want to piss him off to that point? Do you want to be marched through this mall with your arms cuffed behind you?"

The coffee shop was relatively quiet and with a rear table they could keep their voices low. Harold stuck Yo-yo with the bill while he seated himself and Vicka. He laid his business card on the table in front of her.

Without touching it, she glanced at his name and said, "Okay, so I know your name. Get on with this, what do you want with me?"

Yo-yo sat down with the three coffees, when Harold said, "There have been three murders in the last week, and your husband's prints were on the spent shell casings for one of them. In addition, his car and a dress of yours were connected to one of the crime scenes. Maybe he did it, maybe he didn't. Whatever, I need to know the obvious. Why were his prints on the bullets, and why was your dress in the closet?"

Something flashed past her mind and both Yo-yo and Harold caught it. He took a photo out of his coat pocket, sliding it across to her. "Do you know this girl?"

The beautiful blue eyes of Isabelle were dull and vacant, giving her a cold antiseptic stare. The photo ended just below the breast bone, but showed enough of the gore to illustrate what had happened to her. Vicka winced, with her fist to her mouth, gasping, "Oh, no, not poor Izzy. Why would anyone kill her?"

Harold answered, "That's what we're trying to figure out, Mrs. Cherasky. Has she been to your house at the lake?"

Taking a moment to collect herself, Vicka said, "Yes, she was one of my husband's girlfriends. She did some modeling for him also."

Harold reeled at hearing that, "Your husband had a girlfriend? You knew?"

Sipping her coffee, she said, "Detective, I don't know if you are naïve, archaic, or just stupid. You know very well what business my husband is involved in. He deals in beautiful women and sex. Yes, he was fucking the girl. So was I."

Now, totally confused, Harold wrinkled up his brow and said, "You too?"

Yo-yo held a grin, understanding what was being said. "Boss, they were lovers. Lesbo's, man. At least for the photo shoot."

Still in the outfield, Harold didn't catch the drift until Yo-yo said, "They were lesbian lovers, bone-head. Little Isabelle was having sex with everyone." Turning to Vicka, Yo-yo said, "Were there photo shoots and videos? Did this get on the Internet?"

Amused that the man was an idiot, and the black woman was aware of the life of a model, she smiled and said, "Yes, we did about three hours of porn and she got paid well for it. If you can find it in the pile of garbage that's on the web, you will also see her with some other men." Then almost as an afterthought, "And women, other than myself."

Turning back to the flabbergasted Harold, Vicka said, "Is there anything else you need to know?"

He stammered, "Yes. Yes, there's more. Do you know anything about a .32 caliber pistol in your house?"

Her nervous twitch gave her away, and she knew it. Quickly recovering, she said, "Yes, we had one, but it was stolen a couple of weeks ago."

"Mrs. Cherasky, your house is a fortress. How could anyone get in to steal anything?"

"If you want something bad enough, you'll find a way to get it." Her comment told them they should have already known that.

"Why was your dress in Gordon Marks closet?"

This was a revelation that totally confused her. Being honest, she said, "Detective, I don't know what to tell you." Then, she stated the obvious. "If someone broke into our house and stole the gun, they also took the dress. It would have more than likely been hung up in the same closet where the gun was kept."

If Lenny had any notion about the theft, he kept it to himself. However, Vicka was smart enough to know that the gun was stolen on the same night that Petra and Grotzke were murdered.

A vacant feeling of fear crept through Vicka, thinking it could have only been a handful of people able to get into the house. She absolutely did not want to share this with her husband, yet was frightened not to tell him, still unaware of her husband's knowledge that the intruder was Isabelle. Also, her brief clandestine relationship with Darrel Freeman needed to be kept away from any part of Lenny's knowledge.

Harold needed to get all he could before she realized she didn't have to answer any of these questions. He asked, "Do you know Darrel Freeman?"

With her mind still spinning from Isabelle's burglary, she stiffened, thinking this was getting too close to the truth. Straining, she attempted a vacant answer, "Yes, he does computer work for Lenny."

"How about his wife, Amanda?"

With a slight relief, her answer came slower now, but she admitted, "Lenny fucked her also. She put up a fuss about the movies and photos, so he let her go and never called her to come back. Her husband is the one who brought his wife and daughter out."

Now, even Yo-yo was confused, and asked, "Why would anyone's husband whore off their own wife?"

"Darrel bragged to Lenny about how beautiful his stepdaughter was, and how his wife liked to screw. He told Lenny that the mother and daughter were doing each other. Therefore, with enough money thrown at Darrel, he got them to show up. Amanda didn't like it, but Isabelle was enough of a beauty to make up for it. There was some kind of a row between the women, but Isabelle did what she wanted. She seemed to enjoy showing up her mother. Then when Darrel was filmed having sex with his stepdaughter, the mother left."

The two detectives gave each other a fleeting glance, recognizing the conflict between Amanda Freeman and her daughter. Whether it had grown to a proportion to involve murder, was yet to be seen.

Harold was in denial about the next obvious question, so Yo-yo picked it up. "You said that Mrs. Freeman and her daughter were having sex with each other?"

Oblivious of the dismay with the lesbian contact between a mother and daughter, Vicka casually answered, "Of course. I understood it to be just another level of eroticism between them. Why do you Westerners find sex so repelling? Your divorce rate is inexcusable, and it's no wonder."

Yo-yo shrugged and decided to keep her mouth shut.

Harold, upset at the thought of Amanda Freeman having sex with so many people, changed the course of questioning with, "Do you know David Sloan?"

The question startled Vicka. The very idea of Lenny's hired hit man turned her cold, and under no circumstance was she going to acknowledge the killer to anyone, especially not to this rude and obnoxious detective. Suddenly, Vicka stood up, left the table and left them sitting there, mouths agape. With no indication she was done, she just plain walked away, leaving Harold's card on the table.

The two detectives sat speechless for a few long moments, until Yo-yo said, "That went well. Want a doughnut?"

CHAPTER 8
ESCAPE

June 27, the Cherasky estate.

POISED IN FRONT OF LENNY'S COMPUTER, Darrel knew beyond any doubt that he was facing nothing but trouble. Fear was doing its best to churn into hyperventilation. Darrel, muttering nervously to himself, "Oh, God, I'm so totally screwed here. I've got to get a message to Amy before it's too late." A quick glance at the indifferent guard sitting across the room, and then turning to face the unstable Harry Warden, Darrel knew he had only one way out.

Harry's face was in a tight wrinkle with his glasses sitting askew on his nose. Reacting to Darrel's mumbling, clutching the glass of cognac tightly, he chattered, "Huh? Did you say something?"

Darrel thought the man was going to cry, sharply barking at him, "No, I didn't say anything. Shut up and let me think." Darrel knew in his gut that Lenny had discovered what he had done, and that meant it was too late to correct it. There was no doubt at all that as soon as the money was returned, he would die. That was Lenny's way. Intimidate, make the subject squirm, then put the victim through hours of sadistic torture. The unstable accountant was here to be certain somebody was left to show Lenny how to navigate the computer. The reward for that would be following Darrel in the painful trip to death.

The plan with Isabelle made sense at the time, and if he had insisted on doing it himself, she would be alive today and Lenny would be in jail. Then he and his beautiful Isabelle would be . . . No matter, it didn't work that way. His thought, *Fix this and find a way out.*

Seating himself in front of the computer, he looked at the stone-faced man with the gun. Waving his hand to get the thugs attention, Darrel said, "Hey, I need my notes. I can't access anything until I get my notes. Pass words and stuff."

The man sat still, moving enough to shrug, a smirk on his scarred face told Darrel he didn't give a shit.

Harry Warden sat hunched on a wooden chair at the side of Darrel and the computer. He was clinging to the glass of cognac with both hands, tears crawling out of his eyes. Darrel looked at him and said, "Hey, what's wrong with you?"

Harry's hands were shaking and his biggest fear was not the large man with the gun, or the possibility of being on the bad end of one of Lenny's sadistic beatings. He was deathly afraid of shaking so bad he would spill the precious amber liquid he coveted in the glass. The only way to handle the problem was to get rid of the precious amber liquid. He put the glass to his mouth, tipped his head back, and poured it into his throat without swallowing.

Darrel stared at Harry and was amazed at the euphoric glaze that covered his face. Harry's glasses fell off his face to the floor, where he slowly sank from the chair to his knees, crushing them. A mournful wailing came from Harry's throat, "Six months, I was sober for six months. I'm going to die from this." He rolled over on his side, curling into a sobbing fetal position.

Darrel whispered, "Yeah, you're going to die, but not from the liquor." Waving to get the attention of the guard, Darrel whined, "Hey, this guy's no good to me. Look at him."

As the Neanderthal strode across the office carpet, Darrel stared at the huge chest, rippling and rolling under the tight t-shirt. Every move flexed a muscle someplace. The pistol strapped to his chest made his size appear even more ominous.

Grunting, he kicked Harry gently and grumbled, "The boss ain't going to like this. Do what you can with that thing, I'll go get him," and left the room to inform Lenny.

As soon as he was gone, Darrel's fingers quickly flew across the keyboard and accessed the program he needed. With one stroke of his index finger he hit the delete key. Reams of figures and information scrolled across the screen to be sent into eternity, lost forever.

Frantically racing across the room to close the door, he wedged the guards chair against the doorknob. He looked impassively at Harry, not caring at all what could happen to him, and rushed to the window.

The office was on the first floor, so the drop from the window only slightly jarred Darrel, but he was unhurt. Looking up into the room he saw the chair was still in place. He ran towards the road. Pumping his legs as fast as he could across the expanse of lawn, he dove for the bushy undergrowth to hide himself until he could figure out the best way to get over the iron fence at the road.

Darrel's life was over, and there was no way he could salvage any of it. As soon as Lenny brought him to the Gull Lake house Darrel knew his deception had been discovered. His chest heaving to collect air, Darrel hoarsely told himself, "God, I should have never done it. I have to get to Amy and tell her."

Crouching against the tall iron fence, he knew he better move before the dogs were let loose. Grasping the black wrought rails he was unable to hoist himself high enough to go over the top. Dropping back to the ground he became frantic, looking for a way out. He was about fifty feet from the gate when the whine of the BMW approached from the outside. It could only be Vicka. Sprinting along the fence to the gate, he waved and called her name. "Vicka, it's me. Stop."

The motors controlling the gate forced them to open with the BMW following. Darrel bounced off the front fender as she slammed the car to a halt.

Scrambling out, she yelled, "Darrel, for Christ sake, what are you doing?"

Holding on to the side of the car, his breath leaving him as fast as he saw his life creeping away, he stammered, "Vicka, I have to get out of here. Lenny's on to what I did, and he's gonna kill me. Please, take me someplace and leave me, now!"

Astonished, she fell back onto the car, demanding, "How did he find out? Does he know about us?"

"I don't know, Vicka. Please, just get me out of here."

She ran her fingers through her black hair, trying to make sense of what was happening. She grabbed Darrel by the shoulders, "Hit me. Hit me then get in the car and leave. It'll look like you stole it from me, hurry."

Shaking his head, "No, I can't hit you."

Loud and excited, she yelled, "Then die, you bastard. It's all falling apart anyway. I spent the day talking to the cops, and they know about David. If Lenny finds us, I'm going to make sure I'm not connected to you. You'll take what he deals by yourself. Is that what you want?"

Darrel clenched his fist not certain he was able to do this, until he heard the shouts coming from the house.

Vicka, in a panic, looked at where the voices were coming from, shouting to him, "I will never admit I was with you, Darrel. Hit me or die. *Do it.*"

He looked away from the men rushing towards them, then at Vicka, and said, "I'm sorry, honey." He pulled back his arm and slammed his fist into her cheek, sending her rolling onto the grass. With tears in his eyes, he called to her, "Please forgive me. I'll get hold of you later."

Jumping into the convertible, he spun in the gravel backing out of the fence entrance. Slamming the shift lever into drive, the Beemer threw gravel and fish-tailed, with Darrel frantically trying to gain control.

The first bullet shattered the windshield near the center, making him jump. It was the only sign he needed to tell him what his fate would be if he was caught. The second one buried itself into his back, taking his breath away. There was no pain at first, just the impacting thud of the slug tearing his flesh apart.

Racing through the neighborhood, he tried to think which way the highway was. The pain in his back was starting to radiate to his entire body, forcing him to squint to be able to see the road.

The neighbors weren't surprised to see Vicka's car speeding through the asphalt lanes, as she drove too fast all the time. They learned to absorb what the Cherasky's did, finding that complaining led to too many unpleasant dealings with the strange people.

Standing at the gate watching his wife's car speed away, Lenny slammed his fist into his palm, snarling fiercely, "Get that accountant and kill him."

The large man standing next to him holding the smoking pistol, said, "The second one hit him, boss."

Still staring after the convertible, Lenny snarled, "After you wax the geek in my office, get Sloan out here. I want that fucker alive."

He went to his wife, gently picking her up from the ground, "Are you okay? I'll get the bastard, baby. He's going to pay for this."

Holding her broken cheekbone, Vicka on a self-preservation course, sold out her ex-lover in a heartbeat. "He hit me, Lenny. It hurts so much, and I'm going to bruise."

Lenny effortlessly picked her up, cradling her in his arms, walking towards the house. His mind seething, he was planning for the cruelest revenge possible.

June 27, Amanda Freeman's house.

AMANDA, SITTING ON THE SOFA, glad the two detectives had left, looked up at the nurse coming to her with the telephone, "It's for you."

Unsure, she answered, "Hello?" She sat upright, her brow bunching in the middle, with her hand clenching the mop of hair on her head. "Darrel, oh my God. Wait just a minute." Looking up at the nurse, Amy excitedly said, "Why don't you go home now. I really don't need your help anymore. Really, I can get around by myself."

The nurse, skeptical at the proposal, had to be certain, "Are you sure? I can wait outside."

Agitated, Amy pleaded, "No, please, just go."

Rushing through the house to collect whatever was hers, the nurse left, headed straight to a telephone to call Detective Bruntz.

Holding the phone for a few moments until she heard the front door close, Amy breathlessly said, "Darrel, what are you telling me?"

"I've been shot. I don't know what's going to happen now. Just listen, I'm going to tell you something, and I want you to do exactly what I say. Do you understand?"

"Yes, Darrel, please, come home."

Darrel sucked in a deep breath, wincing from the pain, wavered and said, "Shut up and listen. Do you have something to write with?"

Looking around her area on the sofa, she spotted a crossword puzzle the nurse had been filling in. She staggered over to it, and then sat on the floor, "All right, I've got something."

"I'm going to give you some numbers. Memorize them, and then burn the paper. Don't throw it in the garbage. Burn it."

Darrel labored over what he needed to tell her, and then asked, "Do you have all that?"

"Yes, honey, I do."

"Repeat it to me."

She did, with him saying, "Good. Amy . . ."

She interrupted him to plead, "Please, Darrel, come home. I've done some horrible things and I want to make it right for you." Sobbing, "I love you, Darrel. Please don't leave me. I need you and want you with me, forever. We can fix it." The handset of the phone was covered with her anguish, held by both hands.

After a pause, "Amy, honey, I love you too. I always have. I'm hurt real bad and Lenny is looking for me. I don't know what's going to happen now. If there's any way I can get out of this alive, I'll come to you."

Sobbing, "Oh, God, Darrel, don't go."

Loosing his breath, Darrel finished with, "Those numbers are from a bank account in Georgetown on the Grand Cayman Island. The First Caribbean International Bank, remember that name. There's over two million dollars there for you. As soon as you can, get out of town and take care of yourself. Lenny will come there to look for me, but stay in the sick bed to make him think you don't know anything and are helpless. He won't hurt you if he believes you. He just wants me."

Amy was pleading with him until she realized the phone connection was dead. She wiped her face clean with her robe, and then checked the caller ID on the telephone information window, erasing it from memory.

Taking the crossword puzzle to the fireplace, she ignited it, and went back to the sofa. She ran all the numbers through her head until she was certain they were in there for good. Taking the remote in her hand, she turned on *The Wheel of Fortune*. Staring aimlessly at Pat and Vanna, she waited for the inevitable. It couldn't be much longer before Lenny would come bursting through her front door.

SHE WAS EXPECTING IT, yet the crashing took her by surprise, frightening her, which was a theatric in her favor. She played the game as best as she could to convince them she was ignorant. Three men holding horrible looking guns ran through the house, while Lenny stood over her, his gravely voice demanding, "Where is he, Amy?"

Sitting forward, the blanket restraining her, she cried out, "What are you doing? Get out of here. What do you want?"

The three men gathered in the living room and told him, "He ain't here, boss."

Lenny grabbed a hand full of Amy's hair, twisting it in his grip, "Where is he, Amy? You're gonna get hurt unless we find him, soon."

Rising off the sofa to follow his abuse, she cried, "Ow, please don't. I haven't heard from that son-of-a-bitch. If you find him tell him I need help. *Ow, please don't.*"

She slid to the floor when he released his grip, making a point to let them see her holding her stomach. "Oh, God, *that hurts.*"

Lenny bent down grabbing her robe by the collar, ripping it open. Throwing her back onto the sofa, he yanked her gown up exposing her bandaged abdomen. She screamed in pain, "*Ow, God no, please, no. Please.*"

He pulled her up by the front of her gown, winding it around her throat, choking her. Naked from the neck down, the dressing on her stomach was saturated with blood from torn stitches. "If that prick gets hold of you, call me. All right?" Slinging her across the living room floor, she crashed into an end table, the splintered pieces and the lamp falling on her. Gagging and gasping for air, she felt the pain and warmth flow seeping from her wound.

Lenny walked over to her, pulling his foot back, when she quickly cried out, "The cops keep coming here, Lenny. They keep asking me questions about Gordon's murder and Isabelle. They're going to suspect something if you hurt me."

Crouching down to her, he snarled, "If I find out he's calling you and you don't tell me, I'm gonna kill you. I'm keeping you alive so he has somebody to contact." He stood up and brought the toe of his shoe squarely into the bandage on her stomach. She screamed and doubled into his kick, then his foot crashed into the side of her head. The room spun away from her and she enjoyed the blackness that saved her life.

June 28, North Memorial Hospital, Minneapolis

AMY WOKE UP STARING at the stark ceiling of the operating room, with someone mumbling above her. Her face was being tweaked and stretched as the stitches were put in place. An alarmed voice came from behind her, and then she floated away again. Traveling through the surrealistic world of anesthesia, she could feel her body being moved and jostled. If it was Lenny doing this to her, she knew there would be a terrible thing waiting for her. She floated in and out of knowing she was alive, and not knowing.

Wherever she was, she was spinning wildly, with her stomach unable to stay in step. The putrid fountain flowed from her mouth. She heard more mumbling, a lot of bustling took place, and then the darkness overwhelmed her again. Her eyes fought to stay closed, but her will won over them. Blinking at the fuzz, her next vision was Harold Bruntz sitting next to the hospital bed, his head resting on her blanket, snoring. She was too numb to feel anything and just let the miracle of modern drugs take her away one more time.

Waking up to a new level of alertness, the stabbing pain in her gut and the throbbing in her head, she felt this was as bad as it was going to get. For a fleeting instant, she wondered where Isabelle was, and then, remembering, turned her head to sob for her daughter. Thinking it couldn't get any worse, she saw Detective Bruntz sitting in the corner watching her.

Shielding her eyes from the light, she glumly asked, "What do you want?"

He stood up and came to her with a Styrofoam cup of coffee. The odor of the rich brew was overwhelming. She said, "God, that smells good."

He smiled, answering, "You've got some dripping into your arm."

She glanced at the IV tube feeding her, and then felt the stabbing from her stomach again. "Christ that really hurts. Do you know how bad it is?"

"No, I'm just a cop, and they try to ignore me. But, you can't. I need to know who did this."

Talking was an effort, but she managed in short breathless twinges, "How did you know I was here?"

"Your nurse got hold of me and thought you were in trouble. She was right."

"It was Darrel." Her mouth reacted before her brain did, but she thought maybe it was best for her husband to be in custody. She added, "He's been shot. You need to find him."

Harold sat down, "Now you've got my attention. Tell me about it."

"He was angry and beat me up. He said he had a bullet in his back and needed some help."

"There was no blood in your house, except from yours."

Rolling her head, she didn't think she needed to make sense. Just to get Darrel into custody and treated. "I can't explain anything. I told you what happened. Please go find him. I'm not going anywhere."

Detective Bruntz knew she was correct in that last part, and he was only there because of his mental attachment to her shaved pubic area. Darrel Freeman was now on the wanted list, having broken his bail condition, and it was up to Harold to find him. However, the detective's goal was to bury Mr. Freeman and convince his wife that she should run away with an overweight drunken slob. One who was going to put her husband in prison. However absurd that picture was, he had to grin at the possibilities.

Harold stood up, put his hand on her arm, absently caressing the soft flesh. Amy pulled away, putting an end to Harold's dream.

Recovering his dignity, he told her, "There's a guard outside the door in case he comes back." He placed the nurse call button it into her hand. "If anything happens, press the button. I'm going to put an alert on you so they react quicker."

Leaning closer to her than he needed to, he said, "Now, listen to this carefully. If a doctor comes in, any doctor or male orderly, press the goddamn button. Understand? They may come back in any form or disguise."

Amy looked at the disgusting man with an awe of respect, hanging on his use of *they*. He was telling her that he knew who did this and they might not be done with her. She nodded her head as much as she could without causing it to explode.

Harold stopped at the nurse's station, asking, "Who's in charge here?"

The woman at the desk looked up and said, "I'm Helen, the charge nurse."

Harold flashed his badge at Helen, saying, "Someone may come back to try to kill Mrs. Freeman. That will endanger everyone here, so you need to do as I'm telling you. Come with me."

Helens eyes almost popped from her head at the mention of the *kill* word. Outraged, Helen said, "What did you say? We can't have that going on here, this is a hospital."

Harold stopped, telling her, "Of course this is a hospital. There's a policeman at her door, and if you follow my instructions, it *won't* happen. Now, let's go see Mrs. Freeman."

He led Helen to Amy's room, "Amy, this is your nurse, Helen." He looked at the nameplate on her white uniform, adding, "Gambold. Helen Gambold. Every time there's a shift change, Helen is going to introduce the next nurse to you. Any doctor that is to see you will be brought in by her. If there is any change in that, press the button."

He glanced at the guard standing with them, who nodded. "Any guard change will be introduced by this man." Turning to the nurse, Harold said, "Have her put in the room directly in front of the nurse's station."

In the hospital administrator's office, Harold issued more directions. "Notify every hospital and clinic in the Twin Cities and all suburbs to watch for a man with bullet in his back." With that out of the way, Harold Bruntz went home to get drunk, and hopefully, Flo wasn't too busy.

CHAPTER 9
LOOSE ENDS

June 30, the precinct station.

Y O-YO SAT CROSS-LEGGED on top of Harold's desk, ignoring the files and loose papers strewn over it. "Put it together, boss. All this shit is coming in and should point to something."

"Why don't you sit in a chair like a civilized person?"

Elbows on her knees, she leaned forward, saying, "Get me a desk like civilized people get, and I'll sit at it. Answer my fuckin' question. Where are we with this thing?"

Harold's mind told him to steer clear of his issue with the beautiful Mrs. Freeman. Dance all around it and pretend he didn't have a partner he needed to satisfy. Hoping to let Yo-yo create her own direction, he said, "I'm not sure where we sit. There's some stuff that's just not right." He stood up, scratching his head and took a stroll trying to organize his thoughts. Turning back to his desk, Yo-yo had taken his suggestion, planting herself in his chair. Dragging a metal folding chair to his desk, he sat down, telling her, "We need to organize the evidence."

Her mind started clicking like a computer, rattling off what she knew at a lightning speed, "All right, boss, here's what we have. Marks was killed, Mrs. Freeman was wounded. Doesn't that smell a little bit? Why wasn't she killed as a witness? You remember what she told us about not getting killed herself. That's because Marks's killer knew her and didn't want to kill her, or was a dunce with a gun. Mr. Freeman or Isabelle, right?"

At a slower pace, Harold interjected, "I'm thinking Isabelle. She was unstable and had a motive with the competition with her mother. However, I admit Mr. Freeman also had a motive. Then again, Amy indicated it was Isabelle acting out of revenge."

Yo-yo's dark eyes bored into his with his reference to the murder suspect in her first name. She put her objection on the back burner, but was not going to let it get forgotten. She slowly and coldly corrected, "Do you mean *Mrs*. Freeman?"

Acting as dumb as a mud fence, he answered with, "Yeah, that's what I said."

Getting back to business, Yo-yo continued, "The two bodies in the Freeman drive way were waxed out of revenge. It had to be that way. Little Isabelle was too much in love with herself, was a nut-job, and did some bad shit and got waxed for it. The Olson kid was just getting laid at the wrong time. I can put it all together and work around your wet dream about Mrs. Freeman, but can't see why Mr. Freeman got shot, and by who? If he's the trigger man on Isabelle, there's another character in there someplace with a connection to all of this shit."

Harold sat quietly, listening, but she wasn't done yet. "Mrs. Cherasky tied everyone to her husband, and with the sex and porn shit behind it, we have a whole new level of slime to dig out. Personally boss, if you want my opinion, I'd say we need to look at Cherasky, but just not in a boat."

Harold mused, "We don't know how deep this psychotic thing went with Isabelle. If she was a Looney Toon there's no telling what she'd gotten into. Her mother said she didn't have any remorse and did things out of spite. If she was involved with Cherasky, well, let's hope not." That reasoning bothered him. If anyone put up Cherasky as a suspect, it let Darrel Freeman off the hook, and that was not acceptable.

Yo-yo made perfect sense when she suggested, "We need to get a court order to look at Isabelle's file with the shrink."

Harold absently told her, "That's a good idea. Why don't you get on that?" There was no way that Harold Bruntz was going to go to all the trouble to look at Isabelle's mental state. He had her as the Marks's shooter and that was good enough.

Harold sat silently before taking a paper from the desk, wrinkled from Yo-yo's butt. He handed it to her. "They found Mrs. Cherasky's

BMW. There was a bullet hole in the windshield, and blood on the driver's seat. The bullet to the windshield came from behind, and with Darrel walking around with a bullet in his back, I'd place him behind the wheel. Amy said he was the one who kicked her stomach in, but I don't believe her. He's too much in love with her to do that. He wouldn't do that to anybody. However, Lenny Cherasky wouldn't flinch at doing it. Now, we've got a connection to Cherasky. But how do we even get to talk to him?"

Loosing her patience, Yo-yo again corrected, "You referring to *Mrs. Freeman?*"

Confused at the interruption, then catching on, Harold said, "Oh, yeah, Mrs. Freeman."

Yo-yo slid the report back on to the desk, saying, "How much is a Beemer worth? More than I make in two years. We got the car which is titled to Cherasky, so why not send him a message that he has to come and pick it up?"

INSTEAD OF LEONID CHERASKY showing up for the car, a large man with a scarred and frightening face made claim to it. On the weak charge of possessing a vehicle involved in a crime, Peter Wisotskly was put in a holding cell to see if he could be used as bait for the bigger fish they wanted to talk to.

It happened quickly, with the Cherasky lawyer dressed in a suit that cost infinitely more than every single thing owned by Harold. The detective, his shirt tail hanging out of his waistband, his stained tie askew on his neck, greeted the appalled lawyer, "Mr. Anderson, nice to meet you."

Harold's offer at a hand shake was refused, with Mr. Anderson getting to the point, "I want Mr. Wisotskly out, now."

Smiling, Harold offered, "Why don't we go in here and talk for a minute."

Responding to the invitation, the lawyer seated himself in the conference room, glaring at Yo-yo Brown.

She smiled, "This ain't my office. I don't have one yet. I don't even have a chair to sit on, so I just float around. Hi, I'm Yo-yo Brown. Detective Bruntz and I are working together." The new .38 strapped to her gave her a little bit of credence, but not enough to intimidate him. The sly grin on her face told the lawyer that she was just another smart-ass cop.

Mr. Anderson's authoritative manner flowed like fine wine. "Just what is it you want? This whole charge is worthless, you know."

Harold said, "We don't want Mr. Wisotskly. We don't even want Mr. Cherasky. We have a murder investigation that has some strings connected to Leonid Cherasky, and we need to tie it all together."

"Mr. Cherasky has nothing to do with anything you have going here. You're way off base."

Harold leaned forward, putting some sugar on the hook, "I hope so. Mr. Cherasky isn't someone we want to get involved with, and only want to convince our superiors that any connection to him is not warranted. As long as his name is connected to the vehicle, there is no way to leave that alone." Harold gave Yo-yo a courteous glance, continuing, "We think it would raise fewer questions if Ms. Brown and I spoke with him, instead of someone from the DA's office. Those people have too many political motivations and look for headlines before the truth."

Mr. Anderson stood up, "I'll work it out, but it won't be here. You'll have to do it in my office, or at the Cherasky house in Brainerd. Now, bring Peter Wisotskly to me."

Waiting to hear from the lawyer, Harold got a phone report that put another loose joint in the case.

"Yo-yo, we have to go to the morgue."

"You mean where all the dead guys are? Why do you need me there? That's the creepiest fuckin' place I know."

"A couple of bodies have washed up on the shore of the Mississippi, tied together. One has been identified as being connected to Cherasky. All we have to do is make sense out of the connection."

Yo-yo asked, "How do we know they're Cherasky's people?"

Stomping his way out of the precinct house, Harold said, "One was a male who had a record for assault and attempted murder, tying him to Cherasky. The other was is a female—a Jane Doe. But, being duct taped together, wouldn't you think they'd know each other?"

Bopping behind him like a puppy, she asked, "How do you get all that information from one short phone call?"

Tired of explaining everything, he admonished her, "Quit asking so many questions. Please. Just follow me and shut up for a while."

THE TWO COLD STEEL TRAYS holding the large body of Sasha Grotzke and Petra, labeled as Jane Doe, were opened for inspection. The typical autopsy scars despoiled them, but not as much as the open gash in the front of Grotzke's neck. After so much time immersed in the dirty waters of the Mississippi, his wound had opened up enough to cause the head to lazily flop off to the side.

The familiar remnants of duct tape adhesive clung to the sides of his head, prompting the lab tech to explain, "They were duct taped together with an excessive amount wrapping the female's head to his. It appeared to be the most efficient way to transport them. They're legs were the same way. There were no prints on the tape."

Continuing with his show and tell, the attendant pulled the sheets back. Referring to his clipboard, in a nasally monotone he read off the report, "The male bled to death, obviously, and has a deep penetration in the right buttock." He looked up to summarize, "His neck was deeply slashed and then he was stabbed in the ass." Making certain the two detectives were paying attention, he continued, "The female was killed by a deep penetration in the back, but not before she was strangled. There were microscopic fibers in the wound, presumably from a polyester coated fabric. Bruises on her neck were pronounced, indicating a strong grip." The attendant turned Petra's head aside, pointing to the bruise. "The puncture wound in the female has a similar pattern to that of the wound in the male's buttock. I'm saying the same weapon was used on both victims."

Flaunting his laboratory professionalism, he added, "It's obvious, to us anyway, that the killer was a female." In a snobbish display of expertise, he exhibited the four small bruises on Jane Doe's neck. "They were put there by a woman. A strong woman."

Harold asked, "How do you know that?"

Rolling his eyes in a perturbed disgust, he said, "Because they were small. Either a woman or a child, okay?"

Harold pointed to Grotzke, "Turn him over."

Looking closely at the puncture wound on Sasha's buttock, Harold wrinkled his forehead. Standing up, he said, "Why would that happen?"

Yo-yo flagged the attendant, "Roll him over again. Look boss, the bruise at the top of the penetration point."

Still confused, Harold muttered, "So?"

"The hilt of the knife, man." Looking up at the attendant, she asked, "How deep is the cut?"

Thumbing through his notes, "Hmm, it says about six to eight inches."

"That's where they dumped the weapon, boss, in his ass." Before Harold could say anything, Yo-yo continued her chatter, "They had to get rid of the knife, so it was sunk into the dude's butt. That means the blonde chick was killed first. This guy comes along and zip, zip, he gets his neck slit."

Pointing to Jane Doe, Yo-yo commanded, "Turn her over." Running her fingers over the pale skin, Yo-yo said, "The way the bruises on her neck are indicate she was grabbed from behind. The fibers in the wound could have come from a cushion she was lying on. She was killed from behind." Glancing at Sasha, she went on with her observation, "He was gutted from behind as well. The killer was waiting for them."

The coroner's assistant added, "There was a trace of semen in the woman, with the DNA matching the male. There were also slight traces of chlorine in the female's vaginal cavity."

Shattering the lab techs sophisticated demeanor, Yo-yo announced, "No shit, man, they were boinking before they got waxed. They were together, and I'm betting they were both naked 'cause who's going to undress two stiffs, one with his head on a hinge? With them doing the slider gig, they would have thought they were alone."

Harold said, "I still don't get the wound to the butt. It doesn't make sense."

Exasperated, Yo-yo threw her arms up, "How long you been on the force, man? When there's a gangland wipeout, the best way to get rid of the weapon is to give it to the cops right away. There ain't no prints on it, and it's too dangerous and stupid to hide it."

"Do you think this is gang related?"

Yo-yo was right this far, so Harold took great interest in listening to her. "Look at the world that Cherasky guy lives in. This is mob, boss. Or at least someone close to the mob." Then, Yo-yo brought up a new concern, "The weapon was dumped, but it's not here. Someone still has it. Romeo and Juliet were skunked and left as a gift for someone to find."

Harold asked the attendant "Is there a way to get prints from a bruise?"

With an authoritative arrogance, the lab tech replied, "Sometimes."

Harold wrote down Isabelle's name, saying, "She's in here also. See if there's a link to her prints, or at least a match of some kind. Size of the hands . . . something."

On their way back to the car, Yo-yo commented, "The dink in the morgue sure was a snob."

Harold grinned and waved his fingers delicately. "Oh, you think?"

Yo-yo's effort in securing Isabelle's psychiatric records resulted in an appointment to talk with her shrink. Located in a bungalow in the suburban residential area of Brooklyn Center, they checked the address twice to be certain they were in the right place. A pale yellow exterior that was in dire need of a paint job, a lawn that had given itself over to crab-grass, and the street with roving collections of teens, was not what they perceived a psychiatrist's office should look like.

Seated in the living room with a man who identified himself as Dr. George Markham, Yo-yo bluntly asked, "Are you really a doctor? This don't seem like a place I'd expect to find a guy like you."

Dr. Markham crossed his legs, cleared his throat, and said, "This is my home, detective. I have an office elsewhere, but I do much of my business here. A great tax write-off."

Glancing at the well-worn furniture and trappings, Yo-yo was blunt again, "Would you mind showing us proof that you really are a doctor?"

"Of course." Grinning, he stood up and left the room. Harold and Yo-yo exchanged glances and shrugged. Dr. Markham came back with a diploma in a glass covered picture frame stating that he was indeed a psychiatrist in good standing, graduating from the University of Michigan school of medicine. Setting it on the coffee table, he asked, "Is that satisfying enough, detective?"

Nodding, Yo-yo mumbled, "Yeah, looks okay. But you sure don't show signs of being successful."

Dr. Markham smiled and asked, "What can I tell you about Isabelle?"

Harold finally spoke up, "What was wrong with her?"

Dr. Markham paused and bridged his fingers in his lap. Looking up, he told them, "I'm not going to beat around the bush or give you a diagnosis that doesn't get to what her real problems were. To put it simply, Isabelle was astonishingly unstable. She was terribly angry at being conceived in a rape, and had a sexual appetite that couldn't be satisfied. She was deeply schizophrenic and held equal feelings of love and hate towards her mother. I also diagnosed her as being sociopathic which would account for her lack of remorse."

The doctor crossed his legs in a manner which Yo-yo found too effeminate, lowering her opinion of him even more. She took note of the way he held his hands over his lips in an almost praying fashion. In her experience, she took this as insecurity, or lying.

Harold asked, "Could she have killed her mother?"

"I'd say it would fit her nature, and, as I indicated, she wouldn't feel any compunction for it."

Yo-yo asked, "In spite of your modest surroundings, Dr. Markham, you can't be too cheap. Who paid for her treatments?"

His lips clenched tightly together, and his gaze roamed the room. "I don't see where that has any significance."

Harold leaned forward. "Dr. Markham, did you have sex with Isabelle in exchange for her treatment?"

Dr. Markham uncrossed his legs, cleared his throat again, and quietly said, "You've seen her. Who wouldn't?" His voice was hesitant, filled with guilt.

Harold Bruntz was an old police war-horse when it came to his reliance on his gut feelings. And this sleaze-bag sitting in front of him had Harold's gut tied in knots. "Are you married, Dr. Markham?"

The answer was slow to come out, "No, not anymore."

Yo-yo jumped in, asking, "Divorced, huh? How'd that happen?"

Sitting forward, Dr. Markham uttered a weak protest, "I don't see what that has to do with anything," shifting nervously in his chair.

Harold dropped the bomb, asking, "Did Isabelle go to your wife and narc on your affair with her?"

Sitting back, he sighed. "It seems you already have all the answers. Yes, she did. There was no reason for her to do it. She found a way to level pain on someone, and did it." Sweeping his arm to emphasize his living room, he confessed, "After the divorce, this is all I can afford. Is there anything else you need to confirm?"

Harold wanted to cram the photo down the doctor's throat, but instead, he leveled his ire and tossed the autopsy photo on his lap. "Yes, where were you on the night Isabelle and Richard Olson were murdered?"

Sitting up straight, the doctor barked, "Oh, my God. You suspect me?"

Yo-yo attacked next, "Duh, did you have a motive? I'd say so."

Nervously twitching, "I . . . was here. I had a . . . a guest."

Harold asked, "A client?"

Dejected, he answered, "No. It was a . . . a prostitute."

Yo-yo took her pad out, "What's her name and how did you contact her?"

Sitting back, he wheezed out, "Her name's Merilee. Merilee Sward. She comes by every couple of weeks to get drug money. She never lasts in treatment, so I use her. I'm trying to counsel her into getting help and another occupation." He reached over to his desk and handed Yo-yo a piece of paper with a phone number on it. "Here, if you talk to her maybe she'll get serious about treatment."

Yo-yo hesitated, then took the paper. Looking fiercely at the doctor, she admonished, "We'll check. Count on it."

The detectives stood to leave. Yo-yo pointed her long finger at his face, she said, "You are a despicable piece of shit."

Tugging at her before she said any more, Harold pulled her outside.

In the car, Harold said, "We'll run the name and number to check out his story."

Silent for a moment, Yo-yo answered, "No, don't. I know the girl. He's right, and maybe he'll help her. Leave it alone." She wrinkled the piece of paper and threw it on the floor with the rest of Harold's garbage.

July 6, the Cherasky estate.

T HE GATES TO THE CHERASKY ESTATE opened slowly to allow entrance for Harold's Plymouth Reliant. Smoke billowing from the tail pipe, the car dieseled to a stop under the portico at the front entrance. Walking up to the large ornate door, a guard stood at each side. Yo-yo stumbled when she recognized them as the ones who had sunk the rowboat.

When the guards moved to block their way, both Harold and Yo-yo stiffened. Never one to keep quiet at the wrong time, she snidely asked, "What, you gonna sink us again?"

With a smirk, she actually found a tiny bit of comfort when the guard said, "If you didn't have life jackets we would have pulled you out. You're okay. Don't bitch about it. We just want to make sure you don't carry any weapons inside."

Stepping back with her hand on her holster, Harold quickly said, "Just give them the gun and quit talking. We're all right."

A quick shake down produced a back up gun from each of them before the door was opened to find Mr. Warren Anderson waiting for them inside.

Whispering to Harold, Yo-yo spat out, "Where was that back-up when the dude sunk the fuckin' boat?"

Wishing she would shut up, Harold pushed her ahead to stumble on the threshold.

Smirking, the lawyer bypassed the handshaking routine again, saying, "This way, please."

Led through the stately and comfortable house resembling a Roman villa, they ogled the white marble floor, stone arches, and the wide matching stone stairway that curved up to a second floor.

They soon found themselves at the rear of the mansion, on the patio near the pool. Yo-yo looked over the massive expanse of lawn to the lake, wondering if the small aluminum boat was still under water. The yacht was tied to a buoy, and there appeared to be a nude woman lying on the deck of the speed boat.

It was a delightful July day with bright sunshine and a gentle breeze off the lake. A row of white metal patio furniture led to a round glass top table with an umbrella stuck through the middle. A muscular man with the shoulders of an ape sat at the table holding a glass of amber liquid. He smiled, saying, "Detective Bruntz, welcome to my home. Please sit down." He cast a sneer at Yo-yo indicating she should sit also.

Instead, she graciously leaned forward, saying, "Thanks, but I'll stand, if you don't mind."

Harold gave her a sour glare hoping she was going to behave herself.

Mr. Cherasky snapped his fingers and a short thin man with an obvious East Indian recognition, in a white jacket, appeared with a tray holding a carafe of coffee and several cups. Harold took one and tried to show his host he was not the clod he appeared to be.

With his best charm, Harold politely began, "Mr. Cherasky, we thought it would be less conspicuous if we talked to you privately. We have some loose ends to tie up and it's the only way we can clear your name."

In a raspy voice that reminded Harold of a hack saw grinding through metal, "Business so soon? It's a beautiful day. Why not enjoy it? If you want to take a swim, feel free."

"Well, we'd just as soon get this over with and get out of your way."

Yo-yo had wandered away looking over the patio and pool. She turned to the glass table, saying, "This is really nice, it must have cost a fortune. I've half a mind to take you up on the swim offer. Mind if I just put my feet in the water?"

Harold, gritting his teeth, seethed at Yo-yo, hoping she wasn't going to screw this up. He cast an apologetic smile to the host.

Lenny was irritated also, as he seemed to have lost control of what the thin black woman was doing. Nervously, he smiled, "Go ahead. Do what you want."

Looking back at Yo-yo sitting on the edge of the pool, Harold was livid. Maybe for the first time, he would be the one asking for a new partner. Twisting back towards Lenny, "Mr. Cherasky, your BMW has Darrel Freeman's blood stains in it and we know he was hit in the back. Can you explain that?"

"It was stolen. I had to go get my wife at the mall when she was stranded. Really pissed me off. Maybe some punker had an argument and they shot at each other. I don't know, except it's not going to be a cheap repair. Seems like there should have been more cops around, don't you think?"

Harold handed him photos of Sasha and Petra taken at the morgue. "Do you know these people?"

"Hmm, no. Can't you identify them? With all the science you guys have that should be easy."

Smiling, Harold said, "Nothing is easy, Mr. Cherasky. However, if we dog it enough, we usually find out what we need to know." Pushing the photos closer to Lenny, Harold threw him a curve ball. "This one is Sasha Grotzke, and his rap sheet has him listed as having a relationship with you. The female is unknown to us. Now do you recognize him?"

Pushing the photos away, Lenny grumbled, "I got a lot of employees, Detective. I can't know all of them."

The smile fading, Harold asked, seriously, "Darrel Freeman's blood was in your car. You shot him while he was leaving. Was he here? Was he running away from you?"

The lawyer stood up, objecting, "If you're going to . . ."

Lenny put his hand up, "Let the man talk. He came all the way out here for information. I'll tell him anything he wants to know." Looking back at Harold, Lenny said, "Obviously, Mr. Freeman stole my car and was shot doing so. I asked my staff, but I doubt if any of them would do that. Shouldn't you be looking for that guy?"

Harold looked at his lap for a moment, and then said, "Yes, we're looking for him." Looking up at Lenny, Harold pressed on, "What was Darrel's involvement with you? He was a computer expert. Was he helping you in that way?"

Waving off another protest from the lawyer, Lenny said, "Yes, he was setting up some websites for the pornography we deal with." The grin never left Lenny's face, adding, "All very legal, no under age, and it's a pay site."

Harold knew he was getting close. Lenny was looking agitated to him. "I appreciate your honesty, Lenny. How were Mrs. Freeman and Isabelle involved in your business?"

Nervous, he answered, "They made movies for me. They had sex with each other and others to make pornographic material to put on the website. Also, I fucked them both." Lenny finished with a direct challenging look at Harold.

"How did you get them to do that?"

Smiling, gregariously waving his arm, Lenny answered, "Who can tell what a woman will do? You have no idea how easy it is to get a dame to take her clothes off. There are thousands of them on the Internet. They did whatever they were told to do, anything to make the pictures appealing to pathetic slobs viewing them."

Nervously, Harold knew he should never ask, but spit it out anyway. "Do you have copies we can view?"

Rolling his head back with forced entertainment, Lenny chortled, "Subscribe to the website, Detective Bruntz. You can see all of it."

Lenny brought the interview to an end, standing up under the umbrella, saying, "Now, that's all I can tell you. My hospitality has come to a close." He motioned to Yo- yo, telling Harold, "If you will get your partner to quit playing in the pool, you can leave now. If there are more questions, they will be taken by Mr. Anderson, in writing. Goodbye, Detective. Don't forget your weapons on the way out."

Lenny paraded out of sight, but not before Harold caught sight of Vicka standing in the shadows, inside the house. Frowning and curious, he took note of the bandage covering the side of her face. Like a serpent, Vicka disappeared into the recesses of the house with her husband, casting a wary glance at Harold.

Extending his hand to Yo-yo, Harold pulled her to her feet. Upset that he had to do all the talking, Harold admonished her, saying, "You could have been a little more helpful."

Yo-yo snapped a hoarse whisper, "Shut up and get us out of here, fast." She scooped up her shoes and scooted for the door.

Her determination sent a signal he knew he should heed. They smiled to the guards, took their weapons, and left. However, before getting into the car, Yo-yo unbuttoned her pants, stripping them from her legs. Kicking her feet out, she folded them carefully, then pulled her underpants down. Half naked she got into the car, yelling at a surprised Bruntz, "Get the fuck out here, bone head. Now."

The guards at the door were just as shocked as Harold was.

The iron gate yawned open for them and they sped away. Yo-yo held her clothing gently in front of her, frantically telling Harold, "Get to a grocery store, fast."

Confused, Harold made a motion to pull to the side of the road for an explanation, until Yo-yo's bare foot reached over, punching the accelerator, pushing the Plymouth back onto the road. Yo-yo did the best she could to hurriedly explain, "Blood, man. There were traces of blood on the edge of the pool. I sat on them to blot it up on my pants. We need a grocery bag to seal up the evidence."

Coming out of a small grocery store with what would pass as an evidence bag, he congratulated his partner, "I'm impressed, Detective Brown. That was good work."

Smiling, she said, "Now go to that shopping center, you have to buy me some pants, honey."

He nervously looked at her naked thighs sitting next to him, his hand shaking tensely. She smiled, leaning over to plant her lips on his cheek. His hand inadvertently touched the inside of her leg, and then mumbled, "I don't think we're supposed to be doing this, especially in a parking lot."

Whispering into his ear, "Doing what, man? You're the one feeling me up. If it's wrong, then stop."

When Harold was finally able to stand up with no embarrassment, he went shopping for his partner. She gave him a list of exactly what he should to look for, as well as a list of sizes. An hour later, and seventy-two dollars out of his pocket, he returned to the waiting Yo-yo.

Getting dressed in the car, she ignored his complaint. "Seventy-two dollars. Wouldn't jeans from Penny's work as well? You have no idea how embarrassed I was buying those little panty things."

She leaned over him again, whispering in his ear, "If you want compensation, I'll let you take them off me tonight."

Harold's eyes were as big as platters and his tongue wouldn't work. Later, he was able to say, "Yeah, okay. Yeah, that'd be fine."

Leaving the bag with the lab for a DNA comparison with Sasha, Yo-yo instructed him, "Check for chlorine, too. It should match the shit you found in the blonde bitch."

With a dubious sneer, the lab technician told them, "I got the impression the first sample came from pool chemicals. I'll follow the same logic. As for the blonde bitch, as you so aptly put it, there aren't any actual fingerprints. However, the size of the bruise is a remote similarity to the Freeman girl's finger size."

Excited at the connection, Harold asked, "Can we assume that the Freeman girl strangled the blonde?"

The subdued answer from the snot in the lab coat was, "You are free to assume that, Detective, but in court there can be no real proof."

Waving him off, Yo-yo dismissed the lab technician with, "You did good, Fauntleroy."

The vague confirmation that there was a possibility it was Isabelle's finger marks on Jane Doe's neck, Harold mused, "That puts Isabelle in the Cherasky house. If she had to kill the two lovers, it was necessary in order to steal the gun that killed Marks. Thus, it was Isabelle who triggered her mother."

Yo-yo agreed, "If she and Cherasky were doing the badda-bing she more than likely knew where the gun was. Then we agree that little miss fancy-ass was the one who killed Gordon Marks."

"Yup; we'll write it up that way and put an end to that part of this case. That should satisfy the captain. It's all there, motive and opportunity."

Bewildered, Yo-yo added, "I've seen enough shit in my years to not be surprised at anything these bozos do to each other. But, I'll never get comfortable with kids and parents whacking each other. I don't know, boss, your dream of going to Disney Land with Mrs. Freeman just ain't right. She's dirty, man. You know that as much as I do."

"That could be, partner. Maybe before this is over, I'll take a new direction. Maybe. For now, can we leave it alone?"

"Yeah, I'm cool. No shit, mu-fuck, I'm cool."

Back in the car, Yo-yo suggestively asked, "Before we go write up that report, do you want your seventy-two dollars back?"

The smile on Harold's pock marked face traveled from one misshapen ear to the next. His fantasy, however, was short-lived. What they found when they got to his apartment was not romantic and intimate.

CHAPTER 10
THE MURDER WEAPON

YO-YO, RELUCTANT TO REVEAL her own living condition, conducted her business with Harold in his apartment. In spite of the begrimed living space he called home, she felt comfortable there. During her early years at home with her mother and sister, Harold's digs would have been a step up in style, class, and cleanliness.

The odors imbedded into the walls, threadbare carpeting, and sagging sofa were as much a part of Yo-yo as they were of the unkempt Harold Bruntz. On her first visit she had asked him, "Why don't you just clean it up a bit?"

His response was, "That's the cat's job. I can't help it if he's lazy."

Yo-yo had developed a respect for not only the disheveled Harold, but also, his close friend Flo the blow. If she were to become any part of Harold's life, she would have to accept his life style. She had told him once, "This is you, I guess, and that's cool with me." And cool with it she was.

Entering the apartment, Harold went into the bedroom to shed his clothing in anticipation of another romp with his partner. Bouncing on the squeaky springs, he struggled with his socks, adding to the pile of his duds on the floor.

Yo-yo headed for the bathroom to do whatever a lady did before screwing her partner. Pulling the string attached to the bare bulb hanging overhead, she gazed into the mottled mirror, seeing more than herself. Unbelieving at first, she did a double take to be certain she wasn't hallucinating. Staring back at her in the reflection, slumped in the bathtub, was the face of Florence Widholm.

Turning to the apparition she squeezed her eyes to be sure it was real. Gasping, she could only manage to wheeze out, "Harold!" Sucking life back into her lungs, she stumbled backwards to cling to the door frame. With the force of steam through a train whistle, she screeched, "*Harold!*"

From the bedroom, he mundanely answered, "In a minute."

This time, at the top of her scale, she let him know that his minute was not a good option. "Get the fuck in here, *now.*" Throwing herself across the cracked linoleum floor, her arms reached for the body in the bathtub.

Sensing the obvious urgency, in his underwear, Harold raced to see what was going on. He froze when he gazed at the naked body of his best friend, Florence, propped neatly in the tub, her legs draping over the side. She had turned ashen white, slowly moving her eyelids, and the only sound coming from her was a shallow gasping. The luxurious black hair was scraggly and mopped giving an eerie contrast to the whiteness of her flesh against the scum of the tub. Through the eyelid slits she followed Harold as he approached, her parched lips trembling.

Protruding from her abdomen was the wooden handle of a knife, pressed in up to the hilt. Tracks of blood trickled over the folds of her stomach, congealing on her flesh, trailing to the drain, under her. With the precision of a surgeon, Yo-yo carefully pulled the knife out, and then held a washcloth to the wound. Gently laying the knife on a towel Harold was holding, they both stared at the long slender eight inch blade, absolutely certain of where it came from.

Harold made the phone call while Yo-yo did what she could for Flo.

In a short time, the EMTs arrived, with forensics close behind.

Yo-yo stayed behind to cover details with the investigators, while Harold went with Flo in the ambulance, holding her hand all the way. Squeezing a complex of emotions to the back of his head, he whispered to her all the way. "It's going to be all right, honey. You're going to Emergency, and those guys are the best."

Lieutenant Warner sat with Harold and Yo-yo, in a conference room, a recorder on the table, and a video camera running. "Don't make me ask questions, Hal. Spill it all out."

Taking a deep breath, he started, "Detective Brown and I had been out to interview Leonid Cherasky about the killings at the Freeman house. Darrel Freeman's blood was found in Cherasky's car, and Detective Brown discovered blood on the pool edge, getting a sample by sitting on it. We took the pants to the lab, and even with the pool chemicals, they were able to get a vague match to the Russian stiff in the morgue. At any rate, it was blood. It's not positive, and can't be considered evidence, but to us, it's a connection. The bruises on the neck of the female in the morgue are a reasonable match to those of the dead Isabelle Freeman. Isabelle's partial print was also on the knife found in Ms. Widholm's abdomen. Our report states that Isabelle Freeman killed Grotzke and the unknown female. Grotzke's sheet has him as an employee of Cherasky, but Lenny denies it. It's only important as a connection to him,."

In a very serious tone, Lieutenant Warner said, "Your report also said it was Isabelle Freeman who killed Gordon Marks and wounded Mrs. Freeman."

Yo-yo spoke up, "Yes sir, we believe it was also Isabelle. She and her mother were involved in pornography and a lot of sexual dealings with Cherasky. We think it was jealousy driving her to do the unspeakable. Gordon Marks was a target for the two women and Isabelle couldn't take being upstaged. She hated Marks, and found a way to eliminate the competition from her mother in the triangle."

Bob Warner spoke up, "So, Darrel Freeman is still a suspect in the killing of the girl and the Olson boy. Correct, Detective Bruntz?"

Harold, as if in a fog, looked up, and said, "Huh? Yeah, that's correct. Our report states that it was jealousy when he discovered her and Richard Olson in the driveway of his home. The unborn child of Isabelle Freeman was his."

Harold gazed at the floor, tense. Waiting for the objection from Detective Brown, but she remained silent. His eyes met hers, and although seething, she lightly nodded.

Lieutenant Warner held a grave stare at Harold before saying, "That leaves Cherasky clear for the killing of the girl and her boy friend."

Yo-yo, finally speaking, said, "We want Darrel Freeman for that." She shot a glance at Harold, who was struck by his partner's change. Harold's brow wrinkled in confusion, yet he was pleased. Yo-yo slightly moved her head back and forth to tell him to shut up.

Lieutenant Warner said, "It looks like you're not sure about Mr. Freeman. What about Cherasky?"

Yo-yo took charge, saying, "Cherasky is involved, but he didn't whack anyone in this investigation. Like I said, we want Darrel Freeman."

"Yeah, I heard. It sounds like you aren't certain. Is there anything else I should know?"

Harold, seemingly in a quandary over his concern for Flo, vacantly said, "We're still trying to get a good connection to Cherasky, but he's insulated. If anyone takes a fall for murder, he'll have one of his flunkeys do it. Like Detective Brown said, as far as we know, Cherasky is clear and Mr. Freeman needs to be brought in."

Head in his hands, Lieutenant Warner asked, "Well, who the hell stabbed the Widholm woman?"

Harold took his thankful stare from Yo-yo and moved his attention to the boss. "That's something we have to work on. The motive is still up for grabs. The only connection between Flo and Cherasky is me. Whoever stabbed Flo is telling me something, but he just chose the wrong way to say it." Harold's resolve was dark and sinister.

Sitting up straight, with a stern scowl, Warner admonished, "Bruntz, I am ordering you to stay away from the vigilante and self-serving justice crap. Someday, Cherasky will make a mistake, and we'll nail him. For now, as far as you are concerned, the case is done. Find Mr. Freeman and the DA will put him away." Warner's surprising animation held a message that was not overlooked. "The Widholm woman was nothing more than an assault. If she can't ID the attackers, we'll let it go."

Standing up, Lieutenant Warner shut off the recorder and video camera, stating, "Well, that's that. Good job, both of you." Settling unfinished business, the lieutenant said, "I've turned down your request for reimbursement for the boat that was shot from under you, Detective

Brown's lost revolver, and her clothing. You went out there on your own, out of jurisdiction, so I'm not paying mileage either." Rubbing his hands together, he finished with, "Well, find Mr. Freeman, and let's see what other crimes we can put away, okay?"

Harold brushed past him, glumly saying, "I'll be at the hospital with Flo."

Left with a sheepish grin on his face, Bob Warner said, "Sure, fine. Well then, that's a wrap I guess."

Yo-yo stopped the lieutenant at the door, issuing an unwise ultimatum, "It's not over, Lieutenant."

Turning to her with a scowl, Warner knew she was right. He scanned his brain to find a way to shut her up. "Detective Brown, as far as you are concerned, it is over."

In a loud and firm challenge, she leveled her logic at him. "What about Darrel Freeman? Who shot him and where is he? What about Mrs. Freeman getting the shit kicked out of her? And who the fuck is David Sloan? Who shoved the knife into Flo Widholm?" Standing up to face her boss, "No, man, it ain't over."

Back in his office, Lieutenant Warner picked up the phone, telling the connection at the other end, "We've got a problem."

Flo WAS CONSCIOUS AND ABLE TO SPEAK, but really only wanted to go home. "I'm sorry, Hal, I can't tell you anything. Please don't ask me any more. I'm really scared to talk about it." Looking away from the window, with an impish smirk, she asked, "Do you think I could service the doctors to pay for this?"

Harold had already arranged to pay for her bills, but grinned, saying, "They'd be getting the best there is, Flo." He gently held her hand, stroking the back of it.

Flo's face took a detour with a grave thought washing over her. Fear had been planted and there was no way to make her mind clean again. Still smiling but seriously unhinged, her voice sounded garbled, "They were mean, Hal. They made me get undressed and go down to your apartment. It was the first time I had ever been embarrassed at being naked. It was different. I was pushed into the bathtub and they took that awful looking knife out. I was really scared. The one guy pushed the point against me and said to tell you something. They knew who you were and where you lived. He said if you didn't listen he'd come back, and if I lived long enough he was going to kill both of us."

Holding her hand, feeling it tremble, he asked quietly, "What was it, Flo? What were you supposed to tell me?"

Squeezing his hand, she answered, "They said you shouldn't go places you weren't wanted. They said to stay away from some guy but I couldn't understand his name. Then he pushed it into me, shut off the light and they left me. It was painful when it got pushed in, but then I was just so scared. The point was pressing into me and I tried to back away, but there was no place to go. Then it punctured me and that really hurt. I felt it cutting through me and I couldn't scream. I thought I was dying and didn't remember how to pray. I got more scared when I thought a whore couldn't go to heaven. I tried pulling it out but that really hurt and it wouldn't give. I just sat in the dark wishing you would come home."

He stood up and leaned over her to wipe the tears from her cheek. He kissed her gently, saying, "There's a guard outside. You'll be safe, and when you're better, I'll take you home." Before leaving, he kissed her again, telling her, "I really love you, Flo."

Turning to leave, he was startled by Yo-yo standing against the doorframe. "How long have you been there?"

"Long enough to hear what I needed to. Come on, boss, we've got to talk." She took his hand and led him to the coffee shop. With the two cups between them, she leveled the playing field, "It's not done, is it? You know there's still something wrong just like I do. What is it, boss?"

Burning his tongue on the coffee, he winced, saying, "Yeah, there's a loose end or two. So what? Most cases are left with empty corners. Why do they all have to be so damn complete? Isabelle was a killer and got nailed for it, and Darrel Freeman is going to jail for murder. That's all we need to know."

His resolve was far from final, and the disgust in his voice told her he was still in the game. Not willing to give an inch, she pressed him harder, "We don't know for certain whether Cherasky or Darrel killed Isabelle and her boyfriend, and Amanda has dirty hands. What about this David Sloan? Where's Darrel Freeman? He has a bullet in his back with half the communist nation out looking for him. Why does Cherasky want Darrel so badly? You won't sleep any better than I will until we find the prick who shivved Flo. Those are more than loose ends, boss. The whole goddamn sweater is unraveling, and Mrs. Freeman is going to get keelhauled by the Reds if Darrel doesn't turn up. If he does, then he gets the axe. I guarantee that if Darrel is found by Cherasky, Mrs. Freeman is going die with him."

Before Harold had a chance to answer, Yo-yo threw a wrench into the gearbox, "You've got the hots for Mrs. Freeman, boss. If it doesn't get you both killed, then you are going to go through another train load of grief."

His mouth open to respond, she abruptly said, "Shut up. One more thing. If you go for the revenge play to pay back for Flo, you're going to need back up. If you leave me out, I'll walk off the force and start fucking white guys again. In addition, we both know that Flo wasn't killed for a reason. She needed to let you know that Cherasky was off limits so he could go after the Freeman family himself. The dead Russians were killed at his poolside, and he kept the knife. He knew Isabelle did it, but since she was already dead, he left it as a warning to you. If Cherasky had killed Isabelle, wouldn't he have used the knife to do it?"

Harold managed to get a word in, "The knife would put the killer too close to the target. With two victims there would be too much chance of missing." Sitting back looking at her, he affectionately said, "You're right about the rest, though. If you're so smart, why are you just a cop?"

Smiling, her brilliant white teeth sparkling, she said, "I've got an MBA in business administration, as well as a degree in law enforcement.

A skinny black woman ain't gonna be hired by a law firm, though, not anywhere. I got through the academy and went straight undercover in vice. Things went screwy when I got too good at the job. I like to fuck, you know. I was making more than I would in an office, and got too deep into being a whore. When I got made, I didn't want to leave as a cop. You were my last step. I'm not *just* a cop, boss, I'm a *good* cop. However, nobody likes a skinny mouthy sister any more than they like a fat white honkey slob. It was inevitable that we become partners. You and me are like a racial Stan and Ollie. Did you ever see the movie Laurel and Hardy made trying to move that fucking piano up the steps?"

She waited for the analogy to sink in before adding, "That's us solving this case, boss. We're moving the fucking piano up the steps. It's going to take awhile to get it up there, and it'll be sort of funny watching us do it, but it'll finally get to the top. In pieces, maybe, but it'll get there. And, we'll piss off a bunch of people doing it."

Grudgingly, Harold agreed, saying, "We need to get Darrel off the street, and Mrs. Freeman needs to be hidden." He paused for a moment, adding, "Yeah, she got to me, but I know I have to keep the case ahead of me. I'm not the sort of man a person like her would keep around anyway. I know it's absurd. I have a funny feeling that this David Sloan will amount to more than just a name. In addition, like it or not, partner, I'm not going to forget what they did to Flo. You can help if you want. Just don't get in the way." He looked up to be certain she understood.

Then he needed to get something else off his chest. "Don't get me wrong, partner. I can get used to your expanded vocabulary, but I don't like the racial stuff you throw around."

Loud enough to make Harold wince at the attention from other tables, Yo-yo spoke her mind. "Man-shit, mu-fuck, where do you get off telling me how to talk? That's me, dude. Take or shove it. I can call myself anything I want, 'cause it's me." Leaning over the table with her finger pointed at Harold's nose, she grinned and said, "However, you honkey misfit, *you* say that and it's off to the village with bars on all the windows, and ninety-nine percent populated by the brotherhood."

Harold gave her a loving look and just nodded. He really liked this person.

Y O-YO BROWN LOOKED LIKE SHE always had an Ipod imbedded into her brain, with wild rap and offbeat music pounding into her mind. The tightly wound coils of hair sprouting from her head were continually bobbing to an unseen beat, keeping time with the gyrations of her skinny legs. The silent rap in her head kept up the steady beat, but she disconnected long enough to tell Harold, "As for Flo, I love her too, boss. There's some mean shit out there and ain't nobody but us to stop it."

Taken back by the tight knit across her brow, he had no doubt she would stay with him. A calm sensation swept over him, giving him confidence in what they were about to do. Smirking, Harold asked, "So, partner, where do we go from here?"

Pushing away from the table, she let him know, with no chance for a misunderstanding, "Your place, boss. I'm getting in a mood, and I still owe you seventy-two bucks."

CHAPTER 11
FORT YO-YO

YO-YO SHOULD HAVE KNOWN she was not going to get laid as easily as that. Harold passed his own apartment, going straight upstairs to Flo's place. At the top of a narrow staircase, a converted storeroom was the former queen's chamber. There was just enough room for a single bed, a sink with a small water heater, a toilet in the center, and an open burner stove top for incinerating whatever food she had. The main feature of the room was one window, painted shut.

The bed was a fiber mattress over squeaky springs, covered with remnants of her last one hundred customers. Hunched over to scan the floor, Yo-yo thought Harold was going to overcome his center of gravity and fall on his face. He picked up the corner of a piece of plastic food wrap. There were several straight cuts in it, with dark smudges. He carefully folded it between sheets of newspaper. "The knife was wrapped in this. I hope they were too arrogant to think about hiding finger prints."

Yo-yo busied herself examining the bed, but commented to Harold, "Forget it, boss. The case is closed and the lab ain't going to process anything connected to it. Better hang on to it anyway, you never know."

Thinking deeper, Yo-yo added more wisdom, "Boss, the lab already found Isabelle's partial on the knife. You're trying too hard, man. Small shit evidence like that plastic wrap is gonna get us ten miles out of whack. Slow down, Harold. We'll get what we need."

Harold stood upright, his face red from the rush of blood to his upended body. "I know, I know. Keep looking."

Her hands touching the surface of the mattress, she said, "This is where they stripped her." She held up the remnants of Flo's clothing to place on the newspaper. Then, reaching through the dust bunnies under the bed, she came out with a cigar butt. "They always get DNA from these things. Like on TV."

Harold looked back at her, saying, "It's mine, forget it. You really watch that stuff?"

"That's where we learn to be cops, ain't it? Someday, I'm gonna meet that CSI Las Vegas guy. You know, the smart one. Yeah, I'll bang him good. Me and Grissom, oh baby."

Satisfied there was nothing else, he said, "Earth to Brown, earth to Brown. Come on, Yo-yo, I think were done here and besides, Grissom isn't on the show anymore."

Trailing behind, she muttered, "Maybe I'll do Sarah, she's cool. There's always the Stokes guy. He reminds me of Clark Kent."

LATER, BACK IN HAROLD'S APARTMENT, the two naked detectives lay together, holding hands. She asked him, "Was it all right, boss?"

Looking at her, and then rolling over to give her a kiss, he said, "You're the best whore I've ever had, partner. Do you really worry about being so good all the time?"

Running her fingers over his mottled face, she said, "It's all I got going. If I can't give a good fuck, I'm useless."

"You're a smart woman but this time your logic is all screwed up. Stop beating yourself up, Brown. You're an attractive young woman with an education and a great sense of humor. Let a guy get to know you. Set your sites higher for someone who deserves and appreciates you. Be fussy, and don't think a man won't have you if you don't screw them. If that's all they want, move on until a guy comes along who makes you feel good because you are a woman worth feeling good about."

"How about you, boss? You're a nice guy."

Smiling Harold said, "I'm just me, Yo-yo. Since I lost my family, I wake up each day thinking this is when I see the bullet coming. I don't give a shit for myself and take too many chances because of it. No, you need a guy who's going to come home every night."

The inspirational speech over, she crawled on top of him, stuck her tongue in his mouth, mumbling, "Let's go another round."

Moaning, Harold submitted, "Oh, my God, Brown. Don't you ever stop?"

"Just shut up and pretend I'm Mrs. Freeman."

July 15, in the hospital.

Both detectives sat at the bedside of Amanda Freeman. Since the case had been closed, the guards had been removed. Harold asked, "There must be someone you can stay with. You can't go home until this is over."

Amy's face was bruised and swollen. Her midsection was tightly wrapped to protect the bullet wound and a broken rib as well. Sitting on the edge of the bed, she strained to say, "There's nobody. I don't want anyone else involved in this." Wincing, she had to pause to catch her breath.

Yo-yo asked, "What about your parents?"

"Especially them. They won't talk to me. I'm a disgrace to their sanctimonious life. I know they wouldn't care if they knew their only granddaughter had been murdered." Her head sunk to her chest, "Izzy, what went wrong?"

Harold reached out with a wad of tissues to wipe her cheeks. Yo-yo watched, disapprovingly, but she understood. Pocketing the wet tissue, Harold said, "You aren't going home, Amanda." He looked up at Yo-yo, and she caught the meaning of his stare.

Gesturing wildly with her arms, she mouthed the protest, *No, No, No.* Ignoring her antics, Harold generously told her, "We'll take you to Detective Brown's place until we can make sure you're safe again."

With a quizzical look, Amy turned as far as she could to see the reaction on Detective Brown's face. Giving in, Yo-yo sighed, "Yeah, that's okay. My place will do just fine." Stepping over to Amy, Yo-yo allowed a speck of compassion into her hardened demeanor. She put her hand on Amanda's shoulder with a gentle squeeze, "Yeah, that's a good idea."

At ONE IN THE MORNING, IN A WHEELCHAIR, Amy was taken out through the boiler room, onto a loading dock, and then gently placed in the back seat of a waiting rental car. As a secondary precaution, a blanket was drawn over her. Yo-yo followed behind in Harold's Plymouth with contact by radio on a secure police frequency.

Yo-yo had been more successful as a prostitute than she had let anyone know. Pulling into an underground garage of a luxury condo, in the posh Minneapolis suburb of Edina, Yo-yo followed them in after making certain they had not been followed, or caught the attention of a nosey neighbor.

Harold pushed the wheelchair, while Yo-yo followed them backwards, gun drawn, hammer cocked. The elevator took them up four floors to the penthouse, where they were greeted by the soft comfortable surroundings of luxury. The drapes were drawn and the rooms swept, to be sure. Standing dumbfounded, Harold scratched his head, asking the obvious, "Whose place is this?"

Holstering her weapon, and ignoring Harold, Yo-yo pushed Amy into the living room. "You should try walking around to gain some strength. Use the walker the hospital sent to help you, but you need to do as much by yourself that you can."

Amy nodded, "Yes, I know." Pulling herself out of the wheelchair, she stood shakily anchored to the walker, looking around.

Yo-yo caught it, saying, "The bathroom is right over there. Do you need help?"

With a sheepish look, Amy nodded, *yes,* with Yo-yo following the struggling woman in.

Straight from the bathroom to the bedroom, Amanda Freeman was tucked into Yo-yo's bed and fell sound asleep. Tip toeing out, quietly shutting the door, Yo-yo gave Harold the shush sign with her finger to her lips. Quietly, Harold repeated, "Who lives here?"

"I do, boss. I told you I was a good whore. I get a good price for the show I put on. You should know by now. I'm worth a lot of money, boss, and I don't share it with nobody. Not even Uncle Sam."

Settling in the kitchen, she cranked off the top of a Dasani, offered him one, and told him the rest. "I also own the whole building. We're on the fourth floor, sealed by some heavy-ass fire doors. Ain't no-one getting up here unless they know how."

Holding the Dasani up, she offered, "Cheers."

Finishing her explanation, she went on, "This is Fort Yo-yo. I also told you I had a degree in business. A few choice investments, and a luxury condo as a tax write-off, it's easy."

Still confused, Harold scratched his head, "Yeah, but . . ."

"How dense can one man get? You're sitting right in front of me, man. Did you not hear what I told you?"

Finally admitting he was as stupid as she said he was, Harold confessed, "I guess compared to where I live, this is a shock to see another cop living so well. I'm very impressed, Officer Brown."

The comparison was comical, sending Yo-yo into hysterics, "Boss, you'd be moving up by living in the city dump." A few more chuckles and Yo-yo got serious, telling him with quiet sincerity, "You live where you want, boss. There ain't nothing wrong with your pad or your lifestyle. I wish more men were like you. Not as stinky, but just as nice."

Harold was absorbing the compliment when she reached out to pull him out of the chair. Pushing his hulk into the guest suite, she got undressed, telling him, "You can go home if you want, boss, but if you want some clean sheets for a change, get your fat ass in here." Crawling across the king size bed, the satin sheets were folded open as his invitation.

Muttering as he got in beside her, "Don't you ever get tired of doing this?"

Taking hold of the parts of him that she needed to make the game greater, he moaned in pleasure, laying back to enjoy the symphony of seduction from a master.

The next morning, Amy got herself to the kitchen for a cup of Yo-yo's coffee. Easing her body down into a chair, she exhaled in relief, "Whew, that's a lot of work."

Adjusting herself in the chair, she told Yo-yo, "Detective Brown, I can't live off you. It isn't right. I'd probably be all right at home."

"We need to keep you safe and healthy, honey. There's some bad shit out there yet, and we need to find it." Bruntz was still sleeping heavily while Yo-yo asked the questions he was too reluctant to bring out. His attachment was compromising the details they needed. Yo-yo started her inquest, "We need to talk to David Sloan, Amy. How can we find him?"

"Please don't involve him. He didn't do anything."

Getting firmer, Yo-yo demanded, "We'll be the judge of what he's done. If he's clear, super. But we still need to find him. We also need to get your husband off the street and into protective custody."

Sitting next to Amy, Yo-yo leaned closer, firmly saying, "There's more to this than some porno shots, Mrs. Freeman. Your daughter was brutally murdered in your own drive way. Darrel's wounded and being hunted like an animal. If you tell us everything, we can save it all for you."

Gazing blankly into her cup, Amy slowly shook her head, quietly answering, "No, there's nothing else." The vacant look falling across her face seemed to pull Amy into a void that had no bottom. She looked frightened, lonely, and sad.

Needing to get closer, Yo-yo pressed on, "Girl, I don't give a shit what happened with Cherasky. I don't care who fucked who, or what was stolen. I just . . ."

The magic word was spoken. As soon as Yo-yo said *stolen,* she watched Amy stiffen. Bingo. "Amy, level with me. What do you people have that Cherasky wants? Your daughter already died for it. Do you want the same thing to happen to you?"

Amy gave herself away again, the words blundering out of her mouth, "That's not why she died."

Holding Amy's arms to the tabletop, Yo-yo firmly pressed on, "Why did she die, Amy? Why is Isabelle dead?"

The tears flowing down her cheeks, the facial wound turning red, Amy looked into Yo-yo's eyes, her lips quivering, "No, that's all. No." As Amanda's body shook with grief, the broken rib and the ripped flesh of her abdomen tore her to pieces. The flood came like a tsunami, her pain pulling her through a horror that could only be seen or felt by her. The sobbing turned into a wailing flood of tears, her body wracked with pain she tried to ignore. The real pain was in her mind and was not one that could be healed. Yelling as she tore herself loose from Yo-yo's grip, "No more. *There is no more. Stop.*" Wrapping her arms around the destruction on her stomach, she slid off the chair to sit on the floor at Yo-yo's feet. Shaking and tormented, Yo-yo was sure if Amanda Freeman knew anything, she was not going to give it up.

Harold had been watching from the doorway and stepped in to help. Yo-yo stiff-armed him to a stop, with a strength that alarmed him. With a steel-hard resolve, she growled at him, "No, stay back. I'll finish this."

Bending down, she got Amy by the armpits, gently bringing her back to the chair. Pulling the woman to her feet, she placed her behind the walker and guided her back to the bedroom. Amanda was eased onto the bed and assisted to lie down. Sitting beside her, Yo-yo stroked her hair, speaking gently. "We have to get to work, Amy. Forget about the killing of your daughter. We, me and Harold, are only interested in getting to Cherasky." Now planting an illogical seed of reprieve, Yo-yo said, "When we get Cherasky I think this whole thing will fall on him. We're close, but we need your help. Please tell me where we can find David Sloan before Cherasky finds you and your husband. Then whatever it is you have of Cherasky's, you can keep it. My guess is its money, a lot of money. Am I close, honey?"

Amanda peered up into Yo-yo's eyes, held her hand and nodded affirmatively.

"I don't give a shit for the money, girl. We want Cherasky. Don't let you or your husband die for it. The money is yours. Just tell us where Sloan is."

Amanda's lip's quivered and she mumbled, "Bryant Avenue, 3212. The south end, off Lake Street."

"Thanks, you did good. We'll be back in a little while, honey. The phone ain't going to ring, and nobody's going to come to the door. You're safe here, and we're the only ones that know where you are." Tucking the blankets around her, Yo-yo turned the light off and quietly left the room.

Grabbing Bruntz by the loose belt flapping at his huge midsection, she pulled him out of the condo, into the elevator. Back into his Plymouth, she said, "I got Sloan's location. If she's not lying, we're going to bust his balls. He's got to be the connection to Cherasky, and I got a hunch he was Flo's visitor."

As Harold drove his car out of the parking ramp, Yo-yo let him in on what she learned. "The Freemans are on Cherasky's list because they stole a bunch of money from him. Mrs. Freeman doesn't have it, but she knows where it is."

Harold interjected, "The only way to take anything from Cherasky would have to be with the computer. My guess is that Darrel transferred funds to another account, Cherasky found out, and put a hit on Darrel to get it back. That's the only reason Darrel was bailed out of jail." Glancing over at Yo-yo, he said, "Now doesn't it look reasonable for Cherasky to be fingered for killing Isabelle as a warning to Darrel?"

Firm in her response, Yo-yo made chilling sense. "Unless Cherasky did Isabelle in retaliation for killing his guard and stealing his gun. Then again, it could have been Darrel in a jealous rage. Whatever the truth is, if we can find Darrel before Cherasky does, we can nail him for Isabelle and her boyfriend. Then you and your fucking white horse can ride in and swoop Mrs. Freeman off her feet." Letting that sink in, she added, "That little shit knows something that will open up this whole can, boss. When we get back later, we have to squeeze it out of her."

Harold's vision of Amanda Freeman's clean-shaven body was overpowering his sense of judgment. His attraction to the woman had made him inept at doing his job. Driving away from Fort Yo-yo, he sunk into the seat, saying, "I just can't bring myself to push her. I want to keep her from being hurt."

Yo-yo spat back, each word snapping at Harold's perverted logic. "Dump the fucking fantasy and quit acting like a pussy, Bruntz. You're a cop, and if you don't start being the cop I know, you'll be regretting another partner leaving you."

A few moments of silence went by with Yo-yo adding, "She's married, you bone head. Married, and before the day's over, she'll probably be dead. Fucking white men are so stupid." Gazing out the passenger window, she mumbled again, "No shit, man, fucking stupid."

Harold sadly glanced at her, knowing she was right.

Passing the old gray-stucco four-plex on Bryant Avenue, they cruised around the block and down the alley to check out the rear before going in. David Sloan was supposed to live on the first floor, and unless Amanda gave them a bum steer, they planned on just barging in. If they were wrong, it wouldn't be the first false entry.

Coming to a stop in front of the apartment, they did a quick survey before walking up to the entrance. Through a porch with tattered screens hanging from their frames, and into a small dark hallway, they went to the door on the right.

Harold's fist pounded on the door, shaking it in its frame. Almost immediately it swung open, exposing whom they assumed to be David Sloan. Their greeter was a shade less than six-feet tall, had sandy hair neatly trimmed to an Ivy League cut, and was clean shaven. His build was not considered muscular, but he was obviously in excellent condition.

Holding his badge up to validate the intrusion, Harold asked, "David Sloan?"

Not the least curious about the badge or the two people in his doorway, he said, "Yes, I'm David Sloan. Please, come in," graciously stepping aside.

"I'm Detective Bruntz. This is Detective Brown. We want to talk to you."

David Sloan didn't look surprised to see them. In fact, he appeared to have been expecting them. "Bruntz and Brown? Sounds like a comedy team, or a law firm. What can I do for you?"

Harold and Yo-yo cautiously stepped into the dingy apartment, taking note of the squalor. Not too unlike Harold's own digs, Yo-yo thought he and David Sloan could be ideal roommates, except for their personal appearances. Yo-yo looked him over, considering him to be an attractive hunk. If Bruntz could have a fantasy with the married Amanda Freeman, she would snap up David Sloan.

Giving the one-bedroom apartment a cursory assessment, Harold brought his attention to Sloan, asking him, "Mr. Sloan, you were Isabelle Freeman's birth father, correct?"

The grin left Sloan's face, giving him a somber look. Sadly answering, "Yes, I am. Was." Shifting his gaze, he said, "Such a beautiful girl. Why would anyone kill her?"

Harold ignored the question. "Mrs. Freeman claims that when you were kids, you raped her and got her pregnant." It occurred to Harold that he seemed to be a minority when it came to people who had sex with the lovely Amanda Freeman.

Sloan's face turned red, the anger obvious. "We were kids. She was hot and a tease, and I was in love with her. She went along with it well enough. Why would you bring that up?"

Harold continued, "Trying to establish your relationship. You started seeing Isabelle?"

"Yes, of course. She was my daughter."

"You had an affair with her mother at the same time?"

"Yes, I did. So what?"

Harold casually said, "It doesn't matter, other than it could implicate you in Isabelle's murder."

Before Sloan could retaliate, Harold said, "Were you aware Isabelle was having sex with her stepfather?"

David Sloan was clever, but this news put a stutter to his arrogance. "Darrel and Isabelle? Are you sure?"

Bruntz continued twisting the blade, "Evidently, you weren't aware of her being pregnant with his child."

Plopping down on an old mohair chair, he muttered, "Isabelle was pregnant? That son-of-a-bitch. No, he wouldn't do that. Oh, shit no. Really?"

Bruntz leaned closer, "Yeah, really. Where is Darrel Freeman, Mr. Sloan?"

Looking up at Detective Bruntz, David Sloan slowly said, "If I knew, I'd go get the prick myself."

Bruntz suspected that lying was one of David Sloan's best talents, and now he was at his best. However, his anger was not a lie. Harold pressed on, "Who would want Isabelle dead?"

"Nobody, she was . . . she was . . . shit; why Isabelle?" Harold stood back giving Sloan a questioning look. There was a hole in this someplace, something was not fitting right.

Yo-yo got into the act by asking, "Who would be hiding Darrel Freeman?"

With contempt, Sloan said, "The man's poison now. Nobody would be dumb enough to touch him."

Picking up on what Harold considered a slip, he pounced on him, "Why do you think he's poison?"

David Sloan had a worried look that told the detectives, *Screw you.*

Bruntz, moving closer, said, "How are you connected to Lenny Cherasky?"

David Sloan maintained his screw-you look.

Yo-yo said, "Does Cherasky have Darrel Freeman?"

Again, they were met by controlled silence.

Harold, firm with his comment, said, "Look, Sloan, if we find that Cherasky kills Darrel Freeman, or Amanda, we're going to nail your balls to the wall. You have a chance to get out from under Cherasky's clutches and tell us what is going on. Does Lenny have Darrel?"

David Sloan was adamant in his silence, and they knew the interview was over.

As they left, Harold gave one last shot. "You aren't protecting anyone, Sloan. The sooner we find Mr. Freeman, the safer he and his wife are. And don't forget about your own ass. Cherasky has the muscle, but we can make sure you spend eternity in prison."

Looking slowly at Harold, David Sloan, with deep resolve, told him, "That's a shallow threat, Detective." A snide sneer followed.

With the last word, Harold said, "It's not a threat, Sloan. Don't go anywhere. We'll be back." Adding one more comment, Harold's voice came out as a growl, "You were at my apartment and did something you shouldn't have done. At some point, Sloan, you're going to pay for it."

Whatever bravado David Sloan carried, it evaporated. Harold Bruntz had just scared the hell out of him.

Outside, with twilight starting to roll in, Harold and Yo-yo sat in front of the apartment building trying to put a game plan together. Staring at the steering wheel, Harold said, "He's lying." Backed into a corner, Harold had to admit, "You're right, we need to bend Amanda until she talks. If we don't fill up some of these holes we're going to see more people die. Us, maybe."

Holding her leg dance in place, Yo-yo said, "No shit, man, you finally got a little smarter."

Pleased with his partner's evaluation, Harold drove off with Yo-yo commenting, "Not much, but a little bit."

While Yo-yo and Harold were talking in front of the dilapidated old apartment building, their game plan was changing, right under their noses.

CHAPTER 12
BLUFF

O N THE WAY BACK TO FORT YO-YO, the conversation was slow and easy. Harold tried to put all the pieces into place, but there were too many gaps, and they all seemed to center around Amanda Freeman.

Yo-yo had the best answer, no matter how much he disliked it, "We need to put her under arrest, boss. She needs to be protected, and if a jail cell intimidates her, she might spill."

Sighing, Harold agreed, "Yeah, I know. I know. We have to invent a charge that'll stick to her."

Yo-yo punched his shoulder, then told him, "You realize that if the chief finds out we have her in our possession, and the case opens up again, we're fucked." Curious about Harold's connection to Amanda, she asked, "By the way, boss, do you get in this deep on all your other cases?"

Irritated because she was right, and he was wrong, he snapped back, "All right, I know. She needs to be in lock-up." Hesitating, he finally answered, "No, I have always just busted balls and did my job. She just got to me. With Flo being hurt, I've never had a case come so close to home, and I need to do something about it."

"Well, I never mentioned Flo. If it's bothering you that much, remember what I said about the vigilante shit."

"Yeah, you'll be with me all the way." Trying to be logical, Harold changed the subject and added, "But first, we have to dig up enough evidence to show Darrel is Isabelle's killer."

Silent for a few minutes, then with a serious wrinkle in her forehead, Yo-yo spoke up and said, "Have you given any thought to maybe David Sloan whacking his daughter? As nuts as this case is, maybe the kill-your-kin thing is in their genes."

The Plymouth slowed down, with Harold saying, "Yeah, it crossed my mind, but I'd rather save Sloan for something else. I've got another plan for him."

Slowly answering, Yo-yo said, "Save a piece of him for me, boss."

Harold was silent, his mind churning over David Sloan and what he did to Flo. "Maybe. Darrel's already on the hook for the killing, and this case needs an ending. That asshole was screwing his stepdaughter and that's a pretty good motive in any murder. No matter what, he needs to be put away. With a plea, he can get a reduced sentence, especially if we can find him and get him to roll on Cherasky. Hell, he might even become a hero." Harold felt satisfied with his logic, then added, "If he does get out, I've got him on the same list with Sloan."

"All right, boss, I'll make you a deal. If we can get Mr. Freeman to implicate and get a prosecution on the Russian, I'll go along on framing the worm, with a lighter sentence. I gotta agree, boss, incest ain't right. No fucking way."

Harold noticed a drained look on her face. "What's wrong?"

Staring at the dirty dashboard of the Plymouth, digging years back into her shadowy past, she told him, "The incest thing. My dad raped me and my sister. I was too scared, but my sister fought back. She hurt him big time. She told the cops, and they put him away. My mother fell into a hole then and just let her life fade away. Me and my sister had to take to the streets to stay alive. That's when we started hooking. I was fourteen, man. Fourteen fucking years old and a whore. And, I'm still doing it. That's my story."

"Have you had any contact with your father since?"

"He found me a few years ago when he got out. I kicked the shit out of him and charged him with assault. He got sent back and is gonna die in there. Good!"

True confession time was open, so Harold told her, "I haven't been able to work well with partners because I've had a hard time covering up some of the shit I did to nail these bastards. I'm no good at explaining what I'm doing. I want to nail Cherasky, and the only way I see to do that is to use Darrel Freeman as bait. If he gets screwed and lost in jail, then it's just one more prick off the street. Darrel is in deep with Cherasky through the computer. I'm positive that Darrel is as much an accomplice as anyone. The porno, the Russian dames, the killing at the poolside, Gordon Marks and Isabelle, there's just too much of it. And now, we have another player, David Sloan."

Slouching down in the seat, her fists pressing against her forehead, Yo-yo said, "There's another twist to this that's gonna bite us. Lieutenant Warner is sold on this case being closed. I don't like the way he acted when we told him about Cherasky. The Russian dude is a slug, but Warner isn't going to move on that." Sitting upright, she slammed her fists onto the dashboard, forcing the glove compartment door to open. "Why, boss? What good does it do to get involved in the shit? We should be happy the case is closed, and go home. Why are we so mu-fucking concerned about justice? Well, me, anyway." The outburst was rhetorical, but she looked at him for comment, and caught the grin on his face. "What? What's that stupid smile for?"

"Take this any way you want, Brown, but you're the best partner I've ever had. I said just about the same thing to you recently. Except for the true-blue justice part."

Glancing away, she tried to hide her own grin, "Bullshit, I'm the only one dumb enough to stick with you."

Harold sighed and said, "Well, now we have to find a reason to arrest Amanda and get her into custody. She needs to be hidden."

Quietly, with conviction, Yo-yo said, "No, we don't. Just leave her at my place."

Smiling with a side-glance, Harold said, "I was hoping you'd say that. I didn't know how you'd take it."

Yo-yo told him, "I hope we don't get hung out for this shit. We're crossing some thin ice here, boss."

Although not convincing, his answer told her he was aware of her concern, "It'll work out. I'll see that it does. Don't worry."

Pulling into the underground parking ramp to Yo-yo's condo, they both saw something was wrong, but neither could put a finger on it. Yo-yo sat forward, then screamed as she bolted out of the Plymouth, "*The rental. The fucking rental is gone.*"

Yo-yo, hanging onto the open door as Harold slowed down to stare at the empty space in front of them, yelled, "Where are the keys to the rental?"

She heard him say, "I left them upstairs," as she ran to the elevator, leaving Harold alone in the garage. Bursting into the apartment, she flew through all of the rooms, but they were empty.

Harold's bulbous frame, breathless, slowly came through the door behind her. He knew beyond a shadow of a doubt what he had done, and slumped himself into a corner, looking at the floor.

Screaming, waving her clenched fists in the air, "She's fucking gone with the fucking rental car." Turning in circles, helpless, the tirade continued, "Fucking gone, you . . ." But the screaming stopped, her arms quit flying and the smoke quit billowing from her ears when she looked at the pathetic hulk in the corner. Walking over to him, she took his hand, then put both arms around his neck, softly saying, "It's all right, boss. She's gone, so we just have to find her again. We have to find her and Darrel. I'm sorry I blew, Harold. We're partners and whatever we do, we do together. Your fuck up is my fuck up, and my fuck up is your fuck up. I'm sorry."

Letting a moment go by, she quietly added, "Although, you fuck up a lot more than I do."

An APB was already out for Darrel. They added Amanda Freeman. However, they weren't going to be found that easy. David Sloan would make certain of that. A quick check on Yo-yo's phone record showed a number that Amy placed, the address was 3212 Bryant Avenue South. The same place they had just come from, David Sloan's apartment.

Livid, Yo-yo spouted, "That little shit took the rental and went to Sloan. She knows where Darrel is." Striding towards the door, she said, "Come on, boss, we gotta go back to grind on Sloan."

Harold hustled after the erratic woman, breathlessly telling her, "Yeah, but we aren't going to find him there." Once again, Harold's instincts were correct. David Sloan was not there.

AMY AND DARREL LOOKED WAR WOUNDED, struggling to help each other down the rickety wooden stairway at the rear of the old apartment building on Bryant Avenue. The rental car was idling in the parking area, both doors open, waiting for them. "Hurry, Darrel, he's going to find us in a minute."

Grunting and weak from the bullet still buried in him, Darrel told her, "You should have never come here. If Sloan doesn't stop us, Cherasky will."

"Shut up and keep moving, just a couple more feet." Shuffling across the gravel parking lot, panic and fear drove them on. Pushing her husband into the passenger seat, she slammed the door shut and pulled herself to the driver's side. Holding her stomach tightly, the world kept spinning in front of her, and she winced from the pain. Her fear got worse when she saw David Sloan running from his first floor apartment.

Sloan yelled, "Stop, don't go." He managed to get to the car, but Amy's hand was on the gearshift and foot on the gas pedal.

Amanda loudly told him, "Don't stop us, David. We have to get out of here."

Pleading, Sloan tried to convince her to stay, "Cherasky wants to talk to you. He promised not to hurt you. All he wants is his money." Leaning against the passenger door, he looked at Darrel, "I got you off the street, man. You came to me for help, and I did. You owe me. Don't leave."

Darrel impassively looked at Sloan, his eye lids drooping from fatigue and fever. Amy dropped the shift lever into drive and slammed her foot down the gas pedal, spitting gravel from the parking area.

Running to his own car, David mumbled to himself, "Oh shit, I can't let them go." Fear of Leonid Cherasky hung over him. His job was to deliver Darrel and kill Amy. He failed at both and now had to correct his mistake.

The maroon Pontiac rental had disappeared down the alley, but Sloan was able to spot it a few blocks later. Staying back, his best choice was to follow and see where they were going. At some point, he needed to get hold of Cherasky, but he wanted to avoid that as long as possible.

A MOMENT AFTER SLOAN'S CAR had sped after the Freeman's, Harold's Plymouth bounced off the curb in front of the apartment. Yo-yo was getting out before Harold came to a stop, but managed to tell him, "Nice landing, boss."

The door to Sloan's apartment was locked, stubbornly muted to Yo-yo's feeble attempt to force it open. Standing back, she looked for another way to get in, until Harold pushed past her with his shoulder splintering the woodwork. Drawing her revolver, she commented, "Yeah, okay, that's a good way to get in."

Aside from the filth and worn-out furniture, the apartment was empty. As yo-yo made a quick inspection, Harold was on the old black dial telephone demanding information. "Yes, I want a list of all the numbers placed from this phone for the past week. I'll wait, but you have to hurry, this is a matter of life or death."

Holstering her .38, Yo-yo joined him, saying, "I found a 9mm Glock in the bedroom." She held it out, swinging by the trigger guard from her finger.

"Good, put it in something, and we'll have it run when we get to the station." Turning away, his attention went back to the telephone, "Yes, that's good. Thank you very much." Placing the handset back in the cradle, he said, "Just two calls to a private number in Brainerd."

They looked at each other, and in unison, said, "Cherasky."

DAVID SLOAN SAT IN HIS CAR ABOUT a half block away from the Dew Drop Inn. A collection of small rooms built into a strip, it was normally a hangout for prostitutes and drug dealers, and, at this time of day, very quiet. Watching as Amy left the office, he waited to give them time to get settled. About a half hour later, a weary Mexican woman in a white dress was pushing the cleaning cart from room to room. Leaving it outside as she made her rounds, Sloan slid into the room behind her, pulling the cart in with him. Startled, yet not overly upset, the maid thought it was just another rape and made ready to let him do what he wanted. She got paid by the hour, so what was the big deal.

David Sloan was surprised by the woman's complacency. He pushed her onto the bed and was surprised when she just spread her legs, pulling her dress up. "What the hell. No, you bimbo, I've got something else for you."

Amused, he leaned over her, grasping her neck, and then with the other hand covering her face. Panic struck her hard when she realized this was not what she thought. An effort to struggle set in too late, as Sloan's hands worked together forcing her head to snap away from the spinal cord. The last thing the woman felt was a white-hot searing pain shoot through her head. She sank to the floor, her head grotesquely askew and flopping to the side, her legs still parted to accept him. He reached into her apron and pulled out the master key. Looking back at her, he was amused by the way the eyes still had a look of life in them.

T HE GLOCK, RUSHED THROUGH THE LAB, came out with a few interesting results. The bullet markings from the test firing matched up to an open case involving a murder in Chicago, two years ago. Sloan's fingerprints brought up a sheet listing jail time for assault, and two dismissed charges for murder. Digging out the old files revealed the name of Sloan's attorney as Melvin Orenstein, Darrel's lawyer. Taking Sloan's file photo, he made a copy.

Sitting in Lieutenant Warner's office, Harold was locked in combat trying to get the Gordon Marks case reopened. "Goddamit, Bruntz, that case is closed. I don't care what you have. We aren't going to screw with it any more. Now, get out of here, both of you."

Neither Harold nor Yo-yo had any intention of leaving. Yo-yo, tired of complacency for the sake of not having to get off one's ass to do their job, spoke up. Standing up, her fists supporting her lean frame over his desk, quietly but firmly said, "Lieutenant, I realize you hold all the trump cards and make the decision as to what we work on. Hells bells, man, that's why you're a boss and we ain't nothin' but grunts. That's cool though, someone has to be in charge. Let me paint this thing a different color for you. Maybe you ain't looking at all the details."

The red was crawling up the lieutenant's neck, ready to explode into his forehead, "Brown, what the hell do—"

Pushing the button harder, yelling at him, "Shut the fuck up and listen to me, you jackass." Moving around to the other side of his desk, she leaned into his face, still yelling, "The fact is, you moron, that we know about the connection you have with Cherasky. You don't want him pushed because he's making you rich and has his hand on your balls, squeezing. If we don't get your blessing to finish this case, the next office we sit in will be IAD. Maybe they'd like to pull the sheets off you and Captain Hilksman while they're tying your fucking noose."

Walking out of Warner's office, with the blessing, though grudging, Yo-yo had demanded, Harold was having trouble understanding why they both still had jobs. "I know I'm a little slow, Brown, but what just happened in there?"

Smiling, with a skip to her step, she asked, "You don't play poker, do you, boss?"

"No, I don't, but what has that—"

"Well, we didn't have a winning hand, but we managed to win the pot with a bluff."

Stopping, he held her back, asking, "A bluff? That stuff you screamed at him was a bluff?"

"Yeah, boss. I had an idea he was being milked by Cherasky because he got so worried when we reviewed the case for him. And shit, I saw the stuff between him and the captain the first day. Now, let's go get us some bad guys."

CHAPTER 13
DEW DROP INN

July 18, late evening, the Dew Drop Inn, Hiawatha Avenue, Minneapolis.

CONCEALED UNDER THE SHELTER of a large street-side elm tree, David Sloan sat in his car playing with the key he took from the dead housekeeper. At a discrete distance from the motel, he watched the parade of sleazy prostitutes and skuzzy customers barter for price and product. He eyed the ever-present pimps leaning against their Cadillacs and considered any problems from them. As long as he didn't get in their way, what he had to do wouldn't bother them in the least. If it didn't concern one of their girls, they would mind their own business.

Keeping an eye on room seven, he knew that if they needed anything they would wait until the evening darkness rolled in, and he was correct. At eleven, Amy left the room to walk across the street to the Mini-Mart. He watched her enter the store and calculated the time he would need to complete his task.

As soon as she was gone, he quickly left his car and crept to room seven, letting himself in. Although he was certain that the injured Darrel was the only one inside the room, he entered with caution.

Dark and dank, the back-and-white TV cast a flickering gray glow over the bed, the lone light source in the room. The only sound was the soft static sputter from the scrolling ghost-like image on the out-dated TV set.

On the bed, the bulk of Darrel's body cast a shadow in the crumpled sheets, making him obvious in the dim light. Darrel's chest was slowly heaving in a rhythm that kept time to a muted death knoll—shallow and labored and exuding a throaty rasp.

Moving to the shadow, Sloan reached out to see if there was a reaction to the figure. Darrel's low voice startled him, "I'm alive. What are you doing here?"

"You look like shit, Darrel."

Waiting for a coughing spasm to go away, Darrel wheezed out an answer, "Yeah, I feel like shit, too. Ever carry a bullet around, David? You should have taken it out when I asked you to."

Squirming at the thought, Sloan said, "I can't do that."

Arching with a stabbing pain, Darrel gasped, "You're a killer, David. Why would a little blood turn you off?"

"Killing is a different thrill. I don't like blood if it isn't from what I'm doing to hurt someone."

Darrel's next comment held more logic than David was ready to hear. "I know you're trying to get me to Cherasky. With a bullet in my back, I won't be able to run away. Am I right?"

"Yeah, Darrel, you're right. Why don't you just tell me where the money is and I can leave you alone."

Wheezing, Darrel pushed the words out. "No. It's mine now, and you'd never let me live." Darrel's coughing shook his whole body, his flesh moist and glistening in the gloom. "You're going to kill me anyway."

"Don't be stupid, Darrel. If you don't tell me, I'll give up Amy, and Cherasky will grind on her for it. Don't make her go through that, buddy."

Slowly, Darrel answered, "You wouldn't do that to her. You love her and won't hurt her."

"Don't be so sure, Darrel. I don't want Cherasky on me, and I'd turn her over to save my own ass."

The coughing went into a spasm, with Darrel just able to say, "Fuck you, Sloan."

"Sorry you feel that way, buddy. I'm going to kill you and fuck your wife. How does that sound?"

Darrel, fighting the dizziness from the fever, gave his best effort to let Sloan know where he stood. "You'll have to stand in line, David. She'll spread her legs for anyone."

Although expecting it, when Sloan made his move, it surprised Darrel. As decrepit as he was, the only string that kept him alive was the eternal fight to grab at the remotest chance to keep breathing and escape.

The idea that he and Amy could get through this was their salvation—until this moment.

Needing to get this done before Amy came back, David wrapped his fingers around Darrel's sweaty throat, tightening the squeeze. Slowly, hoping the fear of death would make Darrel tell him what he came to find out, the fingers crushed his airway.

Desperate for his answer, David anxiously asked again, hissing, "Where, Darrel? Where is the money?"

The only sound coming from Darrel was a sickening retch. His neck was wet from perspiration, and the flesh was burning with fever. The gagging, writhing body made it difficult to maintain pressure, so he squeezed tighter. Darrel's eyes bulged from the sockets, with his hands weakly, uselessly pushing against Sloan's grip on his neck. To finish the job with a little more satisfaction, Sloan leaned closer, saying, "Goodbye, you dumb shit. This is for Isabelle." Leaning over, David put all his weight on Darrel's throat. Green infected mucus seeped from Darrel's mouth, and ran over his killer's hands.

Darrel's body relaxed, slumping into the bed. Sloan knew that if Amy actually did *not* know where the money was, *he* would become Cherasky's next target. He was about to find out, as he heard the doorknob being worked to open.

Hiding in the darkness behind the door, he watched Amy set her bag on the floor, then move to the bedside. Darrel lay motionless as Amy ran her hand over his forehead, wiping the sweat up into his hairline. It didn't register at first, until she noticed his eyes. They were blank and not normal, gazing past her, empty. His mouth hung open with the green ooze coating his chin. "Oh, my God, Darrel, are you all right? Answer me." She stood up to turn the light on and saw the shadow behind the door. Thinking it was one of Cherasky's goons, her heart fell, sending her backwards with a gasp.

Reaching to flip the light switch, Sloan said, "It's me, Amy. Just me. Don't worry." A solitary floor lamp in the corner cast an annoying glare from the tattered shade.

She stepped back, bumping into the bed, turning to look at the lifeless form of her husband. Sloan said, "He's dead. I killed him."

Sitting down on the edge of the bed, next to the corpse, her fist went to her mouth. She knew she should cry but couldn't. "Oh, no, Darrel, I'm so sorry." Looking up at Sloan, she wailed, "You didn't have to do that. He couldn't hurt anyone."

Her move to turn and look again at Darrel was stopped by Sloan pulling on her arm. "You and me, Amy, we can take the money and disappear." His voice was calm and convincing. "It's always been us, honey. We can go away and they'll never find us." He pulled her up into his arms ready to give her his best sales pitch. She pushed him away.

The sneering contortion of her face held nothing but contempt and hatred. Her lips curled in revulsion, snapping at him with, "You? I've given up everything hoping someday you'd come back and take me away, me and Isabelle." Her voice was rasping from grief with the twist on her face telling the story. "No, David, it's all over now. You can't take anything else from me. Izzy's dead, and now Darrel's gone. Izzy and I played our game and she lost, but Darrel hung on through it all. He watched me with other men and took me home again. He stayed with me because he loved me."

Now, the truth she had held inside for so long came out to hurt more than the piercing pain from her wound. Snidely twisting her words, "He loved me so much, and I never gave it back to him. I forced him to screw Izzy. I watched as they did it, and made him watch while I made love to her. I punished him because I couldn't get to you. I punished Izzy because she was a part of you."

Sitting back on the bed with her head down, she sadly muttered, "You didn't have to kill him."

On his knees in front of her, he lamented, "He killed my daughter, Amy. He got her pregnant and killed her. He deserved to die."

Her face pinched in agony, she looked up, viciously spewing out her anger to him, "You dumb shit, how do you know Cherasky didn't kill her? How does anybody know you didn't kill her?"

Looking at Amanda's face, coated with perspiration and glowing in the ghostly shadows, Sloan's mind was spinning, saying, "No, you know I didn't. It couldn't have been Lenny. He had no reason."

Her grief turned to a sneer, her face awash with tears and told him with snide contempt, "Isabelle killed his guards, you son-of-a-bitch. She was stealing Lenny's gun to kill me so she and Darrel could run away. They were going to live on Lenny's fucking money and thought he'd get blamed for killing that shit, Marks." A convulsive sob passed and she added, "And me."

Leaning onto his shoulder, sobbing, she wailed, "It didn't have to happen. It was all so stupid." Her fists balled she slowly beat on his chest, wailing incoherently, "My daughter and my husband. Stupid, stupid, stupid. Now they're both dead and I'm glad."

Unbelieving, he grabbed her wrists, demanding, "Why, Amy? Why would you want my Isabelle dead?" His face contorted in disbelief, he repeated, louder, "*Why?*"

Amy, with cold determination slowly spit out, "Because I couldn't kill you, and I wanted you to hurt. We'd gone too far and the game had to stop. She tried to kill me, but she wasn't smart enough to do it. She was sick, ass hole. The daughter you created was retarded, just like you. You kill people and smile, and that's the gift she was given by you, a heartless cold killer and a rapist with a demented mind."

David's hand went behind his back to pull the 9mm pistol from its nest in the small of his back. His lips pulled back, snarling with hatred, his own tears dripping from his eyes, he pressed the gun to her head, yelling at her, "My daughter. You heartless bitch, do you have any idea what I could do to you? *She was my daughter.*"

Amy , motionless, drained of fear and logic, was certain she was going to die with Darrel. Quietly and calmly, she told Sloan, "Shoot me, David. Take me out of this. Kill me." She reached up to hold the gun between her hands, pressing it tighter to her head. Screeching, she commanded, "Shoot me."

Shaking and tormented, his finger shook on the trigger. Instead, he whispered, "I don't want you dead. I want you to feel pain. I want you to suffer for my baby."

David pulled the gun away, swung it back and brought it savagely across Amy's face, sending her rolling over Darrel onto the floor behind the bed. She lay motionless, her breathing shallow. Kneeling next to her, he stroked her hair, matted with blood and sweat, and quietly said, "No, my love, shooting you is far too kind for what has happened."

He grunted her upright, laying the limp body over his shoulder, to bring her to a more horrible place than this.

DETECTIVES BRUNTZ AND BROWN stood in the Bryant Avenue Precinct squad room asking for volunteers, but since the altercation in Lieutenant Warner's office, they had become lepers. Bob Warner stepped in front of the assembly of officers, announcing, "No volunteers?" Turning to Harold and Yo-yo, with a smirk, he told them, "This is the game you're going to have to play alone." Leaning closer, he quietly said, "Yes, you had me on the ropes, but I'm still in charge here. Now, you two go do whatever you think is proper procedure. Alone."

Harold looked at his partner, telling her, "You don't have to get involved in this. I'm going to take down Cherasky, and it's going to stink. I won't think any less of you if you stay behind."

Looking at him with a wrinkle in her forehead, she said, "Shit man, you fucking honkey, I already told you I was in. What *is* your problem boss? We're partners, you bone head, and you ain't keeping me from a good hoedown."

Smiling, Harold had a plan, but when the desk sergeant handed him a note, everything changed. Yo-yo saw his face drain and could feel the chill, asking him, "What is it, boss?"

"Darrel Freeman has turned up."

Understanding the gravity of what he said, she remarked, "That ain't good, is it."

T HE PORTABLE BUBBLE SAT ON TOP of the Plymouth acting as a lazy sentinel in front of room seven at the Dew Drop Inn. A couple of squad cars and an ambulance had a more threatening look than the Plymouth. Pimps and hookers waited across the street for the colorful scene to go away so they could get back to business.

The maid's body lay on a gurney with forensics prodding the lifeless form for clues. "Strangled, Detective Bruntz. It doesn't look like she put up a fight. Snapped her spinal cord."

Gazing at the wasted life, Harold said, "I have an idea who did this and I'm sure they weren't acquainted."

The medical examiner told them what he had learned, which gave the two detectives a whole new game to play. "Her master key was found in the room with the dead guy. There are prints on it and we'll rush them." Leading Bruntz and Brown into room seven, he explained, "He was choked, but it looks like it was revenge. He would have died before morning anyway. Look, over here. There're blood pools on the floor with a splatter pattern on the bed and wall. Someone was hit pretty hard here and fell back over to there." Kneeling on the bed to view the spot where Amy fell, Darrel's body rolled into them. Yo-yo jumped back, "Holy shit, man."

Darrel turned to the forensics crew, nodding to Darrel's body, "Get him bagged and out of here."

Yo-yo sifted through the grocery bag, passing a few food items, and coming out with a large box of sterile pads, disinfectant, and a roll of adhesive tape. "Hey, boss, look at this. Mrs. Freeman was here and was trying to take care of her husband. My guess is that Sloan caught up to them."

Disgusted, Harold spouted, "Damn, we were so close."

Harold had a perfect idea of what went on in the room, telling the ME, "Get a DNA on the blood. It's going to be a match to Amanda freeman, the dead man's wife."

Walking back to the Plymouth, Harold leaned against it, telling Yo-yo, "Sloan killed the maid to get her key. He strangled Darrel then hit Amanda hard enough to put her out. That was the only way he could quietly get her out to Lenny Cherasky's place."

They looked at each other with Yo-yo summing it up, "We're going there ain't we, boss?"

Hoping she wouldn't back out, he said, "Amanda is out there and she's the only one left with knowledge on where Cherasky's money is. If she doesn't tell them, they'll kill her."

Yo-yo added, "If she does tell them, they'll kill her."

"That's about it, partner. You ready for some action?"

"Yeah, boss, I'm all set. However, we ain't going in as the Navy this time are we?"

With all the show and fanfare of a Hollywood setting, a large shiny black Buick skidded into position behind the Plymouth. Bob Warner flew out of the door holding his badge out to impress the small crowd. "Move aside. Let me see what's going on here." Uselessly scooting around the crime scene, he cornered Harold and Yo-yo, quickly asking, "Is it true? Is Mr. Freeman dead? What's going on here, Bruntz?"

Slowly, Harold looked up at him, "Do you believe us now? David Sloan killed the maid and Darrel. Now he has Mrs. Freeman and is going to give her to Cherasky so he can torture and kill her."

Hesitating, Warner told Harold, "Look Hal, the captain is the one pushing you. I know what you can do, but she's got a hard on for you and won't let go. Can you find Mrs. Freeman before it's too late?"

Sadly, looking into the lieutenant's eyes, Harold said, "Yeah, I can find her. But, like you said, Bob, we're alone now. This is going to get messy, you know that too."

"I can't give you backup, but I'll go back to the station and make sure the armaments room's unlocked. Will that help? Can you get there in time?"

Smiling, Harold said, "That'll be a good start."

With one last word, Warner said, "Hal, it would be a blessing if Cherasky was put out of business."

Harold nodded, saying, "That's a good idea, Bob, but a blessing to whom?"

Yo-yo stood back disgusted with what she was hearing. Her anger took control. She blurted out to her superior, "You want us to clean up for you? You only want Cherasky gone to cover your ass, you honkey shit."

Astounded at her perception, Lieutenant Warner needed to get control. Yelling and pointing at her, "You watch what you're saying, Brown. I'll have you . . ."

Harold stepped between them, taking the abuse from Yo-yo's flailing fists. In a surprisingly calm voice, Harold told her, "Ease up, partner. Don't say anything stupid. Get in the car, please. I'll handle him."

Harold looked over his shoulder and saw the lieutenant fuming his way back to the Buick. Settled back in the Plymouth, Harold looked at her and put his hand on her vibrating leg.

She glanced back and said, "I'm cool. Let's get the fuck out of here."

Harold nodded, telling her, "We got one thing to do, then we go to war."

Yo-yo didn't ask what.

Striding up the steps to his apartment, he found Flo sitting in the dark on the worn, dirty sofa. He flicked a light on, "How you doing?"

"They won't come back, will they, Hal?"

Setting himself next to her, he calmed her, "No, honey, they won't. We're on our way to take care of that now. I want you to look at a picture for me." He held up the copy of David Sloan's file photo.

She gasped and pushed herself back into the sofa. "Oh, God, no. It's him. It's the man who . . ."

He took her cold shaking hand and kissed it gently. "Thanks. He won't be back, I promise."

Flo watched him leave knowing that he was on the warpath. He would do what he needed to do. It was just the way Harold worked. He saw to it that things like that got done.

CHAPTER 14
THE WAR WAGON

THE LATE NIGHT WAS DEEP AND QUIET, with the precinct house vacant, except for a few on the night shift. Harold made his way along the dark hall leading to the warehouse area of the building. Yo-yo danced behind him like a water bug, her arms twitching out of habit, her head bopping like a chicken. At the chain-link fencing separating the confiscated weapons he pushed on the door, and it swung open, emitting a frightening squeal. A flashlight had been put on the desk, and he handed it to his partner. "Shine this in front of me."

Gazing at the rows of racking filled with sequestered weapons of every imaginable style, Yo-yo whispered in awe, "Man, look at all this shit. We could arm a small country, boss." Stopping to run her hands over a .50-caliber sub-machine gun, complete with tripod, she drooled, "Oh, man, ain't this some shit. What's a piece like this doing in here?" Like a kid in a toy store, she wanted all of it.

Harold hissed, "Come on. Shine that light up here. And don't touch anything."

Among the racks of weapons snapped away from hundreds of evil people, he picked a few that would serve their purpose. Taking more than was needed would raise too many questions. Picking out an M-16 Army assault rifle, he handed it to Yo-yo, asking, "You know how to use one of these?" He slung a bandolier holding six 5.56mm twenty-round magazines over her shoulder. Staggering back at the sudden addition of weight, her smile got bigger. Smiling and trying to suppress her joy at the feel of the awful thing she held, she enthusiastically babbled, "Oh, man. World war three, come on. No shit boss, do you know how fast these babies dance out of the muzzle of this thing? Huh? Do ya, boss? Lemmee tell ya, bubba, 980 fucking meters a second. Man shit, mu-fuck."

Busy arming himself, he scolded her, "For Christ sake, woman, quit making love to the thing. It's a lethal weapon."

After checking the ammunition, armed with a twelve-gauge pump shotgun, a Takarov 7.62 Russian sniper rifle, and Yo-yo's M16, he handed her a Ruger 'P' 9mm. He stuck a Glock 17C into his waist band, and they were almost ready. Before closing the door, he tossed a flak jacket to her, and then took one for himself, sized extra large.

Settled into the Plymouth, Harold noticed the dancing of her limbs had stopped. Her nervous system had armed itself and had the antithetical effect on her. They looked deeply at each other, bone dead serious.

He knew better than to ask her if she wanted out. All he could do was muster up a, "Thanks, Yo-yo."

Smiling, she answered, "You bet, boss. Hell, this is what we get the big paychecks for." Her voice unusually solemn, asked, "Well boss, this is it now, right?"

Driving to the rear of the precinct house, he answered, "No, not quite yet." Slowly cruising into the alley, he stopped at the garbage dumpster. Getting out, he said, "Wait here." Rummaging around behind the trash can, he finally came out with a six-foot piece of two-by-twelve lumber. Wrestling it through the door opening he fit it inside to lie between the two of them and into the back seat. Settling his girth behind the wheel again, he said, "Now, we're ready."

As the little Plymouth rattled its way to the Brainerd Lakes area, Yo-yo ran her fingers over the dirty piece of wood sitting between them. Unable to keep her mouth shut, she asked, "All right, boss, I suppose the wood thing is in case we run out of ammo we have to beat them off. Or maybe we can carve crutches out of it after we get our asses kicked." Her nervous system came alive again, sending her legs back into their familiar spasms.

His face tight and grim, he didn't bother with an answer to her prattling. His mind was on the horror that Amanda Freeman must be facing.

Gull Lake, Cherasky estate.

DAVID SLOAN WAS MADE to stand and watch it happen.

After David had deposited her, Amanda became conscious and saw she was laying face down on the cold white marble floor of Lenny's dinning room. Through a blur she focused on the curving marble steps that led upstairs, just in front of her. The blood on her face had dried and caked, and she avoided assessing what damage Sloan had done to her. Right now it didn't matter. The feet of the men shuffling around her were more important.

She knew that David had sold her out to protect himself from Lenny's temper tantrum. There were no feelings of betrayal towards David. After all, that was his job as Lenny's enforcer. Her lover's profession was to kill people as required.

Lenny's knee appeared, kneeling in front of her. Grabbing her hair, he yanked her head up, screaming in her face, "Where is my fucking money, bitch?"

There was no answer she could, or would, give him. Gasping, she wheezed out, "I don't know. David killed Darrel before he said anything. Please, let go."

He dropped her head on the floor. She didn't see it coming, but when the toe of his shoe buried itself in her stomach, the whole world lit up like a million flashbulbs. The intense light and the pain that followed blinded her. From deep in her throat, she yelled, "Oh, God, don't, please. I don't know." Whatever meager contents her stomach held, oozed from her trembling lips. Flowing onto the white marble, a streak of blood centered the tiny rivulet of slime.

She felt her arms being wrenched backwards, and hauled up, the strain on her shoulders paralyzing her. One large guard was on each side of her, keeping her standing upright, her arms stretched out to the sides. Lenny stood in front of her, his huge fist smashing into her face. The blood and spittle drained down her chin, her torn lip stinging.

"One last chance. Tell me where that prick put my money and I won't do any more to you."

She closed her eyes to wait for the worst. An eternity passed within the time span of a moment. Her body sank with a nauseating tremor running through her rubber legs. Her feeble plea for this to end went no further than the numbness of her mind.

Pulling her head up by her hair, it flopped back, her mouth hanging open. She had passed out. Lenny screamed his frustration.

Backing into a corner, David Sloan became sick, watching helplessly as the woman he loved was slowly beaten to death. He wanted to call out to stop the butchery, but cowardice kept him silent. It was his fault she was here. He justified his logic by thinking that he would have been killed if he hadn't brought her.

Turning to the two holding her, Lenny yelled, "Take her upstairs to the bedroom." They took her away, her head hanging loosely, her feet dragging behind, leaving a smear of blood trailing on the marble floor. As an after thought, he called to his henchmen, "Cut her clothes off and tie her to the bed. I'll be up in a minute."

Wiping the blood from his fist, Lenny walked over to the trembling David Sloan. Calmly asking him, "David, my friend, did she tell you anything, anything at all?"

Lenny's nearness had him shaking from fear, and he nervously answered, "No, she didn't. I did all I could short of actually killing her, but I don't think she knows."

Smiling with an evil twist to his lips, Lenny said, "Well, whether she knows or not, the bitch is going to die today."

To cover his own agony, Sloan wormed a few words out of his mouth, "Yeah, sure, why not?"

As a parting thought, Lenny let Sloan know just where he stood. "Maybe she didn't tell you. Then again, maybe she did. When I'm done with her, I want to talk to you. I'm not sure you're telling me everything. I'm kind of confused why you'd kill that worm Darrel before he said anything. Don't go anywhere." Walking away, he told a nearby guard, "Keep an eye on him."

Lenny finally went upstairs, leaving David Sloan shaking, his mind pounding out the warning, *"Oh shit, no. I've gotta get out of here."* He glanced at the guard hoping for a sympathetic nod for him to escape, but got a smirk and shrug instead.

UNSEEN BY HER HUSBAND, hiding in a dark corner of the kitchen, Vicka pressed herself against the wall shaking and sobbing. Pleading behind her hands pressed tightly to her lips, she quietly babbled, "Please stop, please. Leave her alone."

ABOUT A MILE FROM THE CHERASKY estate, Harold stopped the car, taking the wooden board out with him. Beckoning to Yo-yo for help, he told her, "Hold the board across the front of the car, like this. Good, now don't move."

"Boss, what the fuck are we doing?"

As Harold wound a roll of duct tape around the board and the front of the Plymouth, she caught on. "Oh, no shit, man. A battering ram, how mu-fucking clever."

Standing back to admire his work, he gave the board a few kicks to be sure it was attached well enough. Satisfied, the two stood at the open doors to load and arm their arsenal. The Plymouth coughed into life, charging towards the enemy.

Approaching the entrance, there was a large man in a tight t-shirt sitting on a lawn chair, in front of the gate, a shotgun across his lap.

AMY LAY SPREAD ACROSS THE LARGE round bed, arms and legs stretched, with her feet and hands tied to the ornate metal frame. She was naked, except for the dirty bloody bandage wrapped around her waist. A large red spot had soaked the gauze where her wound had opened up again. Lenny hoisted himself up to the bed, straddling her hips. "Too bad I have to do this to such a beautiful woman. You should have stayed loyal to me, Mrs. Freeman. With you and Isabelle, we could have made some very nice movies. Now, you're all screwed up and not worth a damn to anyone. Are you sure you don't want to tell me where the money is? One last chance."

Amy lay still, bearing the weight he put on top of her. She was too numb to feel the pain from the beating, but she knew that if she lived long enough, it would find her. Her breathing was labored. One eye was swollen shut, the vision in the other was blurred, and her face was a bloody pulp. She mumbled to him, barely audible, "I don't know where it is. Go ahead and kill me. I don't give a shit anymore."

D OWNSTAIRS, DAVID SLOAN was sick at what was happening to the woman he had loved all his life. His stomach eptied out onto Lenny's marble floor. Kneeling in the putrid mess, he wailed, "What have I done. *Oh, God, stop.*"

T O BE CERTAIN THAT THE PLYMOUTH wouldn't cough and die before they were in position, Harold down shifted to a lower gear to keep the RPMs spinning the little engine faster. Roaring up to the gate, the guard heard the screaming four-cylinder engine and stood up to stop whatever was coming. Looking in disbelief at the two-by-twelve board, the duct tape, and a wide-eyed Harold perched over the steering wheel, he brought the shotgun up. He was pulling the pump back to move a shell into the chamber, when the war wagon crunched the guard and his lawn chair against the gate. The iron grating and the lawn chair flew across the grass and driveway as the tires bumped over the guard, crushing him into the gravel driveway. Bump, bump, bump, over the guard and whatever remained of the fancy gate, the car charged on, dragging the lawn chair that was wedged between the tire and fender.

Like a knight's horse charging into the Saracens, the screaming engine piloted by a saucer-eyed Harold Bruntz, kept rolling. It would have driven straight into Lenny's lakeside home if it weren't for the high-powered armor piercing slug that tore through the board and the radiator, splitting the block of the little engine, and the car ground to a halt.

Sitting motionless in the open expanse of the sprawling lawn, steam and antifreeze engulfing the spectacle, the battle plan was now put into play with each detective grabbing their weapons of choice. The next sound they heard was the snarling and barking of the two huge German shepherds turned loose with orders to kill. The first dog was in flight when Harold's pistol sent it toppling backwards, bleeding from its head. The second was scratching and clawing to get into Yo-yo's window. She recoiled from the spit and teeth less than an inch from her face. The explosion from Harold's pistol, in front of her, sent the animal to doggie heaven with its mate.

Harold grabbed Yo-yo, yelling at her, "Goddamit, woman, if you can't shoot a dog, what are you going to do to those guys."

Wide eyed, she yelled, "Sorry, boss. I'm a dog lover."

She then saw that Harold was pointing out at the two armed guards running towards them, guns blazing as they ran. Yo-yo quickly yelled, "Oh, shit, man, they're shooting back."

Calmly, with deliberation, Harold opened his door, pointing the Takarov out the open window, sending two powerful slugs into the closest man. He rolled over backwards, arms flailing wildly. The second guard dropped to his knee to take careful aim, but Yo-yo's M-16 tore him to ribbons.

Harold called out, "Good shot, Yolanda."

Looking at him with a deep resentment for using her no-no name, she caustically shouted, "Be careful, honkey. I'm armed." Just for shits and giggles, Yo-yo raked the front of the mansion, emptying the clip. Dropping the empty clip, jamming in a new one, she looked at Harold, her face lit with pleasure.

Pointing his rifle to the side of the house, he yelled at her, "Go around back and kill everyone that shows up—and hurry."

His pistol tucked into his belt, the Takarov pointed at the front door with the shotgun cradled in his left arm, Harold moved as fast as his girth would allow him. A figure appeared at the doorway, crouched, with his arms over his head. David Sloan came running towards him, breathless and stammering, "They have Amy upstairs. I heard her screaming. We have to . . ."

Holding the grip of the shotgun, Harold pressed it to David's chest. Before the next word got to his lips, pieces and chunks of David Sloan filled the space behind him. The explosion tore out of the choked muzzle, ripping through his chest, his back splattered across the lawn through a twelve-gauge blender.

Seeing movement through the open front door, Harold unloaded the Takarov into the entry, the large wooden door splintered, hanging loose at the hinges. Counting shots, he knew the heavy rifle was useless now, and he tossed it aside. Shifting the shotgun to his right hand, he jerked it midair, one handedly injecting the next shell into the chamber. Marching through the open door, one of the guards who had held Amy during her beating stepped in front of him. Both men fired at the same time, the guard's slug tearing through the side of Harold's bulky midsection below the Kevlar, ripping a six-inch piece of flesh from him. The blast from Harold's twelve-gauge at point blank range disintegrated the man from the chest up. Pumping another shell into place, Harold stepped over the guard's legs, slipping in the goo under his feet. It was all that remained of him.

Harold heard a gun bark behind him, and felt the force of the slug strike the Kevlar vest he was wearing. Toppled off balance by the force, Harold's body went down, with his survival instincts rolling him over to face the man who had just shot him.

The vomit left by David Sloan saved Harold's life. Reaching out to send a bullet into Harold's head, the guard had slipped in it, loosing his aim. In Harold's one free hand, the shotgun exploded, removing everything from the guard's shoulders up. Struggling to overcome his huge midsection, he got his feet under him, and headed for the stairs, stripping off the cumbersome flak jacket.

Stopping at the bottom step, the twinge in his side started barking at him. Looking down at the blood soaking his waist, he said, "Oh, shit, that's bad." Leaning on the railing, he shook his head to force his brain to come into focus. He suspected that the slug that had been stopped by the vest broke one of his ribs, wriggling his back to rearrange the pain.

UPSTAIRS, LENNY STRADDLED the helpless woman. He saw the bruise on her side and pressed it, correctly guessing it was a broken rib. The fragile bone separated again, sending Amy into another level of terror. Unable to catch her breath, she spasmodically retched, her lungs screaming for air. Her eyes rolling back into her head, and she prayed for death to stop the torture.

Lenny realized the game was over now, he could kiss his two million dollars goodbye. And to the miserable piece of shit lying under him, he would enjoy watching her die. Pressing the switchblade knife into the fleshy part under her jaw, he started pushing it in.

The guard standing at his side bolted back, "Jesus, Lenny, what the hell are you doing? Don't do that, man. She's dumb about the money. Just kill her and be done with it."

Snapping his eyes to the squeamish guard, Lenny snarled, "I don't take that shit from you. Go. Get out of here, you pig. I'll deal with you later."

The knife would have penetrated to the depth of death had it not been for the gunfire in his front yard. Jumping off Amy, he ran to the window overlooking the pool, and watched in horror at what was happening below.

YO-YO FLEW AROUND THE BUILDING with her weapon raised. Rounding the rear corner, she saw a figure running away from the pool, towards the lake. A short burst sent the body rolling across the lawn. Creeping up to the form, Yo-yo gasped at the sight of a bleeding Vicka Cherasky. Reaching out to touch her victim, Vicka's last words were, "She's upstairs. You have to get her out." Her eyes wide open, Vicka's life just ended. A short sigh and she was gone, arms and legs spread on the lush grass.

With no time for regrets, Yo-yo sprinted for the house. She heard shots from the front yard and hoped they had come from her partner.

UPSTAIRS, LENNY WATCHED his wife fall from the burst of gunfire, then saw the skinny black woman run to her side. Pulling his gun from his waistband, he bolted out the bedroom door, leaving Amy to bleed to death on his bed, the knife still embedded in her chin.

RUNNING FULL OUT ACROSS THE LAWN, Yo-yo leaped over the pool fence, and pushed her body through the screen door into the kitchen. In a crouch, she moved quickly to the last sound of gunfire. Finding herself in the dinning room, she saw her partner leaning heavily against the stair railing. She yelled, "Boss, you okay?" Yo-yo Brown looked at the mass of flesh and blood strewn across the room, but didn't have time to get sick from the sight.

Harold turned to her voice and watched his partner go down. From the top of the staircase, Lenny sent a bullet into Yo-yo's head, and then watched with pleasure as she sank to the floor.

Up to now, Harold Bruntz had been in control. From the crashing through the gate, to his march up to Lenny's house, he had been fearlessly following a plan. He had a goal, and regardless of what got in his way, he was going to see it to the end. Watching Yo-yo's body go limp and lifeless threw his brain into a whole other orbit. A different force drove him now, one he had no control over.

His eyes wide, nostrils flaring, with fire streaming from his gritted teeth, Harold's chest belched a scream, and he barreled up the steps. With Lenny's bulk as his target, and his arm stretched in front of him, his pistol was blazing and jumping, his finger squeezing as fast as it could. After the weapon was empty and useless, he still charged up the staircase, blaring wildly.

Lenny, in shock from the huge man moving so fast, felt two slugs from Harold's 9mm Glock tear into his shoulder. Lenny's free arm was brought up to point his gun at the ample target racing towards him. Squeezing the trigger six times, he watched as six bullets tore into Harold's flesh, each one spouting blood and tearing flesh.

Harold's gun held uselessly in front of him pulled him up, up, and up. Click, click, click. Lenny watched as the grotesque form rose up in front of him. He lashed out with his own empty weapon hitting Harold in the face and head, again and again. Beating on him savagely, but the monster never broke his step and slammed Cherasky into the wall behind him. Lenny's chest collapsed from the weight of Harold's mass, leaving him breathless.

Harold's arms were waving wildly, the penetrating screech coming from deep within his anguished body, he reached Lenny and grabbed onto him. With muscles that had laid dormant for years, he reacted to the challenge that at one time had made Harold a champion. They flexed in a savage awakening.

He grabbed whatever his fingers could hold and clung tightly with the grip of a pipe wrench. Harold's hands literally tore Lenny's flesh from his face. Crazed and tormented, a raging bull, he ripped his victim to shreds.

Harold's massive body pressed Lenny into the wall. Harold could go no further, but that was far from the end. Unleashing super human strength, Harold Bruntz grunted, one hand crushing Lenny's throat, the other grabbed his crotch, lifting the two-hundred-twenty-five-pound, six-foot Leonid Cherasky over his head.

Roaring savagely, his bellow echoing through the large house, Harold stood at the railing overlooking the ground floor below, a terrified Lenny suspended over his head. With a mighty lunge, Harold threw the horrified man over his head to plummet to the marble floor below. His body heaving and convulsing, begging for air, Harold looked at the bloody heap laying just feet from his fallen partner.

Yo-yo was a cop. If she was dead, there was nothing he could do for her, and if she was alive, she would have to take care of herself until he could get to her. The more important job was next. Where was Amanda Freeman?

Frantically staggering and panting from one doorway to the next, Harold looked into each room, until he found her. The sight made his heart drop. Spread across the bed, her dignity gone, her blood soaked the bed linen deeply. Stumbling, straining to catch his breath, he absolutely could not fail now. "Stay awake, Bruntz. Don't fuck this up like you've done all your life."

Shuffling to the bedside, the vision of little Rachel wandering into the street while he slept in a drunken stupor pierced his brain with the shock of a thousand volts. His mind crammed the picture into his head again, of the truck skidding on the loose gravel, trying to stop before it hit and crushed the little girl.

Leaning over Amy, he gently pulled the knife from her throat, and then used it to cut the bonds at her hands and feet. Wrapping her in the blood soaked chenille bedspread, he tenderly carried her to the staircase. Down one step at a time, his legs crumbling under him, he couldn't fail again. He was going to make it. There would be no jokes about him this time. No snide remarks about the slob never where he was supposed to be. About the father who let his little baby die while he slept in a drunken stupor.

He laid Amy gently on the sofa while he stumbled into the kitchen for clean towels. Holding them at her throat and her stomach, he propped them in place, stepping away to find a telephone.

"This is 911. What's your emergency?"

Breathless, he slurred, "Hurry, she's hurt." The phone dropped from his hand as he turned to his partner, mumbling absently, "They're all dead."

Lowering his body to sit next to her, he cradled Yo-yo's bloody head in his arms and didn't know what to do, so he softly sang to her. "Hush little baby don't you cry, Daddy's here and he won't leave. Hmm-hmm-hmm. Daddy's gonna buy you a mocking bird, Daddy's gonna buy you a diamond ring." Over and over, not knowing the words to one single tune, he kept up the rhythm, "Hmm-hmm, hush little girl, Daddy's here for you. Good night, Irene, goodnight . . ."

It was anybody's guess as how long it took the police to get there. At the first sight of the carnage, they ordered an immediate ambulance call and back-up. Weapons drawn, the officers quickly entered to see the large man sitting on the floor holding the black woman's head on his lap, slowly rocking back and forth.

Nodding towards the living room, Harold told them, "On the sofa. She needs a hospital now. Leave us until she's taken care of."

The helicopter landed on the lawn, among the dead bodies and dead Plymouth Reliant. In a moment, the *thump-thump* of the chopper carried Amanda away. Harold was too large for anyone to carry on a stretcher, but that wasn't necessary. Yo-yo cradled in his arms, he staggered to the ambulance himself. Inside, they assured him she was being cared for, so he finally gave up. He had done it, and nobody was going to laugh at him for it. As the world spun out of control in front of him, the vision of little Rachel was taken into the darkness with him.

The ambulance went screaming out of the carnage-cluttered yard, too busy for anyone to notice the sound of a speedboat disappearing across the lake.

CHAPTER 15
LOVE

July 28

T HE HELICOPTER FLEW IMMEDIATELY to the Southdale Fairview Hospital in Minneapolis, with Amy taken directly into surgery. Her vital signs had all but flat-lined, and she was virtually drained of blood.

Fourteen hours later, Amy was wheeled into an IC ward under constant watch. It was still a gamble as to how long the young woman would be able to draw life into her shattered body. If she was able to stand the stress, two more surgeries were required. After that, she was to see an oral surgeon, a plastic surgeon, and if one was available, a psychiatrist.

Harold and Yo-yo were taken to the Hennepin County Medical Center in Minneapolis. As police officers injured in the line of duty, the medical staff viewed them as heroes, providing the best attention available. Harold's heavy body was able to absorb the damage, but Yo-yo was not expected to live through the night. The medical staff worked feverishly to prove themselves wrong.

Harold's flesh was sewn together, his broken rib set, and all of Lenny's slugs fished out of his body. Using a wheelchair he spent his time sitting at Yo-yo's bedside, waiting patiently for her to wake up. Day after day, Harold sat quietly at her bedside, waiting.

Her doctor told him, "Detective Bruntz, there's nothing you can do for her. Go back to your own room. We'll call you as soon as she shows signs of responding. Also, you have to understand that she could very well never regain her faculties."

Harold looked blankly at him, saying nothing, and returning his attention to his partner. He was not going to leave, for any reason. Cops didn't do that. A good cop would never leave his partner.

When the duty nurse asked him what his relationship was to her, he simply told her, "She's my partner." He lovingly and sadly looked at the wiry springs covered by white wrappings, wishing she would start twitching and bopping again. Straining to reach over, he absently brushed one of the black springs away from her face, not wanting it to make her uncomfortable.

WHEN IT DID HAPPEN, Harold was not surprised. He had been waiting a long time, and knew she wouldn't leave him alone. Late one afternoon, Yo-yo's eyes cracked open, trying to focus. Unsure if she was dreaming, in heaven or hell, she let her mind pull her along. The swimming objects she looked at started to slow down, and come into focus. The first thing she saw was an angel in the form of a large man with a bulbous nose and pock-marked face, sitting in a wheelchair, smiling at her. With a great deal of effort, she rasped, "Some fucking party, eh, boss?"

He wrapped his hand around her little fist, saying, "Yeah, some fucking party."

Barely audible, she asked, "How are you, boss?"

"Shot up a bit. I've got a plastic gadget on my back that makes me feel like a turtle, but that should come off some day. I know how you are. I've been asking so many questions about what's going on with you that I might be able to take a medical exam. Between you and Flo, I could spend all my time on you two."

Smiling, she said, "No shit."

"Yeah, no shit."

She twisted her hand so she could hold his also, and then looking deeply into his eyes, she sincerely told him, "Harold, I love you."

There was no way he could react to that, so he just sat dumbly looking at her, his face still swollen and bruised, his pale blue eyes blinking in bewilderment.

With considerable effort, she went on, "I was dying, Harold. I felt the chill running through me and everything turning bright. I mean really bright, but it didn't hurt. I wasn't even scared. I said goodbye to my sister and waited. Then I heard an angel sing. It was you, Harold. I heard you singing to me and felt you holding me. It was the most beautiful fucking thing I ever heard."

She squeezed his big hand, and told him, "No matter where either of us goes from here or what we do, together or alone, I will always love you, man. You're beautiful, Harold, just fucking beautiful."

Smiling, her lids closed and she fell into a peaceful sleep, leaving Harold with a wet mess collecting in his eyes. He softly told her, "You have such a way with words."

September 2

ABOUT A MONTH LATER, Harold was home on medical leave. Yo-yo had gone to Duluth to visit her sister, telling Harold she wasn't certain if she would be coming back. Flo was back in business, living in Harold's apartment for many reasons—economy, convenience, and mostly too afraid to go back upstairs. He took care of her, always treating her with respect, trying to make her feel comfortable. She had separation anxiety every time Harold left her alone, so he gave her a small revolver as a measure of security.

He was deathly afraid to visit Amy, not knowing how she would react when he saw her. The police reports were routed to him, and he was able to see the medical records. He was aware of her health, and by some miraculous twist, her bones would mend, the wounds would heal, and the torn flesh would react to plastic surgery. Aside from the scars, the most damage was to her mind. That would be a little more difficult to mend.

However, he needed to get over this hump. He stiffened up and made the visit to the Fairview Hospital. The Plymouth was dead and sitting in a pile of scrap in the junkyard. He upgraded to a 1985 Chevy Cavalier. This one even had a radio that worked, and all the windows opened and closed. The heater worked, but the air conditioner was just something to keep the fan belt tight.

For Amanda Freeman, confined for over a month, the outlook was bleak. The reports on her that Harold got from the hospital staff were not encouraging at first. Once in a while he would send a few flowers, but that was only to make himself feel better. Amy had no connection to life around her, dipping in and out of consciousness. Now, for at least a week, she has been opening her eyes, managing a few words with the doctors and nurses.

The staff learned to make a special effort to keep the hall noise to a minimum. Every time a pan dropped, or a loud voice rang out, she would go into hysterics, thinking the beating was going to happen again. An infrequent visit from a staff psychiatrist did little more than annoy her. After screaming obscenities at him for digging too deeply into her mind, he decided it was better to leave her alone.

HAROLD WAS NOT GOING TO ARGUE. Either he got the help he needed, or he would do it by himself, again. Lieutenant Warner sat behind his desk, knowing he was wrong, but with his strings being tugged by Captain Hilksman, he was hamstrung. "There's nothing I can do, Hal. The case is closed and all the bodies have been buried. Either go home and retire, or get back to work."

With as much conviction as he could muster, Harold answered, "Cherasky's body was never found, Bob. He was on the floor right next to me, but when the clean up started, he was gone. He's on the loose, and he's coming back. He knows his money's gone, so all he wants is revenge. That'll make him even more dangerous."

"Yes, I know all that. So what?"

Harold stood up to leave, giving his superior one last thought to dwell on. "Who is he going to root out, Bob? You were supposed to be his protection, and now it looks like you set him up. Then, after he kills you, he's going to find Mrs. Freeman. She's worth saving, Bob. As for you, well you don't stand much of a chance. Maybe you're right, and I should just let Lenny get to you. You aren't worth a shit anyway."

Harold sat in the Cavalier for a long time before starting the engine. The problems racing through his head were more than he could handle. It would be so easy to just drive home and leave it all behind. But, he knew that was not going to happen. The woman lying in the hospital had crawled into his head, and wouldn't leave. Pulling away from the curb, he was guided by his stupid fantasy.

A tan Toyota pulled out behind him, following all the way to the hospital.

AMY APPEARED TO BE SLEEPING, yet the twitching in her arms told him she was frightened, even now. He stood at the window watching the leaves blowing away, leaving the raw beauty of the naked trees behind. The season was changing with the unwelcome winter snows and cold waiting to blow in. He turned away from the window and glanced at Amy to find her quietly watching him.

Her voice a whisper, "Detective Bruntz, what are you doing here?"

Smiling, Harold pushed a chair to her bedside, saying, "Just seeing how you were doing. You've been in here a long time."

"I'm glad you're here. I want to thank you." Her voice was soft and followed by a mellow smile that made Harold feel warm.

His head moving in denial, he told her, "You don't need to thank me for anything."

She held her hand out, reaching to touch him, "Yes I do. The nurses told me what happened, and some people from the police department were here to fill out some reports. They said you really made a mess of Lenny's house."

He gently held her hand, marveling at the soft warmth, "Your blood was there also. Have you been able to think about what happened to you?"

She pulled her hand away, turning her face away from him, "Yes, I remember all of it. I almost died, and sometimes I wish I had. I'll never be the same again." The chilling remembrance of that day was permanently running through her veins and kept her on the edge of hysteria.

Instinctively, he reached out to gently stroke her hair. In spite of the swollen and bruised face, laced with tracks of scars, she was still beautiful. The beauty and the beast, brought together by a violence that would haunt them both forever. They had both bathed in the blood of battle, but there was no winner, just victims. They had been drawn together by a tragedy yet were held apart by reality, and Amy knew she had better let him know.

Looking sadly at him, she said, "Detective Bruntz . . ."

"Harold, call me Harold, please."

She gave him that smile again, the one that made him want to pick her up and hold her. Her voice soft, but firm, she went on with his destruction. "Harold . . . I know what you want, and I can't give it to you. I'm used up and destroyed. I can never get close to anyone, ever. Don't let yourself get involved with me."

Surprised at her observation, he lowered himself into the chair, saying, "I didn't realize it was obvious. Sorry."

Her voice was hushed, and she forced it painfully out of her mouth. "Don't be sorry. Just understand what I'm trying to tell you. I've been hit by the wrecking ball too many times. I have nothing to offer anyone, and all I can do is bring you more hurt."

He was in pain also, and it all came from his heart. Harold knew what the boundaries were, and he knew he had to stay on his side. "Amanda, regardless of what shape you think you're in, I know a woman as beautiful as you would laugh at a slob like me. If I just know you're well and safe, I can live with that." His words were clean and simple, as simple as he was himself. As each one fell from his lips, it tore his heart into little pieces because he knew she was right, and the separation between them was right.

Smiling, and drawn to him by his sincerity, she said, "It isn't you . . ." and then the flag went up, turning her cold inside, the fear launching into her brain like a comet of ice. Deciphering what he had just said, "What do you mean *safe*? Why wouldn't I be safe?" It had to be Lenny. It was always Lenny and his control. Lenny sitting on her, ripping her body and mind into pieces. Her face contorted with doubt. He had to answer. He hesitated a moment too long, and the alarm went off with her yelling, "*Tell me.*"

He sighed, sat down and leaned close to her. "All right. I'll tell you everything. You deserve that. Cherasky got away. His body was gone, probably in the speedboat. The boat was found across the lake with blood in it. He had a storage locker near there filled with get-away and survival gear. Two more lockers were uncovered in different places. It was an escape network he had set up."

Her fists pressed into her face, pulling her legs up for fetal protection, she wailed, "Oh, God no. He's coming back."

Leaning over, he held her shoulders firmly, telling her, "No, Amy, he's not. I won't leave you for a minute until I know he's dead. I'll make sure you're safe. That's a promise."

Her agitation set off an electronic alarm to the nurse's station. Two nurses, one a male, stormed into the room, brushing Harold's massive frame aside. A sedative was injected into her IV line and they recorded her vitals. As the drug worked its way through her brain, Harold was severely told, "You need to leave her, now. Her condition is precarious, and these outbreaks will set her back too far. Do you understand?"

Holding his shield up, he softly told them, "Yes, I'm sorry. I need to stay near her to take any information she has. The man that did this to her is loose, and she may have details that will help me locate him. I'll be more careful, but understand that I'm here on police business." His voice was hushed, yet urgent and firm.

As Amy slipped into another fog, her vital signs leveled out and Harold was left alone with her again. She remained awake, yet in an artificial state of reality. Now, Harold's job was to convince her she was safe and he would stay by her side. That was little comfort, but at least she was not alone. The ordeal wore on her, sliding her into an agitated rest.

He stood at the door to the room, his mind blank, when a passing nurse smiled, and then retraced her steps to tell him something. "You're the detective, aren't you?"

Harold's response was abrupt, "Yeah, I am. Why?"

"Well, I know that Mrs. Freeman was in a gangland brawl, and this bothers me."

Pushing the nurse into the hallway to keep frightening news from Amy, he frantically asked, "What? What bothers you?"

"There was a man at the nurse's station asking what room she was in. Instead of going to the room, he left in a hurry. I didn't like his look one bit. He was nasty looking, you know. Like really mean and ugly."

"Yeah, I know." Glancing back at Amy's bed, he asked the nurse, "Is there someplace else she can be put, another room?"

Pensive, the nurse said, "Yes, we have a room down the hall."

"Do you have a room that can be locked?"

"Not really, but if it's just for a while, we could put her in the staff room. It's just over there and we can lock the hall door. The only other door is from the watch desk."

Harold's mind was busy and racing to be a good cop. "Good. How do we keep her a secret from all the staff that uses the room?"

With authority, she said, "I'll just tell them to stay out."

When Amy woke up, Harold told her what was going to happen, and she went ballistic. As she was wheeled across the hall, another miracle of science was injected into her IV tube. She was far too agitated to fall asleep, but it forced her to calm down.

Amy's mind was teetering between a surreal world of drugs and the terror of Lenny's torture. As the day turned into evening, her body was incapable of sustaining the stress any longer, and shut down. In a fog, she lifted her hand, hoping the detective was nearby to see it.

She felt the rough security of his hand wrap around her own, and knew she had to trust him. Her eyes were open enough to look at his bulk hunching over her, faintly telling him, "Harold, I can't do this anymore. Go ahead and do what you have to. I'll be all right."

He leaned over and kissed her forehead, making her feel very safe, and oddly, comfortable.

THE TRAPPINGS OF MIDNIGHT hung over the hospital. As the dark and sinister character worked his way up the rear stairway, he took the knife from his pocket. Pressing the tiny button to release the blade, the click making a small echo in the deserted stairwell. If he was confronted before he finished his mission, he would use it to silence any obstacle. With a deft grip on the hilt, the extended blade was hidden in his coat sleeve. The 9mm pistol with the long silencer was tucked in a holster under his arm, just in case.

Reaching the third floor, he cracked the door open to gaze along the hallway. The corridor was dimly illuminated by nightlights to provide serenity to the patients, and safety to the staff. He counted the doorframes of patient's rooms and located the one he wanted. Sliding from the stairwell, he worked his way along the wall to the target's room.

The duty station was in the middle of the empty corridor, with the sparse night crew absently doing paper work. All but one was concentrating on hospital procedure and record keeping. Concerned for his own safety, Lieutenant Warner let Harold talk him into placing an undercover policewoman, dressed as a nurse, at the desk to keep vigil as only a trained officer could.

At about two in the morning, seated at the duty station, Officer Cynthia Madden spotted the man slowly creeping along the wall. Mumbling softly to herself, "You arrogant and ignorant asshole." Turning to the two nurses sitting behind her, she softly told them, "Get in the staff room, lock it and stay on the floor. He's in the hallway now."

Swiftly and quietly, the two nurses fearfully crept into the room adjacent the duty station, closed the door and hunched on the floor. Officer Madden pressed the call button to Amy's room and reached under the desk to wrap her hand around her weapon.

With a quick check up and down the hallway, the only danger the intruder saw was a nurse seated behind a counter obviously engrossed in her job. "If she noses down this way, I'll get rid of her."

In front of Amanda's room, one more quick check, and he cracked open the door. Quickly surveying the room he slid in, pushing the door shut behind him. The room was dark except for the dim glow of a safety lamp at floor level. A small flashlight lit his path to the curtain pulled around the bed. He stopped for a moment, listened carefully, and slowly pulled the curtain aside. Gazing at the mound in the bed for a moment, he slid up to it and placed his hand on the form under the blanket. His free hand came from the cuff of his coat with the blade of the knife extended. Slowly and methodically, he worked the steel point through the blanket into his victim. Once more, just to be certain, he plunged it in again. Easy as pie.

Stepping back to admire his craft, the next thing he saw was Harold's huge fist, on a powerful swing, smash into his startled face.

As his body thumped onto the floor, Officer Madden pushed through the door with her gun at arm's length, ready to execute deadly force, and almost shot Harold. The muted light from the hallway cast over the figure on the floor, with Officer Madden remarking, "What the hell?"

Kneeling down to cuff and arrest the intruder, the policewoman looked up at Harold. "Good job, Bruntz. Why didn't you let me shoot him?"

Grabbing the man by the hair, Harold pulled his face into the light. "Shit, it's the wrong man. It's not Cherasky."

Looking at the heap in front of her, Officer Madden said, "Son-of-a-bitch, what am I going to tell the lieutenant?" Then a strange realization came to her, and looked quizzically at Harold, "Bruntz, let me ask you something. The lieutenant told me to shoot to kill, but now that I think about it, the gunshot would send this entire hospital into orbit. Why would he tell me to do something so stupid?"

With a great deal of contempt, he answered, "Yes, it is stupid, and why didn't you think of that a long time ago? The lieutenant wants Cherasky dead, no matter how it's done."

With three uniformed officers on the scene, the confusion was kept to a minimum. The officers handcuffed the assailant to a wheelchair, and he was taken for booking of attempted murder. Groggy from Harold's blow to his face, the man was still unaware of what happened.

Outside, the scene of flashing colored lights and an accumulation of squad cars in the street at the hospital entrance was witnessed by a shadow in a tan Toyota.

Put in a different room, Amy now had two uniformed officers at her door. Harold spent a few moments holding her hand and gently talking to her, letting her know she was safe, or at least let her see the pretense of safety. Still encased in the euphoria of the sedative, Amy was as zoned out as the man who tried to kill her.

After the assailant was gone and relative peace returned to the floor, Officer Madden, still dressed as a nurse, confronted Harold. "Bruntz, there's a big question mark sitting over this whole thing. I know all the guys think I'm 'Bimbo Cop,' but I'm bothered by the open audacity of what went on here. It's got 'set-up' written all over it."

"What do you mean set-up?"

"I've seen that guy before. I think he's been in the cage a few times. Or, I've seen his face someplace. I can't place it."

Harold pondered this and felt the same reaction. "Yeah, it does seem strange. But, it's Warner's problem. Don't get close to it or you might get involved."

In the nurse's locker room, changing back into her uniform, she was startled by a visitor quietly coming in. "Captain Hilksman, I didn't expect you to be here. The perp was taken already."

Her deep voice gave the impression that she ate hot rivets, washed down with malt liquor. Quiet and commanding, the captain said, "I know. He'll be booked and questioned. I just wanted to thank you for doing such a good job. I'll see that it gets on your record."

Embarrassed, Officer Madden stammered, "Gee, thanks. Just doing my job, Captain."

Smiling and turning away, Captain Hilksman stopped and asked, "By the way, weren't you supposed to shoot him to be sure he didn't harm anyone?"

Surprised and uncertain, she answered, "Detective Bruntz had him under control by the time I got there. Anyway, deadly force would have been too alarming in a hospital. Besides, Bruntz said it wasn't the guy he was looking for."

Momentarily startled, the captain asked, "What? Not . . ." The realization hit her hard. With a snide smile, "Bruntz, huh? Oh, I see. He did it himself. Hmmm. And you say that it wasn't Cherasky?"

"That's right. Oh, before I forget, Detective Bruntz told me to give Lieutenant Warner a message."

"Message? What message?"

Officer Madden carefully repeated, "With or without his support, tell him I'm going to nail Cherasky. Tell him to pray that I do it before Lenny gets to him."

Nodding, the captain said, "Interesting. I'll pass the message on to Lieutenant Warner. Good job tonight. Thank you. Goodnight."

The captain's fury at Bruntz's interference burned through her body. Stalking out to her car, she clenched her fists in frustration. "Bruntz, you son-of-a-bitch. I'm going to fry your ass for good." Added to her frustration was the absence of her target.

CHAPTER 16
SAFE HOUSE

November

AMANDA FREEMAN WAS DISCHARGED from the hospital, physically healed, but still in an emotional war zone. It now became Harold's job to keep the woman out of harm's way, and Yo-yo's condo was the only secure place available. It became all too clear that there was no help from his superiors, so he was on his own, which had always been the way Harold preferred to work. He could do what he wanted with no explanations. Harold knew Lieutenant Warner well enough to realize that he and Amanda Freeman were the bait required to snare the big fish.

HAROLD BRUNTZ WAS A TERRIBLE baby sitter. All he understood was that he needed to keep Amanda Freeman out of sight, away from Leonid Cherasky, for as long as possible. After that it was anyone's guess as to what would happen. As far as Harold knew, their location at Yo-yo's condo was unknown by anyone else. The only option open to them at the moment was just to wait. And that was something Harold was not very good at.

He understood that Cherasky was too vindictive to leave retribution sit idle for very long. He had already sent in a substitute assassin, so it was obvious Cherasky was ready. Sooner or later a confrontation with the violent gangster had to take place. Cherasky would make a move, but there was no telling how or when.

Before she left for Duluth, Yo-yo saw to it that Harold had the key to her condo, as well as the security pass codes. The condo blinds were usually kept drawn, blotting out the daylight, but it gave Amanda a secure feeling. Amy needed constant tending and attention to keep her from climbing the walls at every sound. Harold was warned to keep the medication to a minimum lest she would become addicted, or worse, too groggy to respond.

Forced to deal with the frustration of being hamstrung by having to watch Amy, Harold knew he should be out looking for the sinister Leonid Cherasky. His partner was gone, and there was no help from the precinct house. All he could do was to wait for something to happen.

HAROLD AND AMY SPENT their days playing Skip-Bo and watching Dr. Phil and Oprah, until the rubber band got wound up too tight, with Amy yelling out in protest, "This is bull shit. What are we doing? I have to get out of here. If I see Dr. Phil one more time, I'm gonna puke."

Startled by the outburst, yet not surprised, he told her, "We can't let you go out, Amy. When Cherasky is caught, or better yet, dead, you can do whatever you want. Please, until then, try to stay calm. I can only imagine how you feel being shut in with just me as company, but it can't last forever. If there was somebody I could trust to stay here with you, I'd go pull Cherasky out of whatever worm hole he was hiding in. While you were sleeping this morning, I called Yo-yo in Duluth. She said she'd come as soon as she could, but I guess she's got some problems with getting around. We'll just have to wait and see."

Amy gave Harold a long look, then told him, in not too gentle a manner, "Harold, ease up on yourself. True, you aren't Brad Pitt, but I can't think of anyone I'd rather be with, I think. You're a nice guy and let's just leave it at that."

Shyly smiling, Harold picked some crumbs off his stomach shelf, and said, "Thanks." His tongue froze in his mouth, leaving him to look and feel very stupid. Being so close to a woman he admired so deeply gave Harold a schoolboy bearing, believing he was just out of place being so closely confined with her. All he had to do was keep his distance so he wouldn't scare her and embarrass himself. As enamored as he was of

Amy, there were moments when he wondered how he could finagle a trip to see Flo.

Harold got as involved as he could in making her comfortable, fixing her meals and spending time talking to her. He enjoyed the casual contact, and in another fantasy, they could have been married, doing just this, however ridiculous that thought might be. He had brought in some weights and worked with her to build up her strength. Before long, she was getting her figure back and was feeling more confident.

Telling him with admiration, "You know, Harold, you're pretty good at this work-out business. You seem to know a lot about nutrition. You should try it for yourself."

Sheepishly, he said, "Naw, I'm too far gone. I don't care about myself, I just want to see you get better." His buried past was going to remain buried.

Any other inquiry by her to get him to start exercising was squashed as soon as she brought it up. Relenting, she said, "Fine, suit yourself."

One gloomy day while watching a commercial on TV, Harold realized it was Thanksgiving and had an overwhelming inspiration. Putting on his coat he told her, "Amy, I have to go out for a few minutes. I'll be right back."

Pleading, she implored him, "Take me with, please."

Holding his hand up to stem her enthusiasm, he said, "Absolutely not. Stay here. I'll be right back."

Resigning herself, she called after him, "Bring back some liquor."

Coming back about an hour later, he set the brown paper bags on the kitchen table while she snooped through them to see what kind of game he was playing. "Come on, Harold, what are you doing?"

"Happy Thanksgiving, Amy. Why don't you set the table for dinner. This won't take but a minute." Sharing several glasses of wine while the cardboard containers from a local Deli were torn open, Harold had provided a traditional dinner.

Her thrill and gratitude were beyond what she could show. Stuffed to the gills, nursing some more wine, she held her glass out to him,

"Cheers, Harold. Thank you from my heart. This is so beautiful. You know, I can't cook worth a damn. Darrell would rail on me constantly to learn how, but the few times I was home we had pizza delivered."

Amy had been toying with men long enough to see what her guardian was going through. She began to look at this human shipwreck as the sensitive and caring person he could sometimes be, viewing him as a big pock-marked teddy bear.

Amy knew he had fallen in love with her, or at least had some sort of attraction, but to her that was old-hat. Men always fell for her. She knew she had captured Darrel in the supermarket the first time he looked at her. The first time Gordon Marks looked at her she was permanently imbedded in his mind. David Sloan's emotion in the yard was visceral with no control or reasoning, so he raped her even though he loved her deeply. She knew Sloan was driven by his fear of never being allowed to love her if he didn't force it on her. Her attraction to a man was nothing more than a notch on her list of the men she had dealt with. Men fell in love, and, to her, it was no more important than a grocery list. However, after all Harold had done for her, she held an emotion for him and what was festering in her mind was better than another card game.

She looked long and hard at him, and then stood up, saying, "What the hell. If I play one more game of Skip-Bo, I'm going to explode. Come on, Harold, let's get this over with. You know you want to." She reached out taking his hand to pull him up.

Harold, as aware as a tree stump, followed her into the bedroom. When she started removing her clothing, his head spun out of control. "Uhm, ahh . . . what?"

With the underwear following her shirt and pants, she looked at him with a slight smirk, and then held her arms out to exhibit her wares. Very smooth and softly, she said, "Do you want to? I'm not the woman I used to be, but if you overlook the scars and red splotches, it might be okay."

Amy was surprised when she felt a sensual emotion shiver through her body. Standing naked in front of a man, or a camera, was just about the biggest turn-on she could conjure up. Even a man like Harold Bruntz. He wanted her, and there was a deep satisfaction knowing she could do that just by letting him look at her.

His quivering lips managed to utter, "Oh, my God, are you sure you want to do this? With me?"

Naked, and on display for his benefit, she slid across the floor to unbuckle his belt, letting his huge trousers fall to the floor. His mind raced back to the first time Yo-yo did this in the shower. He felt his knees shiver, and all he could do was dumbly let her undress him. "Oh, my. Ohhh."

Unbelieving, Harold Bruntz was making love to the beautiful Amanda Freeman.

When Amy's game had played itself out, she estimated they had consumed no more than a half hour and the sensual fantasy was gone. Now, they were just two naked people. Willing to do anything other than play more card games, she lay next to him, cuddling into his huge body, feeling small and safe.

When she stretched herself out, he recalled the night at Gordon's house when he became enamored over her shaved pubic area and wondered if he would ever be able to dismiss the sight. His eyes traveled to the denuded intersection where her thighs met, and he lived it all over again. And now, as unreal as it was, he was in bed with her. In an extreme state of spent pleasure, he reached out to finger the red splotch and scar on her stomach, asking, "Does it bother you?"

She glanced down to look at his fingers and sadly said, "Some, but not as bad as how it got there." The discoloring covered most of her stomach as a result of Lenny kicking and abusing the wound. Candidly, she softly added, "It's numb and sensitive from all the jabbing that asshole Lenny did." After a reflective pause, she said, "I used to be soft and all in one piece, without the scars and stuff. I'll never get into a bikini again."

His comment was direct, and she knew it came from his heart, which made him a little more special to her. "No matter what's been done, you're a beautiful woman."

Lamenting, her voice trailed off, talking to no one, "Isabelle had a perfect body and breasts that anyone would envy. Mine used to be like that, sort of. But Isabelle was flawless. It became a curse to her."

The beauty and the beast lying naked together could have been a comical sight, if it had not been for the tragedy that had brought them together. Reality, the always glaring truth, brought the intimate moment to an abrupt ending. Harold, calm and slow, said something that hit with a horrible force. "You knew all along it was her, didn't you."

Startled, sitting up and wincing with a strain, she said, "What?" The reaction that came from her was quick and hard. She heard what he said but was fishing for a different meaning to it, hoping beyond all hope that he meant something other than what it sounded like. "Did what, who?"

"Isabelle shot you."

The fear of his knowledge swept through her body leaving her flesh with tiny bumps. Looking at him, she shakily asked, "You know?"

"I think I knew it right away, I just had a hard time understanding why."

Desperate for an explanation, she babbled, "Look, Harold, Izzy and I played games with men. When it came to Gordy, she was glad to be rid of him, but she didn't want me to enjoy him also. Nobody was supposed to be better than she was. She had a real problem dealing with other women who made more of an impression than she did."

Trying to understand the female logic, Harold scratched his head in an attempt to say something clever, or at least not stupid. "I really don't understand." He said something stupid anyway.

Arching her back to relieve the strain, she decided finally to let him hear the rest. "We loved each other as a mother and daughter should have, but as she got older and more beautiful each day, we became adversaries. Darrel was fondling her years ago, and I knew about it. It kept him away from me, so I could do what I wanted. In a sick way, we were all punishing each other. Then when she got older, Darrel started more serious stuff and screwing her. She used it as a way to hurt me. They screwed openly, and I knew what she was doing. Since my feelings for

Darrel had never been real love, instead of stopping it, I stepped up the game."

Lying back down, she continued, "I tweaked Izzy's libido by flirting with her. It wasn't long before we were into full lesbian action with Darrel watching. It was a nasty and dangerous game, but once we started, we couldn't stop. And, I didn't want to. Looking back, I can see where I might have been doing it to get her away from my husband."

Harold rolled to his side, facing her. The mattress heaved, moving them closer to each other. He started, "Wanna know what I think?"

Cautious, she said, "You seem to know a lot already. Go ahead, tell me more."

He rolled back onto his backside. "I think Darrel transferred a lot of money out of Lenny's account. Somehow Isabelle gave him the idea that if you were dead the two of them could run away. She broke into Lenny's house thinking she could frame him for the killing. She was pregnant and wanted to make sure Darrel stayed with her."

Chilled at what she was hearing, she could only say, "That seems to make a lot of sense."

As long as she was talking, Harold asked for more, "What happened at Cherasky's? Why the pictures and videos and stuff?"

With a grimace, she went on. "That was nasty. Darrel told that pig what we were doing, and since Lenny was making porn, he paid Darrel to get us out there to make some movies. At first, Lenny did each of us, then Izzy and I rolled around for the camera. Then Lenny suggested a threesome with Darrel. It was creepy for me in front of so many people, so I got out of the picture and watched my husband have sex with my daughter. David Sloan took me home that night and stayed until morning. Lenny was captivated by Izzy. Why not? She became one of his girlfriends. She photographed well, and would do anything without whining. As long as she had an audience, she'd perform. Not long before it fell apart in Gordon's yard, she said Lenny asked her to go to Chicago for prostitution. She was seriously thinking about it. In a perverse way, she didn't take him up on the offer because she didn't want to get that far away from me. In spite of her feelings for me, she needed me. She would deny her mental condition, but she kept me close as a crutch. She never gave a thought to being alone if I was dead."

Turning to Harold, she asked, "Are you sure you want to hear this?"

"Please, I need to understand."

Slowly, Amy continued, "Isabelle got the wrong idea about Lenny. She never saw his dark side like some of the others did. She didn't understand that the pig was surrounded by beautiful women, and she was just another naked performer. One of his favorites, but he would cut her loose like any of the others. She never got that. Sneaking into his house and killing people was another high for her. She had an instability that clouded right and wrong."

She paused while a slight nausea rolled through her stomach. Sitting up at the edge of the bed, bluntly telling him, "My daughter was brutally murdered and I don't want to go into this anymore. It just gets slimy, and I'm trying to push it away. Everybody is dead, and I'm the only one left to live with the memories." She turned her head to him, her eyes watering, weakly pleading, "Please?"

Reaching out to run his fingers over her back, absorbing the softness, he asked, "One more thing?"

The tear fell from her cheek to land on her shoulder. Nodding slightly, the sadness lined into her face told him to go ahead. What was one more hurt.

He shifted himself to sit next to her, the edge of the bed sagging under his weight. "Do you think that maybe her unborn baby was fathered by Lenny?"

His body touching hers made her skin shiver. Thinking that her nudity was the only resource she had, she put her hand on his leg. His arousal was obvious, yet she was not certain he could be controlled. Would he bend as Gordon Marks had? Unsure and deathly nervous, she slowly and cautiously said, "Didn't the police say it was Darrel's baby?"

He picked her hand off his leg and put it to his lips, then said, "Yeah, they did."

He ran his hand down the course of her hair, still finding it incredible that he had just made love to her. Tracing his finger along the red track on her cheek, he saw the shiver give birth to tiny goose bumps.

His voice a hoarse whisper, he uttered, "I'm sorry. I'll leave it alone." He stood up, went into the closet picking out a long terry robe, and held it out to her.

Following his gesture, she stood and felt strangely embarrassed at her nakedness now. She was grateful and more comfortable when he wrapped the robe around her. His arms circled her from behind, talking softly into her ear, but his words were confusing and sounded like a warning. "Don't worry, Amy, I'm not going to do anything to harm you. All I want from you is to ask that you don't make fun of me. I am what I am and I can't do anything about it. I'm going to kill Cherasky and then I can leave you alone."

Feeling her tremble under the terry fabric, he turned her around to face him, adjusting the robe to cover her, "You're afraid. What is it?"

Desperate to cover the overwhelming urge to tell him more, she covered with, "Lenny. It's always Lenny. I hope you do kill him, but please be careful. He's a sadistic monster." Looking up into his eyes, a frown on her forehead, she said, "He thought I knew where the money was. I held out hope that he'd keep me alive to get me to tell him. When he had me in his house and . . . and did those things to me, I knew I was as good as dead."

Holding her tightly, he said, "Those things he was doing to you, it must have been horrible."

Her body shook harder. "I'll never forget that. Oh, God, I'll never be at peace again. And David was the one who put me into it. He said he loved me, but he sold me out because he'd rather have me killed than him."

Quietly, yet firmly, he said, "Where is it, Amy? Where's the money?"

She pushed away, wiping her eyes, "I don't know, and don't worry about it."

Sniffling, she bent to recover her clothing, loudly and curtly telling him, "I'm incapable of loving a man, Harold. That was beaten out of me.

I'll give you whatever I can, but please understand that all I have is admiration and sincere thanks. I'd like you as a friend, but that's all I have left. I know what you did for me, and how you feel about me, and I'll never denigrate you. I learned who you are on the inside, and I hope you can accept my respect. That's all I've got for you."

He smiled and kissed her forehead, grateful for any crumb.

Penned up in the condo for two weeks, sex with the fat man was getting difficult for her. Boredom set in again, until a shock wave rolled over them. It was Saturday afternoon when the rumbling noise from the elevator stunned them both. Amy ran to the bedroom, slamming the door shut, and Harold stood still, his pistol pointed at the sliding door. He was alarmed, but had a hunch who it was. Only one other person knew the code to get the elevator to climb up here.

As Yo-yo bopped through the door, her first comment was, "So, where's the fucking party?"

Amy was convinced she could come out of the bedroom, extremely happy to have a different person to talk with. After greetings and small talk, Yo-yo looked at Amy, "How are you, honey? You're looking good, girl."

"I'm healing, the body anyway. But please don't tell me you want to play Skip-Bo."

Quizzically, "What the hell is a skip whatever?"

Delighted, Amy purred, "Oh, thank God. No more card games."

Harold had a question burning inside, and needed an answer. Tell me, partner, how's it going. Are you all right?"

This was not something that made Yo-yo comfortable to talk about, but she owed the man the truth. "I have some bad days. I can't aim a gun anymore, and I get some dizzy spells. What bothers me most is that I don't crave dick anymore. That ain't right."

Harold solemnly told her, "I'm glad you came back. I called because you are the only person I can trust, and Amy can't be left alone. There is something I have to do."

"Yeah, boss, I know. I'd come with you, but right now I'd be in the way. I was offered a job at the precinct shuffling papers and shit, but I told them you needed back-up before I started. It ain't done yet, and I know you won't stop 'til it is."

Chills ran through Amy, "Is that really necessary? Can't you just forget him?"

He looked at her and wanted to pull her into his arms, but only said, "You know that can't happen. I'll leave tomorrow."

Yo-yo caught the look that floated between Harold and Amy, and left it alone. She saw them talking quietly together, thinking the old fart had scored with her. "Well, good for him."

Before he left to finish the affair with Cherasky, he privately told Amy, "The issue with the money is over, and I'll never bring it up again. You'd better bury it so you don't slip and say something wrong."

Giving him a quizzical look, she nodded slightly and kissed him goodbye, watching the door long after he left. She wanted to trust him, but she would be very cautious.

EVERY TIME HAROLD TALKED TO Lieutenant Warner, he got more bad news. His visit today was no different. "I want to talk to the guy we nailed at the hospital. We need to find out where Cherasky is."

Warner pushed back from his desk looking at the floor, then up at Harold. "You can't."

Short and sweet, the comment sent Harold into an angry frenzy. "Bob, don't give me any shit. I'll make you a promise . . . when Cherasky's caught, I'll retire and never bother you again. That should make both you and the captain happy. I want to see the man."

"First off, you dumb shit, I don't want you to retire. Second, you can't talk to him because he's dead."

Stunned, Harold asked, "Wasn't he in lock-up?"

"Yes, he was. Yesterday, when his breakfast was brought to him, he was found on the cell floor, a bullet in his head."

Standing, his huge hands leaning on the desk, Harold yelled, "Murdered under your nose? Did you pattern the slug? Is there a match?"

"Sit down, Hal. I don't like it when you get serious. Yes, we checked out the slug, and I'm afraid we know where the gun is."

Confused, Harold demanded, "Why don't you just spit it all out to me. You're trying to avoid telling me everything, and I'm not going to take it. Just level with me."

Slow and deliberate, Bob said, "The gun used to kill him had a silencer, and it came from the confiscated weapons section and was the same gun we found on him when he was arrested. It was put back after the job was done."

Bordering on revulsion, Harold hissed, "There's someone inside, and the killer could just as well be one of us. Cherasky is here."

Leaning forward in his chair, Harold told Warner, "You were Cherasky's stooge, Bob. Who else were you working with? What was your connection?"

"I thought I was alone. I honestly don't know of anyone else in the department who has a connection to him."

"How did you get involved with him? What was the first contact?"

Lieutenant Warner saw his career slowly swirling down the drain, with this bumbling oaf sitting in front of him, in control. Slowly, knowing there was no easy way out of this, he confessed, "One of his henchmen caught me with a hooker and threatened to tell my wife. Later, I realized it was all a set up. The girl was planted. Cherasky came to my house and forced me to do what he wanted. My wife left me later anyway, but I was on the hook, and it was too late to get off. When you said you were going to raid his place, I saw a chance to get away from him."

The pieces started sliding together for Harold, with a picture starting to form in his mind. "Bob, you tell me everything, and I'll keep you out of the final episode. There are some loose ends that need someplace to go."

"I've told you everything, Hal."

Firmly, Harold pressed for more. "No, you haven't goddamit. There's another person here with the key to Cherasky." His head swimming in confusion, the next puzzle piece hit him. "Bob, who denied the help I needed when I went to Cherasky's place?"

"That came straight from . . . oh shit, Captain Hilksman."

"You and the captain are close, aren't you?"

The puzzle came to Bob Warner now. "Since the shootout, she's been staying away from me. I was happy, because I never wanted to be mixed-up with her anyway. She knew everything I was doing, and even told me how to deal with you and Yolanda."

"Where is she now?"

"The last thing she said to me was to keep the place running for a few days. She said she was going to take a vacation."

"We have to find her, Bob. She's the only way to find Cherasky." Not done tying up the loose ends, Harold asked, "Who was he, Bob?"

Warner knew what the fat man was asking, but couldn't bring himself to admit it. "What are you talking about?"

Harold, fuming, yelled, "Cut the crap, ass hole. Who was the guy that got killed in your jail? Who tried to kill Mrs. Freeman?"

Dejected and scared to death, Bob Warner said, "All I know is that he was connected to Faye through Cherasky. The only one who even knew his name was Faye Hilksman."

CHAPTER 17
INVASION

December

HAROLD WAS GETTING AGITATED with Bob Warner. "I have to find Captain Hilksman, Bob. I need to know where she lives."

"That's a bad idea, Hal. If you did get to her, what the hell could you do? She's in charge of this place and controls everything."

"No, you ass-hole, she controls *you*. I can't believe there aren't still good cops who'd do the right thing." Hoisting his body out of the chair, he left Lieutenant Warner sitting behind his desk. With one last comment, Harold turned to him, "Piss on you, Bob. Don't forget that you're in Cherasky's sights also."

Watching the large man walk out of his office, Warner picked up the phone, pressing his speed dial. Responding to the muted voice on the other end, "Faye, we need to talk. Bruntz is getting close and if he doesn't get it done, we're going to have to do it ourselves."

It wasn't difficult to get Captain Hilksman's home address, but he took a detour first. Standing on the front step of the small suburban bungalow, he pressed the button next to the door. It opened slowly to present a trim and attractive young woman with a dishtowel in her hand. She knew who Harold was, but impassively asked, "Yes, can I help you?"

"Hi, Evie, I need to talk to Jim."

Stammering for an answer, she fumbled with, "Ahh, I don't . . ."

Jim Haggard pulled the door away from her, saying, "Never mind, honey, I'll take care of it." He stepped outside into the frigid weather closing the door behind him. Two little faces peered out the window at the curiosity that had come to their home.

"What the hell do you want, Bruntz?" The vapor from his voice hung between them.

Bypassing the apologies and trying to sound reasonable, Harold came right to the point. "I need help, Jim."

"Yeah, so take a shower."

"I didn't come here to argue, Jim. I need your help, and if you say no, I'll leave and never bother you again." From the determined look on his ex-partners face, Harold knew he at least had his attention. "Leonid Cherasky is loose, and he's going to kill Mrs. Freeman. Captain Hilksman is helping him, and I need to get to her."

Jim's stomach rolled over leaving him with a feeling of helplessness. "I can't help you, Bruntz. I don't doubt what you say, but if it goes wrong, and I manage to live through it, I'll be out on the street for rousting the captain."

"I understand, Jim. Sorry to have bothered you."

Harold smiled and turned to leave, when Jim stopped him, asking, "Why me?"

Harold turned, looking first at Jim's two little children staring out the window. Without looking at Jim, he said, "Because you're honest and a good cop."

Ready to turn the key in the ignition of the Cavalier, the passenger door opened and Jim Haggard slid in. "You realize that if this doesn't go right, we're both screwed."

"I'm screwed anyway, Jim."

He hadn't closed the door yet, so Harold had no idea if Jim was going to join him or not. Something was trying to worm its way out of Jim's mouth, but he had trouble with it. Finally, he said, "I was told to request another partner. I don't think Bob Warner was behind it, so it had to come from the captain."

"It figures. She was trying to dump Detective Brown as well as me. I've been around too long and Yo-yo was, well, she was just considered garbage like me."

Jim added what he had suspected from the beginning, "Hilksman knew Cherasky was involved with the Freeman women. With you on the case, there was a good chance you'd dig up something. And, you did."

"She's not good, Jim. With help or not, I'm going to take down Cherasky and the captain."

"I'll help as much as I can, but if it looks like the bottom is dropping out, I'm leaving you alone. I've got a family to worry about, and I'm getting static from Evie about the dangers of the job."

Jim got out and before closing the door he leaned in, with a somber tone, told Harold, "I go on my shift tonight. Meet me at the station, and we'll see if we can find the captain. Is that going to work for you?"

Smiling, Harold told him, "It's better than nothing. Thanks."

Watching the Cavalier pull away, Jim mumbled softly, "Son-of-a-bitch. Why me?"

THE TAN TOYOTA IDLED silently in the underground garage of Yo-yo's condo, its driver patiently waiting while the work was being done. Late in the evening, there was no traffic to interrupt their clandestine meddling. The elevator had been momentarily put out of commition, leaving the stairway the only way to get to the garage. Since the steel fire doors were firmly locked shut to the top floor, this was the only route open to them.

Two of them were dressed in service coveralls to give them reasons for being there as elevator repair men. One man stood by the elevator listening and watching the stairway, his pistol held under his coat. The electronic surveillance technician had the control panel removed, the small flashlight clamped between his teeth to light up his work. A couple of jumper wires strategically hooked in place, and he whispered, "All right, just push the button, and you'll get up there."

The man he was talking to was difficult to see in the darkness, save for the glow from the flashlight. The deep heavy voice commanded, "Fine, now get out of here."

The techie packed his equipment into a small case and climbed into the tan Toyota, along with the man on watch. The driver made certain there was nothing left undone, asking, "Did you double check everything?"

"Yeah, don't worry, I showed him what to do, and if he can follow directions, I'm done."

She handed him an envelope, adding a last comment, "This buys your silence." Adding a comment to assure his allegiance, Faye Hilksman warned, "If you screw me and say anything, I mean *anything*, I'll burn your balls with a blow torch. Understand?"

Startled by the warning, he answered, "Jesus, Captain, how stupid do you think I am? I'm not gonna do anything."

Her stare was evil and bore straight through him, giving him the chills. He nodded in agreement as they drove off. Stuffing the envelope in his pocket, the technician asked, "Where are we going?"

The man in the back seat had removed his coveralls, answering, "We need an alibi. We're going to get noticed by a lot of people. Don't worry, the drinks are on us."

Protesting, the techie said, "Why can't I just go home?"

"Shut up!"

T HE EIGHT O'CLOCK SHIFT STARTED, and Jim Haggard logged in. He had seen Harold sitting in the Cavalier outside, but made a phone call before going out to meet him. "I'm going out now. He's waiting outside." In response to the voice at the other end, he said, "Yeah, I know, but I still don't like it. Are you sure this is going to work? Why don't you just fire his ass and get it over with?" Finalizing his conversation, he said, "Don't worry, I can follow directions."

From there, he stepped into the chilly evening to join Harold Bruntz on one more caper.

In response to Jim's call, Bob hit his speed dial again. "Faye, they're on the way. Are you at the bar? Good, make some noise to be sure you're noticed. Jim will time it to work in with the bar closing."

In the warmth and comfort of Yo-yo's condo, Amy had just thrown the entire deck of Skip-Bo cards at Yo-yo. "Damn-it-to-hell, you're a beginner. Why do I always lose at this stupid game? You sure you never played this before?"

Rolling back with a bellow of laughter, Yo-yo assured her, "No man, I ain't never heard of Skip-shit or whatever it's called." Settling into the large cushy sofa, Yo-yo in a smiling calm state, asked Amy, "You really screwed Harold?"

Still angry at losing, Amy had a stern look, answering, "One more game of this Skip-Bo bull shit and I was going to scream, what else was there to do?" Mellowing her attitude, "Yeah, I did him. I thought he'd enjoy it, and I at least owed him that for what he did for me." Amy stopped herself before she said too much. Keeping her mouth shut now was all she had to do. Shut up and it would all be over.

Running her toe through the pile of blue cards strewn on the floor, Amy added, "I had to stay on top though. I don't really like it there, but what the hay. It burned up a couple of hours and he really got into it."

Yo-yo's vision blurred on and off, but she had enough control to know what was going on around her. In a calm voice, she told Amy, "I did him in the shower the first time. Man, he stunk. He's been staying clean now. The poor man just never thought about stinking so much. He's carrying a trainload of shit with him, and I try to give him some slack. In spite of him being a pig, he's one decent guy."

Wanting to hear more about Harold Bruntz, Amy opened up, "I think he fell in love with me. I felt bad because I don't want any more connections, ever. I'm done with all of it."

"He's a really nice guy, you know."

Amy stood up to stretch, telling Yo-yo, "I know."

"He turned this whole case upside down to protect you."

Surprised, Amy asked, "What do you mean?"

Stretching her arms, Yo-yo kept Amy in sight watching closely, telling her, "He had this fantasy about you and him. You got under his skin, and he couldn't get you out. He kept you out of the loop 'cause he was goo-goo over you. Just like a school kid." Watching Amy carefully, Yo-yo added, "Of course, I thought all along you knew some shit you weren't telling."

Amy's body twitched nervously, confirming Yo-yo's suspicion. Her face drained of color, Amy stammered, "What?"

Yo-yo respected Harold enough to give him what he wanted, a free Amanda Freeman. Leaning forward, she put the lid on the accusation, closing it for good. She told Amy, "I don't care what you did or maybe didn't do. I don't care anymore. Your husband took the truth with him. It don't matter anyway. Someday I'd like to hear more about David Sloan, but I don't really need to."

Amy looked at Yo-yo with a dreaded fear, "Please, I don't . . ."

Yo-yo stopped her, saying, "Don't worry about it, girl. I'm cool with it. Let's forget it."

Sighing, Amy managed a small smile, "That's it?"

"Yeah, babe, that's it. Done."

The blood started flowing into Amy's brain again and she softly said, "Thanks." Holding her hands to her face, she added, "Oh, my God, I was so worried. Thank you."

In a calm voice, her eyes narrowed and straining to focus, Yo-yo told her, "I did it for Harold, not you. I hope you respect him enough to not crap on him when you're out of here."

Amy brought her hands down, letting a few moments pass, then saying, "I wouldn't do that to him. I know what he did, and I'll never forget it."

"Okay, and before you say any more and fuck this up, let's both shut up."

"That's what Harold told me." Giddy with relief, Amy, feeling a lot better, turned to go into the kitchen and asked, "Do you want a Pepsi or anything?"

Stretching her arms up, Yo-yo yawned, "Yeah that sounds good."

Since she got out of the hospital, Yo-yo had been dealing with a change taking place in her. For the first time in her life, her body was relaxed. The twitching and nervous tension was gone. Occasionally, she'd reach back to caress the bald spot on her head, with the whole scene coming back, scaring her terribly. There was a dent where the skull was removed to get the bullet out. She fingered the stubble, relieved that at last that the hair was growing back.

Thinking Fort Yo-yo was as safe a place as anywhere, Yo-yo's alertness took a nap in the back of her mind. Her edge was mellow now, and besides, she felt like crap. The sound of the elevator was nothing more than a distant hum, parked inside her head with the rest of her problems. Going permanently blind was grating on her, but she kept that to herself.

Turning her attention to the closed elevator doors, Yo-yo knew it was in motion. The elevator hit the stops with a gentle bump. Pleased that Harold would be coming back, she turned to greet him with a smile as the door whooshed open. However, what stood in the open elevator was the worst possible thing, turning her to stone.

Lenny was as shocked as Yo-yo was. They both froze, staring at each other, until Lenny spoke, his gravelly voice threatening, "You're the bitch that killed my wife."

Stepping into the room, he moved to her, the anger racing up his spinal chord and exploding in his head.

Yo-yo's smile turned upside down, her mouth hanging open, the only sound that came from her, "Ohhh, God, no." Her knees gave out, sending her into a dip, and she felt naked knowing her gun was in the bedroom.

Lenny, in his own state of shock, walked slowly and menacingly to her, "You fucking bitch. You killed her. You fucking killed my wife."

Snapping his arm out, he caught her throat in his iron fist. Pulling her into his snarling face, he growled, "Where's the fat guy?"

Stunned with chilling fear, hanging from his fist, Yo-yo gasped, "He ain't here."

Squeezing her neck tighter, Lenny put her fear in capital letters by pressing the muzzle of his pistol against her head.

Amy dreamily sauntered from the kitchen with two cans of cold Pepsi, thinking she'd give Skip-Bo one more chance. Feeling light and euphoric, thinking she was clear of suspicion and free to go get the money, there wasn't much that could upset her now. "Just keep my mouth shut and everything will work out."

Looking up, her small smile still in place, her euphoria slid away. The sight in the living room wasn't right, that much she knew, not being able to register what she was looking at. His back to her, she could tell the tall man dressed in black was not Harold. She knew who it was, but her mind denied it. Her mouth agape, the gears in her head started whirring and meshing, forcing the truth. It was . . . "Oh my God," the devil.

One of the devils hands wrapped tightly around Yo-yo's neck was squeezing her throat shut, and she was gasping for air. She had both hands wrapped around his wrist, clinging tightly. His other hand held the automatic pistol pressed to her forehead, boring it savagely into her.

Frozen in fear, Amy muttered, "*Oh, my God.*" Mesmerized, she shuffled across the carpet, still not believing the horror that held Yo-yo by the neck. The black woman, gasping, was slipping to the floor, her eyes bulging, frightened and huge. Her hands clung to the devil's wrist uselessly pushing away.

Stunned to awareness Amy dropped the two cans of Pepsi on the carpet, stumbled once, then ran screaming at Lenny's back. She leapt into the air wrapping her arms around his head, with her legs clamped around his waist.

Screeching into his ear, "Aaaaahhhhhhh . . ." the muscles on her arms bulged, flexing to tighten with numbing uncontrolled rage. Her fingers digging deep into his cheek where Harold had torn his flesh, the other hand scratched at his eye socket. Her legs became deadly, tightening so fiercely, he lost his breath. Her scream ended giving her one more weapon to use. Biting into his ear, pulling back her head, the flap was torn from his head.

The unexpected onslaught threw Lenny into a moment of terror. He screamed in pain as ear was savagely ripped off. "Aaaghhh."

Releasing Yo-yo, he grabbed at Amy's arms, the tightness clamped frighteningly to his head. He shook his body to free himself from the frenzied creature tearing him apart, but she was attached firmly. Staggering to collect his balance, he lunged backwards forcing her into the wall with a shuddering thud. The sheetrock gave way revealing the outline of the studs that crushed into Amy's body. Fear became her weapon, tightening her clamp on him tighter than anyone could with a sound mind.

Amy's lungs gave out as her breath was frozen in a vacuum, but she clung to him. Her mind was racing at the speed of light on how she could kill him. Her finger nail clawed at his eyelid, and then pierced through to squeeze and pinch the hard lump inside the socket. His fear and agony launched from his throat in a terrifying roar, his arms waving wildly.

Frantic, as blood and juices flooded his face, he flexed his muscles, squeezing Amy's tiny arms, and pulled with all his might. She felt her arms giving in to his strength, and desperately tightened her grip, but he had too much power. She knew she was loosing to him, until Yo-yo became her tag-team partner.

Shaking herself back to this world, Yo-yo forced herself to focus on the apparition staggering in front of her. Straddling her legs to gain support, she brought one foot back and swung it viciously into his crotch. The sickening destruction of his scrotum, his testes squashed like grapes, he slunk forward, retching. He fell to his knees with Amy tumbling backwards to the floor.

Reaching out, Yo-yo grabbed his hair with both hands, took a deep breath, and pulled his face down into her knee, raising her leg to meet it with the force of a splitting maul, his nose instantly flattened against his face.

Lenny leaned over, covering the sickness in his groin, moaning with tears from his remaining eye mixing with the blood. Amy stood, shaking life back into her arms and leaped on him again, pounding his head with her fists. She stood back and lunged again pushing futilely to topple him over, her feet skidding on the carpet.

She stepped back, her chest heaving for air, her fists balled into tiny rams. Looking frantically for what she needed through wild red eyes, she saw it on the end table. Running to it, she tore the heavy lamp from its mooring, racing back. Feet apart, she raised it over her head and plunged it into his skull. The metal and ceramic pieces flew everywhere, stinging as they bit into her flesh.

Lenny groaned and slowly fell onto his back. Yo-yo stood over him, muttering, "I paid a hundred dollars for that lamp."

In a panic, Amy had to get Lenny wrapped up before he got enough strength to fight back. Screaming at Yo-yo, "Fuck the lamp, we have to tie him up, quick." The vision of Lenny hitting her again was more than Amy could handle. Grabbing her hair and pulling it, still screeching, "We need some rope. *Get some fucking rope, please.*" Amy, stamping her feet and twisting, to find something—anything.

Yo-yo quickly pointed to the window, "The blinds. Use the rope from the blinds."

They both worked at ripping the custom-made bamboo slats from the window. Wooden pieces flew all over, with piles of rope collecting at their feet. Unwilling to wait for all of it, Amy grabbed what they had, winding it around his feet, straining to tighten the knot. Breathlessly, she ordered, "Help me move him, quick." Together, they dragged his body across the floor, to the heavy sofa.

Speed was her ally now, tying his feet tightly to the sofa's stubby legs. His right arm was forced to his side, then the left one. Rolling him over, the rope was wound tightly around his arms and body, from the neck to his ankles, making him look nearly mummified. The last of the rope they tied tightly around his neck, then pulled under his body and tightened to the ankle ties.

Amy stood up pacing, while Yo-yo gave the bonds a confirming tug. Thinking it was over, Yo-yo got up to do what she thought was the right thing. That was not what Amy had in mind.

His head rolled, followed by a low moan. Amy screamed, "He's waking up." In a frantic moment, she swung her foot back, bringing it solidly into the side of his head. He went out again. Breathless, her body heaving and gasping for relief, she ran into the kitchen to grab what she needed. Her body lurching uncontrollably, she stood over him, on the verge of hyperventilation.

Trying to be a calming influence, Yo-yo, her voice hoarse from the destruction to her throat, beseeched her, "Girl, he's tied now." Pointing to what Amy held in her hand, she asked, "Why do you need that? Let the police take him."

Amy didn't have an answer, but glared at Yo-yo, her head bowed slightly with her hair wildly circling her face, her eyes glowing red and lips tight. Yo-yo looked at the muscles flexing in Amy's arms, her nostrils flaring with the determination of hatred and fear. The devil had entered a new body, and Yo-yo knew that Amy was going to have her way. She rasped in a terrifying hiss, "Get away from me."

The blackness that came from Amy's eyes sent Yo-yo stumbling back, her fists clenched at her mouth. She had never seen such terror.

CHAPTER 18
AND JUSTICE FOR ALL

CAPTAIN FAYE HILKSMAN LIVED in a two-story Colonial in a Minneapolis suburb preparing itself for urban blight. Neither man knew the captain very well so her habits were a mystery. Sitting shivering in the dark of the street, they watched for about an hour, with nothing happening.

Totally pissed at his involvement in this fiasco, Jim broke the silence, "The place is dark, Bruntz. If she's not in bed, she isn't home. Let's wrap this up and leave. I'm freezing." To Jim, this caper was a farce intended to corner Detective Bruntz, and he was tiring of it.

Harold tried to be congenial, offering, "Maybe, if you want to go I'll take you back."

Jim knew the captain was not home, but he played the charade anyway. His phone call to Bob Warner before joining Harold at the station house told him to placate his ex-partner. It would be over soon, and was a nice easy gig. Now he was bored of the silly game, wanting to go back to the station and spend the rest of the night safely and warmly attached to a coffee cup. Small talk with Harold was uneasy, as he knew the large man was going to be destroyed tonight. That was the plan, and the captain assured him he would be rewarded for his part in it.

THE BAR CLOSED AT 1:00 A.M. and the techie was finally able to go home. Whining his objection, "This has been the most boring night of my life, captain. I'm blitzed and you aren't taking me home?"

Her last-call drink in her hand, she sneered at him, "Quit sniveling, you worm. You'll get a ride home." She looked past the crowd leaving the bar and signaled a man standing by the door. "Follow him, he'll even tuck you in."

Exasperated, he complained, "Finally. I never wanted to come here in the first place."

She grabbed his arm with a grip that surprised him, "Just keep your mouth shut and remember what I've told you." She watched him leave, thinking that she needed to get rid of him, soon. "He can join the scrap heap with Bruntz and his partner."

Later, sitting in her tan Toyota, she answered the cell phone ringing in her pocket. "Yeah, what?"

The excited voice on the other end asked, "Where the hell are you?"

Irritated at the question, Faye said, "At the bar. What's your problem, Bob? This is where we're supposed to be, you dumb shit."

"Ease up on the insults, Faye. You'd better get home fast so they don't leave. Jim thinks this is going to be a simple break in, and might get tired of sitting with Bruntz all night. Play your end, and Jim will make sure they step into your trap. Anything else?"

A sleazy sneer on her lips, she asked, "Thanks, are you busy?"

"Oh, for Christ sake, Faye, it's after one. No, I can't now. Just go home and be glad your ass is covered."

"I'd rather it would be in your face, Bob." There was no response, so she put the phone away. Wondering if Cherasky had finished his part of the purge, she thought she could send him after Bob Warner, next. "What a set up that would be. I'll put another clown in Warner's place, and me and Lenny can run this town." An evil chuckle rolled out of her mouth. Her next plan was already forming in her mind—how to get that Neanderthal Lenny taken down after she was done with him.

The Toyota pulled up to her garage, and as she got out, she lost her footing at the sight of Harold's Chevy parked up the block. Slurring her revulsion, "Son-of-a-bitch, they're sitting there waiting. Fuck you, Bruntz. I'm finally getting rid of you." The bar booze had worked its way to her brain, slowing her reflexes. Slamming the car door, her frosty breath clouded in the cold night air. She stumbled into the house, not caring what the fat man was going to do. Confident that her orders were in place, she knew Jim Haggard was with him and would make certain everything happened the right way. Her vision of Jim spending the night with her when it was over put a smile on her distorted face.

ACROSS TOWN, IN A BETTER NEIGHBORHOOD, Bob Warner was sitting alone in the dark, getting drunk. That was the only way to keep his nerves in place. He poured another bump, waiting and watching With the network he had set up tonight, no matter who got wiped out, he would benefit. Sitting alone in the darkness his sly grin slowly turned to a sneer.

LENNY WAS BECOMING CONSCIOUS, twisting and pulling at his bonds. A terrible pain was shooting through his head, and he could feel warm fluid collecting on his face. The fog left his remaining eye enough to see Amanda Freeman sitting on his stomach. The pain in his groin had become an annoying numbness, but there was a problem with his face. He tried blinking, but the focus only got worse. "What's wrong? What did you do?"

Struggling to sit up, he was held firm. Then he realized, "My eye! You fucking bitch, you gouged out my goddamn eye." Infuriated, he thrashed his body, but the pain and the ropes held him back. Barking, "You're going to die, woman. You are going to fucking die."

Quietly, but with a sadistic twist, sitting on his stomach, Amy answered, "You already tried that once, Lenny. It didn't work." Her hair, wildly skewed about her head, framed a face that held no fear. If evil had ever looked into Lenny's face, it was now. Her eyes glowing red, bored into him with fire streaming from her nostrils, she leaned closer, hissing to him, "Payback, asshole."

He squirmed again, but to no avail, he was tied tightly. He laid his head back, realizing what destruction had been done to him. He'd been tortured before by the KGB and the Israelis, managing to live through it. Whatever had been done to him now, he would live through it, and then exact his revenge. Wheezing, he whispered, "You piss ant bitch, you're nothing. You can do nothing. Give it your best shot, then you die."

Amy straddled his chest leaning forward, looking from his remaining eye to the bloody hole on the other side. Her breath hot and wheezing, she spoke into his mutilated ear, "You're a mess, Lenny. You look like shit." From her cache of household supplies she had garnered, a long serrated steak knife. She brought it out. Flashing it in front of him, she said, "A knife, Lenny. Isn't that the weapon of choice? A knife to make the dumb bitch afraid and tell you where your fucking money is?" At this point, she leaned into his good ear, whispering quietly, the numbers to the Grand Cayman account. "There it is, honey. You want the money, go get it."

He snapped his head away from her, but the restraints held him fast. Bellowing, "Goddamn you . . ."

Before he could yell any more, she poked her finger into the gaping hole in his face. Recoiling, he screamed, "Stop. For Christ sake, stop."

Amy's confidence came out in caustic humor designed to humiliate him. "You're angry. Does that mean it's over between us, honey? After all we've been through, how about one more romp for old-times sake?"

Despite the new pain her finger was causing, his mind was processing what had been done to his left eye. He knew it was gone, thinking he would wear a patch, after he dismembered Mrs. Freeman. Uncertain as to what she was doing, he felt his strength waning, unable to fight back as he used to. His breath was coming in short quick spurts and he felt a severe spinning. Horrified and unbelieving, he gasped, and then roared, "Aaaaahhhhgggg!" His stomach pushed a column of burning bile up through his throat to seep from his lips.

Yelling in fear, he gasped, "You're sick, bitch, fucking sick." His breath was spasmodically rasping with his chest heaving in pulses.

FROM SOMEPLACE IN THE ROOM, Amy heard Yo-yo yelling over the maddening uproar, "Stop, no don't. Oh, my God, Amy stop." She tried to pull Amy from her perch on Lenny's chest, but she was planted firm.

His screams pounding off the walls, the tormented body going into spasms, with Yo-yo waving her arms uselessly, yelling, "*Stop, stop.*"

Moving up to his face, she leaned to the open flesh where his ear used to be, calmly telling him, "Now, let's see, honey, what's next?" Pressing the knife blade to his throat, she sliced across the larynx, deep enough to open it. Moving the point up to his chin, her words were echoes in his throbbing head, "According to you, if I push this up far enough, it will kill you. Am I right? But let's not spoil the fun by going too fast. I want you to feel the blade enter that mush in your head."

Amy was in a wild frenzy, her eyes blood red and searing, the lips drawn back tight from her teeth. She needed to hurt as much as possible and was immune to Yo-yo's screaming protests. The ability to protest was dying within him. His body lurching wildly, the pain and fear tore through his throbbing head, a searing hot pool of bubbling blood and acid.

Amy pressed deeper, until she felt the cold pressure against her temple, looking up to see Yo-yo holding Lenny's gun, pressing on her. Trying to stop Amy's aggression, Yo-yo quietly told her, "Stop, Amy. Stop or I will shoot you."

Amy's eyes were plucked from the face of the Devil, rolling in fire, wide open with tears flooding down her cheeks. Her teeth clenched, lips still pulled back in a snarl. Her face was framed by wild hair. Amy was beyond killing. She was destroying, hurting with as much pain as evil would allow.

Yo-yo reached for the knife, telling her, "Stop, Amy. I will shoot you, girl. Give me the knife."

Amy snarled, snapping her teeth together, and Yo-yo pulled her hand back, shuddering with absolute dread. The deep guttural growl coming from Amy did not belong to her. She was possessed with forces of hate and contempt beyond all human understanding. Screaming through clenched teeth, her voice pitched to its limit, Amy demanded through a growling snarl, "Then kill me, shoot me. I'm dead anyway. I'll go to hell twisting the pain into his black heart and drink his blood to spit back into his face." Amy leaned into the muzzle, her eyes burning in pain and hatred, shrieking, "Kill me, please. Let me rest . . . in . . . peace."

Pressing her weight on the handle of the knife, the blade shakily progressed slowly into Lenny's head. The explosion from Lenny's 9mm filled the room with the final deafening sound.

JIM AND HAROLD CREPT through the darkness to the Colonial, both wondering what they'd do once inside. Jim, knowing that Faye was aware of them and was waiting, with her plan in place, led the way. Remembering his instructions, he went in first. His hope was to diffuse any radical plans Harold had. He'd been sent here to protect the captain, hoping to be able to set up Harold with a bogus breaking-and-entering charge.

Ominous blackness engulfing the rooms made it difficult to navigate. Bumping into furniture and household trappings, Harold whispered, "Upstairs. She's probably in bed." Unknown to Jim, Harold's plan was to force the captain to reveal her connection to Cherasky, using whatever intimidation and force was necessary.

Jim looked at the shadow next to him, deciding to do as he was told. His silhouette crossed the huge living room picture window, starkly outlined against the moonlight outside. Moving cautiously, his stealth was all he could rely on, thinking he was involved in a childish game of hide and seek.

Faye knew where they were, following their progress from her spot deep in the darkness. The form passed the large picture window and her need to strike came before she was able to think about what she was doing. The blinding flash filled the room. Once, twice, three times, each burst punctuated by an ear-piercing explosion, followed by the shattering of the window glass.

Harold yelled, leaping towards the front door, groping where there had to be a light switch. The sudden illumination from a series of lamps blinded everyone for a moment. Gaining control of his vision, Harold stood looking dumbly at his ex-partner, lying grotesquely against the wall under the big window, shards of glass covering him. His eyes were wide open in an unbelieving stare, looking at nothing except eternity. His chest was saturated with blood.

The curtains framing the window fluttered in the cold breeze wafting into the warm confines of the house.

Captain Faye Hilksman stood in the center of the room, both hands stretched out in front of her, the smoking revolver held shakily. Staggering from the realization of what she had just done, as well as the effects from the booze, she mumbled, "What? Oh, my God, no. Jim?" Looking pathetically at Harold, she incoherently let him find out, "That . . . that was supposed to be you." The gun dropped to the floor, and she pointed to Jim's bleeding corpse, "He was bringing you in here to get caught. I was going to kill you."

Slumping dumbly, staring at the bleeding body in her living room, her mind pulled itself in to hide from the truth. All logic and reasoning was spinning, twirling out of reach.

Harold's entire body slunk on his frame. The total revelation of the deception by a man he trusted was a shock to him. He walked over to the body to press his finger to the pulse, but there was none. "If he was plotting to get me killed, why should I give a shit about him?" Jim's wife and kids flashed through his mind, and he felt sorry for them, but held no remorse for the dead man. He looked at the shocked captain, still planted in an unbelieving pose, staring at the tragedy, swaying from the booze.

On one knee, over Jim's body, Harold looked at the woman, calmly asking, "Faye, where is Cherasky?"

Unbelieving, she stood still, raising one arm to point, "Jim?"

Louder, Harold demanded, "Faye, where's Cherasky. Tell me *now*."

Her eyes wandered to Detective Bruntz, contempt and disgust rolling across her face. In a sneering voice she said, "Fuck you, Bruntz. You fat fucking slob, you don't deserve to be on my police force." With the awkward grace of a drunk, she leaned forward to stab her fingers into the space between them, followed by her incoherent words, "You dumb shit, Lenny's a man. A real man. And right now, asshole, he's waxing your black whore. Then he's going to kill that Freeman bitch for good."

"He's at Yo-yo's?" Panic struck Harold, cramming his brain with what he could imagine Lenny was doing to the two women.

With his handkerchief, Harold reached inside Jim's coat to remove his service revolver. Glancing at Faye, seeing she was still inanimate, he placed the gun in Jim's right hand. Pulling the dead arm up, he aimed the gun at Faye. She was still unbelieving at what was happening. Then, all of a sudden, it dawned on her that she was going to get shot. She stooped over, picking up her own weapon to point it at Harold.

Too late, Jim's gun barked in his hand, sending Faye backwards with a red hole in the center of her chest. Standing up Bruntz looked at the pathetic carnage, commenting, "You both deserved this." Going out the door, he thought about the nice cleanup job on a double homicide, he was leaving for the forensic crew.

The time frame was close enough, so everything would fall into place. Back in the Chevy, he called Bob Warner, "Bob, Hal here. Listen, Jim got out of the car and hasn't come back. There's nothing going on at the captains house, so I'm going to leave. Jim will find his way home, or maybe you could send a car out here to get him."

The lieutenant, still sitting alone in the dark, listened to Harold's message embed itself onto the answering machine. His failure to destroy the message would give Harold Bruntz an ironclad alibi.

Slamming the Chevy into gear, Harold raced to Fort Yo-yo, scared to death of what he would find. The portable bubble on top of the car did little to move traffic away from his course. Bars had just let out, and all the drunks were wending their winding way home.

THE CONFUSION AT FORT YO-YO was calming down. Yo-yo pushed Amy away from Lenny, toppling her backwards. Amy, on her back side blinked slowly and asked, "What happened?"

Yo-yo, amazed at the comment, said, "You don't know?"

Amy stared at the bloody man stretched across the floor, her mouth hanging open, totally bewildered. She looked back at Yo-yo, in a whisper she wheezed out, "I did that didn't I? Why didn't you shoot me? I thought it was all going to end." Holding her temples, Lenny's blood smearing her face, she moaned, "Why didn't I die with that son-of-a-bitch?"

Yo-yo crawled over Lenny to put her arms around Amy. "I was going to shoot you, but it hit me what you were doing. That wasn't you, honey, there was something evil in you that did that. Your voice, man, your voice was bad, bad and fucking scary. I shot him instead. I couldn't stand his screaming, and I knew you weren't going to stop. I put the gun to his head in the same spot he shot me. I went ballistic with you, babe. We both killed the dude."

Amy reached out with her foot to kick the lifeless Leonid Cherasky. "You're sure he's dead?"

"Yeah, man, he's dead." A moment later, Yo-yo said, "Look what you did to his face. Man, that's ugly."

Rolling the body onto a shower curtain and tying it tight with the ropes from the blinds, they pulled him to the elevator. Yo-yo wiped his gun clean, slipping it in with him and asked, "How are we going to get rid of him?"

Amy's infantile answer made perfect sense. "We'll screw Harold, make him feel real good, and he'll do it for us."

Yo-yo looked at Amy for a moment, finally saying, "Be careful with Harold, honey. He's not stupid." Turning to the destruction in her condo, Yo-yo said, "Let's get this shit cleaned up. Then you and me need to wash the remains of Mr. Cherasky off us."

Amy stood still, her bloody arms clenched around herself, started to cry. Yo-yo, with as much compassion as she could muster, held her tightly, whispering, "It's over, honey. There's nobody left to hurt you now. Come on, we have to move fast."

Amy stumbled, doing what she was told. Every move she made was punctuated by a glance at the blood smeared shower curtain, checking to be sure it was not going to get up.

HIS GUN DRAWN, HAROLD BOLTED into Yo-yo's living room, tripping over the shower curtain. Catching himself, Harold stood looking at the lump, the blood in a puddle around the corpse. "Did he suffer?"

The women's hair, wet from the shower and both wrapped in towels, looked at each other without answering. Amy walked away to sit on the sofa, staring at a piece of rope lying on the floor, her fingers absently playing with the edge of the towel.

Yo-yo quietly told him, "Yeah, he suffered. A lot. Don't ask any more." She reached out to tug on Harold's sleeve, with a nod of her head towards the sofa, she indicated he should go to her.

Sinking into the cushion next to Amy, he put his arm around her, pulling her into his chest. She buried her face in his neck and let it all come out. Shaking and sobbing, she clawed at him, wailing wordlessly. He leaned back with her, willing to sit with her forever if she needed it. After a long interval of convulsing, she fell asleep in his arms. He sat motionless for hours letting her mind and body find the peace and freedom they needed. With care and concern, he pulled the towel up to hide her nakedness.

Yo-yo covered them both with a blanket, and then disappeared into her bedroom.

In the morning, Amanda was in terrible shape, shuddering over the gruesome lump enclosed in the shower curtain. Harold and Yo-yo pulled Lenny's body into the elevator, disabling the controls. If anyone inadvertently pushed the call button, there would be a highly explosive reaction when Lenny's body appeared.

Through the day, Amy was kept stoned with pain killers and booze. That evening, she was weaned from the cocktails. She had avoided seeing and thinking of the body in the elevator, but there was a price to pay for it. Yo-yo summed it up, telling her, "No shit, girl, you look like crap." Her face was bruised and beet red, her hair was totally out of control, the eyes matched the color of her face, and she couldn't stand up without support.

"Oh, God, I feel terrible. What did you do to me?"

Settling Amy onto a kitchen chair, she pushed a cup of coffee in front of her, and said, "Let's just put it this way, honey, it was a lethal combination."

Harold sat next to her, as gently as possible telling her, "Amy, we have to get rid of Lenny, but you should stay here. This isn't going to be pleasant, and we have to be very careful to not be seen."

She blankly looked at him, nodding, and with a soft voice, said, "I just need to know he's dead." Reaching out to touch his arm, Amy pleaded, "Harold, please don't let him come back."

With a wry understanding smile he told her, "He will never come back, Amy. He's dead, and we're going to put him in a place he belongs." That evening, under the safety of darkness, they put the body in the trunk of the Chevy.

Yo-yo had gone to the garage earlier to move the car into place and make sure nobody was around. Amy descended in the elevator with Harold to make absolutely certain he was where they said he was. Harold went to close the trunk, but was stopped by Amy putting her hand out. "Wait." With no further explanation, she looked at the plastic shroud and sneered. Reaching out, she poked the lump, then backed away. She quietly said, "I'm done."

Watching Harold's car leave the garage, Amy stood hugging her body against the cold evening chill. A slight uncertain feeling nagged at her, thinking she should have gone with to be doubly certain that Lenny was indeed dead, and his body was never going to be found. Digging deeper, she pulled up the thought that Harold would see to it that it would happen. He would do it for her. Standing still for several minutes, her body softened, and she smiled, ever so slightly. Her mind was on a different path now. She was running the number of the account in the Grand Cayman Island through her head. Reliving the beating she received from Lenny, she acknowledged that the only thread that kept her alive during the ordeal was by repeating that number in her mind, over and over . . . and over.

Leonid Cherasky was where he belongs with rats devouring his remains. Harold would be sure it happened. Feeling calmer, she muttered, "He loves me, he'll see to it."

On a more somber note, she mumbled, "It's Yo-yo I need to worry about."

HOURS LATER, FAR OUT IN THE western Minnesota farm land, Harold stopped on a deserted gravel road. With lights out and no moon to guide them, they pulled Lenny from the trunk. Dragging the body to the roadside ditch, they covered it with weeds and piles of snow.

Yo-yo leaned against the side of the car waiting for Harold. He had walked ahead to stand in the road gazing to the dark sky. He wanted some words to come, but there were none. All he could bring up was a softly spoken, "Good night, Rachel."

EPILOGUE

My favors you received
May you be pleased
Tho loved with ease
Thou be deceived

LIEUTENANT BOB WARNER WAS SKILLFUL at devious tricks, especially when it came to protecting himself. His affair with his boss, while distasteful, put a protective shield around him. He could navigate in and out of situations with the overbearing presence of the captain taking the superfluous elements into her camp. The underlings, like Jim Haggard and Harold Bruntz, were pawns to push into battle ahead of himself. He remained in the middle, keeping his feet dry and his hands clean.

He issued a statement that Captain Hilksman and Jim Haggard were having an affair and shot each other during a quarrel. This was circulated through IAD with the story being buried to make certain his widow would receive the insurance money. The investigation was routine, with most of the officers pleased at the demise of the abrasive captain. The message on Bob's answering machine was played for IAD and the district attorney, with Harold getting a reprimand for leaving an officer at the time of need. Not much was made of it, but Harold remained an outsider with the rest of the squad. Nothing new for him, and he preferred it that way.

Faye Hilksman and Jim Haggard were laid to rest as heroes. Sunset Memorial had a special section devoted to service people who gave their lives in the line of duty. An impressive affair to the living that held honor in their hearts—or on their sleeve.

Jim's widow, dressed in a form-fitting black dress, had the little fur collar of her coat pulled up, an ineffective shield to the cold air. She must have cried herself out earlier, as she shed not a tear at the funeral. The generic expression on her face gave Harold the impression she was here because she was supposed to be here.

It was a typical emotional affair with the rifles blasting their respect to fallen comrades, bagpipes wailing into the cold winter air, and the folded flag was handed over to the widow. Words of condolence by a minister paid to do it glossed over the brave souls he never knew.

Captain Faye Hilksman had only one person at her gravesite, but nobody knew who he was. Nobody went to offer their condolences, or to introduce themselves. As the crowd dispersed, the stranger tossed the funeral flag into a trash can before walking away.

At Jim's gravesite, Harold remained behind until he was the only person left. The frigid air was a small matter to him. He could warm up later. Watching Jim's casket being lowered into the hole, his anguish was for his own daughter, recalling her funeral so many years ago. When he had to stand alone, ostracized by his wife and colleagues. When he had to stand alone, to absorb their stares and condemnation. When he had to stand alone to witness her tiny casket disappear into the earth, never to come back.

The outstanding difference between that day and this was that today, he was sober. And, once again he was responsible for the deaths. Harold's seventh sense told him she was standing behind him. He knew he should talk to her, but he didn't want to. She was invading his sorrow, but she at least deserved his respect.

Turning to her as she walked to him, he groped for something decent to tell her, but there was nothing. The children stayed several feet behind her, just watching, stamping their feet to find warmth in them. Her question was an obvious one spoken in a calm definitive manner, "Where did you two go that night? I know he left to meet you."

"It doesn't matter, Evie. He's gone and you have to be brave for your kids. Don't listen to what the stories are. He wasn't having an affair, he loved you too much."

Just staring at the ground made him feel like he was lying to her, so he relented, and told her the truth, "We went the captain's house because she was involved in some terrible things. I needed someone with me as a back up. As it turned out, she knew we were coming and had Jim help her set me up so she could kill me. I think she would have given the blame to him if it had worked out that way. If he didn't get killed, he would go to prison for my murder. Either way, when he left your house that night you were going to lose him."

She pondered this, and then slowly let her mind unload the truth, her voice fogging into the frigid air between them. "I don't think he was having an affair either. This worked out all right though. I was going to leave him anyway. No woman should ever marry a cop." She nodded, turned, and went to her children.

Watching her walk away with a child clinging to each hand, the small boy clutching his father's flag, the sad vision of Gladys walking out of his life came back. She had told Harold the very same thing.

A few yards away, Evie stopped and turned back to Harold. Speaking loudly over the distance, she said, "He really did like you, you know. He was forced to ask for a new partner. He told me he wanted to be as smart as you were, and how you were a natural at seeing things he didn't. I thought you should know that."

Harold smiled and nodded his appreciation.

The little boy, clutching his father's flag, looked at Harold and put two fingers to his forehead. Harold smiled and returned the salute.

Back in the Cavalier, Harold finished the half-pint and drove home to Flo, to cry his heart out, all night long.

Yo-yo went back to her sister in Duluth on a leave of absence to sort out the good stuff from the bad. A shrink and therapy helped her get back on track, and she decided to take the offer from the police commissioner, filing and shuffling paper. She was told it was a reward for her service.

She knew the office routine wasn't going to last long, but kept it a secret, as she started getting horny again. Things in her head started falling back into the spaces they belonged, and the Yo-yo of old came back to life. Boredom in Duluth brought the vibrations back to her limbs, and she could be seen bopping her way along Superior Street and Canal Park looking for romance, for a price. A black wiry woman on the prowl in Duluth was an oddity, but she managed to keep busy.

AMY SETTLED HER AFFAIRS, selling the house and seeing that her daughter and husband had decent headstones. She also made sure that Richard Olson had a marker. Her parents told her they would pray for her, but she was sinful and needed to leave them alone. She held no animosity towards them, understanding their ignorance. As she left their home for the last time, she told them, "I don't need your prayers, but I hope you will be forgiven for not accepting your granddaughter. She needed you more than I did."

Harold was a frequent visitor, and Amy allowed him to satisfy his lust because she felt she owed it to him. However, she told him flat out, "I'm sorry, Harold, I'd love to have you here as a friend, but that's all I can offer you. I'm empty." Eventually, the lack of passion turned their relationship into an unusual but close friendship. The Amy that used to be a seductive brawling woman reeking of self-confidence was gone. She had become just a woman who lived from one day to the next. Her connection to Harold Bruntz was addictive. A paradox. She couldn't live without him, yet needed to if she was going to survive on her own. Something was waiting for her, earning interest, and all she had to do was claim it.

Harold drove Amy to the airport, she kissed him goodbye, and he watched her plane leave.

He went back to work and wormed his way through a few cases, but seemed to have lost the fire that drove him before. His lack of enthusiasm bothered him, but he knew it had nothing to do with law enforcement.

He missed Yo-yo Brown and her erratic gyrations, but most of all he was miserable thinking about Amanda Freeman. Making certain Flo was established, and seeing that she was sent a check from his bank account once a month, he had a need to run away. He had accumulated so much vacation time that the police union forced him to use it up.

At that time, he got a letter from Amy inviting him to visit her on Grand Cayman Island.

AMY HAD BOUGHT A SMALL VILLA close enough to the beach to be considered close to the beach. For the first few days she and Harold had continuous sex. With nothing else to do, they toured the island taking in the sights and enjoying the calm warmness and tropical beauty. Exotic foods, silly drinks in coconut shells, and hours lying in the sun, became their way of life. Amy had taken on a tan that covered some of the disfiguring. Able to get back into a bikini, she became a favorite flavor for locals and tourists. She played her games and granted her favors, except her old kamikaze hit and run were abandoned for just the pleasure of attraction. Wrapped with a white shawl over the bikini bottom, she blended with the regulars.

Harold, dressed in Charlie Brown shorts and an obnoxious red shirt adorned with flowers, looked like a beluga that had been dressed for a holiday. He knew his vacation, as well as his welcome, was coming to an end. Other than to have sex with a gorgeous woman, he had one overriding thing to get out of the way, the second reason for making this trip.

After a mid-morning dip in the ocean, the beauty and the beast walked slowly back to the villa. Harold marveled at the shimmering sleek body he knew he had to say goodbye to. "I have to leave, you know."

Amy answered, "Yeah, I'm ready to be alone again. It was nice having you here, but I agree, it has to end."

Reaching the villa, Harold suggested, "One for the road?"

"Sure, why not. Let's do it out here on the patio."

Harold smirked, asking, "Like in the back yard?"

Stiffening at the implication, Amy shot back, "That's mean, Harold. If you want to get laid before you leave, you better be nice to me."

"I'm sorry, Amy. Come into the bedroom. I want it to be dark this time."

After a mechanical show of emotion from both, Harold, satisfied, opened the can of worms. Lying with her folded in his arms, he caressed her flesh, calmly saying, "You really are a beautiful woman, Amy. I know if it weren't for the nasty business that brought us together you'd never be doing this with me. I'll never forget it."

Looking up at him, she said, "You'll be back some day won't you? I really have grown fond of you, Harold. Making love to you is not a chore. Although, if Brad Pitt walked in the door I'd kick you out in a minute."

Smiling, Harold said, "Thanks."

A few minutes washed by and Harold tipped over the can of worms. "Why did you do it, Amy?"

Reacting slowly, she didn't catch on right away. Then the chill crept through her, forming little bumps on her flesh. Not wanting to say anything, she relented and asked, "What?"

His answer welded fear and despair to her brain, "Isabelle, why did you kill her?"

There it was, in plain open language with no room for misunderstanding. She pushed away and sat up, "I don't know . . ."

He reached up to trace his finger tips across her back, feeling the trepidation under the skin. "Yes you do. You killed your own daughter and her boyfriend. How could you do that?"

She bolted up from the bed, grabbed a shawl, and left the room. Finding her on the lanai, her feet up on the chaise with the shawl protecting her nudity, he sat next to her.

"I knew it from the beginning."

"Wh . . . why didn't you do something about it?" She didn't have the nerve to look at him.

"I did. I wrote in all the reports that Darrel killed them."

Finally looking over at him, a serious frown across her face, "Maybe he did. There's no way to prove otherwise is there?"

"Not anymore. The case is closed, and you're not implicated, nor will you ever be."

The scowl meant that she was frightened and unbelieving. He finished, "I had you embedded in my mind and didn't care who did it. Darrel was easy to put in your place, so it worked out."

Gathering whatever her mind could process, she stood up, went back into the bedroom and got dressed. When she came back she tossed Harold's clothing to him and set his filled suitcase on the floor. "I think it's time to take you to the airport." The silence between them was heavy as Harold covered his bulk with the same clothing he had arrived in.

Before they got to the terminal, she pulled the little 4 Runner over and shut off the engine. Turning to face him, with tears drenching her face, she unloaded. "You know the game we played. It went too far, and Izzy actually tried to kill me. She was pregnant with Darrel's baby and insanely jealous that Gordon dumped her for me. She wasn't capable of thinking things out. She reacted on impulse, thinking that being beautiful would get her whatever she wanted. She had the same sick genes her father did."

She accepted a handkerchief from Harold and went on. "Darrel told her about the money he diverted to the island and that, if I was out of the way, they could leave and raise the baby. He was finally at the end of his tolerance for what I was doing with all those men, and wanted out. A divorce would only get him maintenance payments and lose his house to me. He couldn't see past the young body that Isabelle kept taunting him with. Her screwing the Olson kid in the driveway was just another way to mock me.

"I flew into a rage and ran outside. Darrel came out, took the gun and pushed me back in the house. You know what happened then."

"Where did the gun come from?"

With a sardonic slur, she babbled, "Oh, that's a good one. David gave it to me to kill Darrel with so he could be with me." She slowly added, "And I almost did."

Harold took the handkerchief back, wiped a drip from her cheek, and said, "We better get to the airport."

Shocked, Amy loudly recoiled, "What? What are you going to do? How is this going to come back and hit me? What do you want?" She pressed her fists tightly against her temples.

Calmly and sincere, Harold told her, "I don't want anything, Amy. Just be a friend and don't make fun of me. I don't think I'll ever come back. Being around you is too hard for me knowing I don't deserve you as a wife. And, you don't deserve to be married to a person like me, anyway. The case is closed and nothing will ever be any different."

WATCHING THE PLANE RISE and slowly circle back to the States, Amy held her hand over her mouth to stem back the emotion. She couldn't begin to count the number of men she had taken and set out to destroy. Using sex as a weapon of mass destruction, her vengeance on the male population had become legend. All of that was behind her now, destined for celibacy, until she narrowed her sights on the next man. Or woman.

Harold Bruntz, an outlandish display of inconsistent ambiguities, was leaving, the only other person alive who knew the truth. Someday, she thought, she might have to deal with that.

On the plane, nursing a whiskey from a tiny bottle, Harold played it all over again. The scenes of blood and death, all going back to the erratic actions of a depraved sick girl that never got the treatment she needed. Beauty and a remorseless soul—a deadly combination. Dangerous—like loose gravel.